Two Trains to Tamarind

The Mountweazel & Mondegreen Mysteries ~ Volume 1

Wm. Brett Hill

FIREWORDS

First published 2025 by Firewords
Copyright © Wm. Brett Hill 2025

ISBN 979-8-218-75682-6 (paperback)
ISBN 979-8-218-75684-0 (epub)

Book Cover by Wm. Brett Hill and Dan Burgess

Typeset in Caslon by Dan Burgess

www.firewords.co.uk
www.wmbretthill.com

For Carrie and Katie,
who were there every step of the way

Two Trains to Tamarind

Chapter One

Jeremiah Mountweazel rubbed his eyes and took a deep breath. In all of his days he had faced a plethora of dangers, from deranged killers to vicious cutthroats, from scheming criminals to psychotic debutants, but nothing he had ever encountered had prepared him for the scene in front of him. He opened his eyes, dropped his hand into his lap, and forced a smile onto his face, knowing full well that the assembled group was not the slightest bit fooled.

"You don't seem pleased to see us, Jeremiah. One would think there would be some benefit to being the best of friends to your dear, departed mother, and that would merit one some special consideration. But it would seem not."

The trio had forced their way in, led by the speaker, and occupied the two leather chairs in front of his desk, leaving one of them, a sheepish woman with a plump face and glasses that perched impossibly on the tip of her nose, to stand behind them, her hands folded in front of her.

"Mrs. Dunning, I assure you—"

"Dunning-Kruger, Jeremiah. I'm sure I told you once already," she interrupted with a sharp sniff.

Jeremiah groaned inwardly. She had not told him, but she expected him to know. Of course she had remarried as soon as old Dunning had no doubt gratefully departed this world. He didn't know much about her new husband, but he was certain the man was either deaf or regularly comatose.

"Right, Mrs. Dunning-Kruger," he corrected. "I assure you that I saw you as soon as humanly possible. Now what can I—"

"And in such disgusting premises, as well. I shudder to think what your mother would have had to say about the fact that you live and work above that horrid eatery." The sneer cut across her face like a permanent scar and she crossed her arms and sniffed with distaste.

Her companions stared, one with shock and the other as though waiting with eager anticipation. Jeremiah imagined they regularly saw their friend berate people in this fashion.

"Who are your friends?" he asked. He had no desire to discuss his living arrangements with a woman whom his mother had once referred to as 'that loathsome battleaxe with the taste and sensibility of a feral chihuahua'.

Mrs. Dunning-Kruger flinched as though struck and then, realizing her error had been rightfully pointed out, resigned herself to the social niceties that were expected.

"Mr. Jeremiah Mountweazel, son of my dearly missed friend and confidant Lillian Mountweazel, allow me to introduce Mrs. Mildred Weber-Fechner," she said, gesturing to the woman sitting next to her, "and Mrs. Agnes Baader-Meinhoff," she added, gesturing over her shoulder like she was shooing a fly.

Mrs. Baader-Meinhoff, suddenly conscious that she had been mentioned, started and flashed a smile as she performed a quick bow.

"How do you do?" she said quietly.

The other woman's face split in an enormous predatory smile and she began to nod repeatedly to an inaudible beat. Jeremiah smiled back at her, unwilling to break her gaze for fear she would be at his neck in a moment.

"I bid you both welcome," he said.

Mrs. Dunning-Kruger snorted. "Some welcome. Not even a pot of tea. What would your mother think, honestly?"

Jeremiah bit back the retort that rushed forward in his mind that his mother would have nothing but sympathy for his current predicament and would likely tell the offending woman exactly what she thought of her. His mother could get away with that sort of thing because she didn't care what anyone thought. He was not so fortunate. Rumor and gossip, especially at the hands of such a skilled craftswoman as Priscilla Dunning-Kruger, could destroy a business like his that depended on word of mouth.

Jeremiah held his hands up. "I apologize, ladies, but it seems I am ill-prepared to receive guests at the moment. I can offer you a glass of whisky, but I'm afraid that is it."

Mrs. Baader-Meinhoff began to nod eagerly but stopped when Mrs. Dunning-Kruger snorted with derision and shook her head.

"No respectable person would be drinking such a repugnant liquid at this time of day, Jeremiah, and you should know that by now," she said. "You're certainly old enough to have obtained at least a little good sense. What are you? Twenty? Twenty-five?"

"I'm thirty-five years old, Mrs. Dunning-Kruger, as of last month," he said, stifling a sigh.

"Well, hardly a grownup at all, but you should still know better. Whisky! As if women of our caliber would allow that filth to cross our lips."

Mrs. Baader-Meinhoff blushed and looked at the floor.

Jeremiah forced another smile. He felt as though his face might shatter if he forced it any harder. "Indeed. My apologies for my thoughtlessness. As to what I can do for you?"

Mrs. Dunning-Kruger sighed dramatically and snapped her fingers at the woman behind her. Mrs. Baader-Meinhoff pulled a ledger from her bag and placed it in the impatient hand.

"We three pillars of society are members of an elite organization known as The Pansophic Order of the Belletrist. I'm sure you've heard of us," she said with a sharp nod.

Jeremiah's eyebrows furrowed. "The Panso—what now?"

Mrs. Weber-Fechner exploded in a barrage of titters. "I told you it wouldn't make sense to anyone else, Pris, but you insisted." Her eyes were wide as she covered her mouth to try and hold in the uncontrollable laugh. Mrs. Baader-Meinhoff tried her best to stifle a smile.

"Yes, well, that's neither here nor there, Mildred. I would never expect someone as pedestrian as Jeremiah here to understand the subtleties of our name," Mrs. Dunning-Kruger hissed. "No offense, of course, Jeremiah."

Jeremiah shook his head and smiled. "None taken, I assure you." He forced a thoughtful look on his face to try and assure her he was taking things as seriously as she wanted. "And what service can I provide the Order today?"

Mrs. Dunning-Kruger, irritated by the impropriety of her friends, slammed the ledger down on Jeremiah's desk more forcefully than she had intended, startling herself and the others. She took only a few seconds to cycle through the list of possible reactions before finding herself back at condescension.

"You can help discover what villain is absconding with our funds. Mrs. Weber-Fechner has been our bookkeeper since the beginning, but it was only when I took a look at the books that I saw there were discrepancies." She cast a judgemental glare at her companion.

Mrs. Weber-Fechner shrugged. "I never said I was good with numbers. Once they get all big I can't tell what's what anymore."

Mrs. Dunning-Kruger snorted. "Clearly we made a mistake in our choices at the beginning. It's a good thing I'm in charge or nothing would get done properly."

Both of the other women rolled their eyes in unison in the split second before they were both met with Mrs. Dunning-Kruger's challenging glare. By the time she locked eyes with each they were smiling and nodding.

"Anyway, it's all there in black and white. I'm sure you can figure it out. Your mother always claimed you were clever," said Mrs. Dunning-Kruger, doubt etched on her wrinkled face.

Before Jeremiah could respond the door to his office swung open and a whirlwind of hair, fabric, and complaint came whirling into the room.

"Honestly, Jerry, if I have to do one more job where I have to pretend to be some doe-eyed imbecile I'm going to shave my head, pluck my eyes out, and join one of those ludicrous cults where all I have to do is make flower chains all day and sing absurd hymns," said the twister. "Oh!"

The blonde wig that had been on the woman's head at the beginning of her entrance now sat in the lap of the now-even-more-irked Mrs. Dunning-Kruger, who stared at the newcomer with a look that showed nothing but disdain, likely due to the fact that the younger woman was halfway through removing her over-dress corset when she saw the assembled company.

"Excuse me, Miss, but we have an appointment with Mr. Mountweazel at the moment and would appreciate it if you waited until its completion to initiate whatever depravity you had in mind," she said, standing up. She handed the wig to Mrs. Baader-Meinhoff, who took it wordlessly, and turned to glare at Jeremiah. "Honestly, Jeremiah, what would your mother—"

"Ladies, may I take a moment to introduce my business associate, Ms. Millie Mondegreen," he interrupted with a gesture to the woman who had managed to put her dress back into order and stood smiling innocently.

"Millie, may I present Mrs. Dunning-Kruger, Mrs. Weber-Fechner, and Mrs. Baader-Meinhoff," added Jeremiah, gesturing to each woman.

"Ah," said Millie, her face showing she had taken in all she needed to know of the situation. "My apologies. It has been a long night and I forgot myself." She managed a curtsey before fixing Jeremiah with a stone stare.

"I should think you did," said Mrs. Dunning-Kruger sharply. "Ladies, we should take our leave before things descend into further inappropriateness. Jeremiah, I expect a report back from you with great haste."

She turned and stalked out the door without looking back, followed closely by Mrs. Weber-Fechner.

Mrs. Baader-Meinhoff stood holding her bag and looking back and forth between the two. "It was very nice to meet you both," she said quietly, her cherubic face gleaming with a smile. "Thank you for your help."

"Agnes, now!" came a shout from the stairs. "Before I catch something just from breathing the horrible air in this place."

Mrs. Baader-Meinhoff shrugged and, almost as an afterthought, handed Millie the blonde wig she had been holding. "I like your hair," she said, grinning at Millie, and then she shuffled through the door and closed it behind her.

Millie burst into laughter and turned to look at herself in the mirror on the wall by the door, laughing even harder when she saw the wild tangle that her red hair had been left in when she had ripped off the wig.

"So what did the Hyphen Ladies want, anyway?" she asked after smoothing her errant locks.

"Hyphen Ladies?"

Millie nodded. "The Double Barrel Club? The Name Collectors? I'm not sure which one works best," she said, tapping her chin as she walked over to the drinks cabinet. "Ladies who collect names like others collect umbrellas, then wave them around so that everyone knows how important they are."

Jeremiah laughed. "Just more missing money claims. Thank you for the timely interruption, by the way. I thought that would never end." He fell back into his chair and rubbed his face. "Has it really come to this, that sussing out penny-filchers for a group of penny-pinchers is the only work I can find?"

Millie cleared her throat, and when he looked at her it was to see her blue eyes twinkling over a glass she held out in front of him. "Perhaps this will cheer you up."

He took the drink and sipped it as he thumbed through the mail that had amassed in both of their absences. "How did the Flage situation turn out?"

"Not as fruitful as we had hoped. It turns out Mr. Flage, or Percy as I'm, or rather Daphne," she said, holding up the blonde wig, "is now allowed to call him, isn't quite the villain his boss suspected him of being. Pity, since the payoff was so low as a result. Very chatty fellow, though, Percy. If he had been up to no good he likely wouldn't have been able to keep from telling me as his mouth never seemed to stop moving."

"So that's another job with no large reward, and the coffers are running dry," sighed Jeremiah. "Enjoy your whisky. We may be cutting back soon."

Millie tossed back her drink and fell into one of the chairs, twirling the wig around her finger. "Something will come up, Jerry. I can feel it in my bones."

Jeremiah stood suddenly, staring at the letter he had been reading. He slapped the desk and let out a whoop of delight.

"Your bones, my dear Millie, are entirely, utterly, and magnificently accurate!"

Chapter Two

The office in which the unfortunate meeting with the ladies of the Pansophic Order of the Belletrist had taken place sat on Jeremiah's half of the center floor of a three-story building overlooking the frigid waters of the Torri River. While Jeremiah's living quarters occupied the top floor, the base of the structure was filled entirely with a restaurant run by the affable Ivan Panglossian.

Panglossian, a slightly hunched elderly man brimming with youthful energy, had his apartment on the other half of the center floor. The restaurant had long ago spilled from the confines of the front of the building and filled the area to the street with an eclectic assortment of tables and chairs restrained only by a border of planters filled with lush greenery. Combined with the bright yellows and reds adorning the building's front, the entire place had a chaotic feel that perfectly matched its cuisine.

The place was inexplicably named Cobbler's Rest, and it should be said that it never once, to anyone's knowledge, saw the recumbent form of any sort of shoe artisan. It did have an apple crisp known all over the city to be the best in existence, especially if you asked the effervescent proprietor, so most theorized that it was from this the name arose.

Cobbler's Rest was the seventh restaurant known to occupy the building, and coincidentally was the seventh restaurant opened and run by Mr. Panglossian. His tenacity in the face of multiple failed attempts to discover what type of food would appeal to the masses led him to the latest incarnation, which gave the customer the ability to choose from the menus of numerous cuisines despite the fact that they may not sit well on the plate together, or indeed in the stomach of the eater.

"So, your friends were nice," said Millie, a smirk on her face. She had changed out of her dress and corset into a more comfortable blouse and trousers, an act that lifted her mood but also drew curious stares from passersby, mostly women wearing what was deemed the more appropriate dress for a lady. Her mane of wild, red hair also didn't fail to distract most people from what they had been occupied with before.

"Those harpies are no friends of mine," Jeremiah groaned. "Hell, I only know the one, and though she claims to be a friend of my late mother the truth is I never heard a nice word uttered about her. I'm still not convinced she didn't kill her first husband."

By comparison to his companion, Jeremiah would be considered plain, though that fit with the expectations of society and suited him just fine. He made every attempt to dress like the more affluent members of society in an effort to elevate his status and attract clients who were more willing to compensate him greatly. They didn't need to know that he only had two suits, and that his pocket watch had long ago stopped working. He always had his hat and cane on hand, ever looking the part.

The two sat at a corner table on the patio of Cobbler's Rest at a table which could be considered 'theirs' save for the fact that the seating, like the food, was as mercurial as the river that flowed within view of where they sat. While the furniture was changeable, however, their claim on the corner has thus far gone unchallenged.

Millie laughed and stirred her soup, trying to identify the pieces that floated in it. As always, Millie quickly abandoned her investigation and ate it regardless, opting for ignorant enjoyment over informed horror.

"She seems the sort. Nothing direct, of course. No knife in the heart or bullet in the eye," she said, dipping her sandwich into the stew before taking a bite.

Jeremiah laughed. "No, she's the poisoning type, that's for sure. Poor old Mr. Dunning never stood a chance." Catching Millie staring at him with a cocked eyebrow, he added, "But I'm kidding, of course. As I hear it he died in his sleep at the theater.

The horrible woman waited until the play was finished to tell anyone so she wouldn't miss the show."

The waiter came by and refilled their glasses, bringing a halt to the conversation. They had learned long ago that everyone had ears in the city, and it could be detrimental if the wrong thing was overheard by the wrong person. As a result, the wait staff of the Cobbler's Rest likely thought the two of them continually sat in silence.

"Enough about them, though," said Millie when the young man walked away. "Let's talk about the letter." Jeremiah slipped it out of his pocket and skimmed it again as if looking for something new to leap off the scented page. When Millie gestured, he handed it over to her.

"Quality paper, expensive perfume," she said, holding it up to her nose and taking a sniff. "The handwriting is legible and deliberate, like they wanted no chance for misunderstanding." She held it up to the sun. "A watermark of their family name, too. This looks to be the real deal."

"Do you know anything about the author of the letter?" asked Jeremiah. He regularly depended on Millie's knowledge of the upper crust of society, especially in matters originating in Fleis where she had the, according to her, misfortune of being raised.

"I know the name Sudworth, but I'm unfamiliar with these particular members of the family. Still," she shrugged, "if they're Sudworths then they have the coin they're offering."

Jeremiah shook his head. "Yes, but you and I know their son is more than likely dead, so how willing are they going to be to pay to hear that confirmed?"

Millie held the letter up. "You don't know that for sure. It says here he was an Authority recruit. That's a pretty clear lead. Maybe he got here and flunked out and was too ashamed to write home and tell his family. If his parents are anything like my mother—"

"Then failure would be unthinkable," Jeremiah finished.

Millie's mother was the sort of member of the upper class that felt the need to remind a person that they were far more important than anyone else. Lady Mondegreen had, as Jeremiah recalled from his one encounter with her, a way of looking down her nose at you that made her seem ten feet tall despite being shorter than her daughter. Having witnessed her treatment of her daughter firsthand, he could only imagine what a sort of person like her would think of a child that flunked out of the Authority's grueling entry process.

As if on cue the light of the sun was blocked, and the two looked up to watch the underside of an airship lazily pass overhead. Jeremiah squinted and studied the markings.

"Yet another Authority ship, by the looks of it," he said.

"Leaving this time," agreed Millie. "Always good to see them going away."

Jeremiah scratched the stubble on his chin. "So, the young man leaves Fleis on the train, waved off by his proud parents and all full of piss and vinegar for his future with the Authority, and somehow doesn't end up at the other end of the rails here in Tamarind. Or he does end up here and disappears."

"Well the letter says Commander Rantallion told them their son never reported in," said Millie.

"Yes, well, I'm not sure he would divulge information to the parents if it might damage the reputation of the Authority. How would it look if they couldn't even get a recruit safely moved from their Capital to our lovely city? It would certainly challenge their tenuous hold here in Tamarind."

The Authority, the main controlling body in the Western Reaches, had been trying to claim some portion of Tamarind as their own. The city council had resisted their platitudes but had allowed them to establish a stronghold in the northern part of the city with the understanding that while Tamarind did not fall under their jurisdiction their assistance would sometimes be called upon if needed, but only if requested. The cockiness of the young Authority soldiers who paraded through the city in their crisp, white uniforms made most people in the city hope they would eventually be sent packing, and any excuse to shame them or show how ineffectual they were was grasped with feverish glee.

Millie nodded. "And they can't take any challenges as it is, with their presence here not even being completely ratified by the city council. You may be onto something. So how do we proceed?"

Jeremiah took a bite of his pizza and chewed thoughtfully. "I have a friend that may be able to get me in to speak to Rantallion, although I'm sure I'll get the same denial the parents got. Still, it's a start."

"So are we taking it on?" she asked.

Jeremiah nodded. "I can't resist a payout of this size, assuming they pay in the end. I'll write them back and arrange a meeting. Meanwhile, you, dearest Millie, get to look into the missing funds from the Pansophic Order of the whatever the hell it was."

Millie laughed. "Oh, Jerry, you silly man, you forget yourself, as usual." She held up the letter and waved it at him. "You play the role of a gentleman, but you haven't a clue how to talk to people of this caliber. Plus, this is bigger than a one person job. The Hyphen Ladies will wait. You need me on this."

He sighed. "Fine. You can't blame a man for trying." He shrugged and held up his finger to call the waiter. "But the next time I have to talk to Mrs. Dunning-Kruger, you have to be in the room. So far her disgust with you is the only thing that tops her disgust with me, and I need that defense."

"You say the sweetest things," she said, tucking the letter into her shirt pocket. "I'll write the Sudworths back and tell them we're on the case."

"What would I do without you, Millicent?"

Millie glared. "Call me that again and you'll find out."

Chapter Three

The city of Tamarind, it could be argued, was actually four cities that met in the middle. Divided first in half by the Torri River, which flowed from the northwest out of the Stelin Mountains, through the city, and then disappeared to the southeast into the Morlin Mountains, and then again by a canal, which had been cut through going southwest to northeast to tie in to the Tarsain River flowing up from the south. This allowed trade, whether coming in from the south or transferred over from the railway, to be transported through the city without clogging up the roadways.

In the middle of this aquatic crossroads sat an island of sorts that held only one building, a seven story towering structure, called The Centre, which functioned as the hub of administration for all of Tamarind. It was connected to each of the four sections by individual bridges wide enough to allow for carriages but only in one direction. Traffic flowed around The Centre in a counter-clockwise fashion, as dictated by the city council, but more out of habit than following the rule.

Most things in Tamarind went on out of habit. It could be argued that precedent was set by the notion that something was done a certain way because it had always been done that way. Change came slowly to the mountain city, as the Authority was finding out. The people in Tamarind recognized one law, the Constabulary, as being in charge. The crisp white uniforms of the Authority officers meant nothing to them.

The Constabulary held such importance that it took up three floors of The Centre, with the street level story and second story being offices and courtrooms while the below water story, sealed against the frigid waters of the Torri and Tarsain, held the cells. If a person was said to be 'under the river' you could be assured that they had been locked up for some reason.

As Jeremiah crossed the western bridge on his way to call upon his friend he watched another airship, this one privately owned by its markings, untether from the spire on the top of The Centre and drift westward. He could see the workers at the top retracting the gangplanks back into the side of the building and his stomach churned. How they managed to work at such a height and not lose their lunch escaped him. He was happy with his feet planted firmly on the ground.

Jeremiah didn't recognize the young man behind the counter when he got inside, but as he approached, the man looked up and gave him such a huge smile he felt like he should.

"Welcome to the Constabulary, Sir. Would you like to report a crime?"

It was the clothes that garnered him such a warm welcome. If this man knew that Jeremiah was nearly penniless he would likely give him a completely different reception.

"Not today, no, at least nothing of which I am aware. If you could, my good man, please tell Sergeant Ward that Jeremiah Mountweazel is here to speak to him about a matter most urgent."

The clerk was a corpulent man, and this, combined with his round eyeglasses gave him a strigine appearance that Jeremiah had an even harder time shaking when he replied, "Who?"

"You must be new here, Constable—?"

"Filcher. Constable Filcher, sir. Pleased to make your acquaintance," said the young man.

Jeremiah smiled. "You're a policeman named—?"

"Filcher. Yes, sir. The irony has not been lost on anyone in the department, believe me. 'So, do you ever accidentally arrest yourself?' they say. Endless fun. Still, it could be worse," said the man with a pained smile.

Jeremiah forced the smile from his face. Growing up with a name like Mountweazel did afford him some familiarity with the young man's suffering at the hands of others.

"Yes, well. That's the spirit," he managed. "I'm looking for Sergeant Ward."

He was once again met with the quizzical look.

"Sergeant Radclyffe Ward. Been here for years. Tall, burly gentleman. Big, bushy mustache. His desk is just over there," offered Jeremiah, as he pointed to one of the many desks behind the front desk. As he did so, he noticed things looked different in that corner of the room. Gone were his friend's deer antler coat rack and pipe stand. The desk looked organized, and he had never seen it in that state the entire time he had known Ward. Jeremiah began to suspect the worst.

"Sorry, sir, I'm new here," answered Filcher. "We have an Inspector Ward upstairs, is that who you are looking for?"

Jeremiah had a hard time keeping the surprise from his face. Ward had never been one for doing what was necessary to rise up the ranks. They had always joked that the man would die at his desk one day.

"Yes, that's the one. Apologies. I wasn't aware his promotion had gone through," Jeremiah lied. "It's been a while."

"I should say," answered Filcher. "He's been an Inspector the whole time I've been here, and that's nearly been a year." He pushed his glasses up his nose, picked up a telephone receiver, and punched a button before waiting for a response.

Jeremiah smiled at the man and tried to guess what sort of welcome he would get. He hadn't realized it had been over a year since he had made contact.

"Front desk here. I have a Mr.—?" Filcher raised an eyebrow at Jeremiah.

"Mountweazel."

"A Mr. Mountweazel here to see Inspector Ward." The surprise that registered on the constable's face nearly made Jeremiah burst out laughing. "Did he just—? Miss Slater, what did he—?" he said nervously, turning away from Jeremiah. "Oh dear."

Jeremiah decided not to wait, he left the man at the desk and bounded up the stairs before Filcher knew he was gone. He thought he might have heard the man calling after him but he didn't stop to make sure.

Where the downstairs was mostly open, affording very little privacy to the constables with desks there, the upstairs was a maze of hallways. Jeremiah stopped at a crossing of two hallways and, not certain which way to go, opted to stop and listen. Before long he could hear the familiar shout of Ward echoing down the hallway.

"That son of a bitch thinks he can just tell me to put everything on hold and run his errands? Well he's got another damn thing coming if he thinks I'm going to cave!"

As Jeremiah rounded a corner he saw through an open door the hulking form of Ward storming away from the desk of a distraught secretary. He passed through a nearby doorway and slammed the door so hard the glass nearly shattered.

The lady took a deep breath and let it out slowly, focusing her eyes on the desk in front of her. After a moment the tension in her face melted away and she took notice of Jeremiah, regarding him with kind eyes, though her lips were still pursed with irritation.

"You must be Miss Slater," said Jeremiah, removing his hat as he entered the room. "The man downstairs said to come on up."

"Mr. Mountweazel, I presume? Please take a seat. I'm certain Inspector Ward will be happy to speak to you once he—"

"Whoever it is, send them away!" came a shout from the closed office.

The woman sat up straight and forced a smile. "Please take a seat," she said, then she stood, smoothed the front of her blouse, and walked through the door, closing it behind her. Jeremiah could hear hushed voices but was not able to make out what was being said.

He hung his hat on the deer antler coat rack and slid his cane into the elephant foot shaped container below. Years ago, when Ward's wife was merely his fiancée, she had insisted that the hunting, and the trophies it garnered, would have no place in her life, so these two pieces of furniture had been relocated to the Constabulary and were now as associated with Ward as his bushy white mustache.

A moment later the door to his office flew open and the man, his countenance now completely cheerful, came through with his hand extended.

"Jeremiah, my friend, no one told me it was you that was here!"

Miss Slater cleared her throat loudly as she slid back behind her desk. "Perhaps if you would allow a person to get a word in edgewise," she suggested.

Ward's crushing handshake had taken down many a man before, leaving them whimpering and clutching their damaged hand, but Jeremiah had long learned his lesson. He met brute strength with forced vigor, trying to crush the other man's hand to keep his intact.

"Come in, come in," Ward said, pulling him toward the door.

Miss Slater cleared her throat again. Ward winced.

"Miss Slater, I apologize unreservedly. You were absolutely correct. I did, in fact, want to see this guest. Satisfied?"

She managed a small, but lethal, victorious smile.

"I am. Will you be taking tea?" she offered, making it clear that all offense was foregone for the immediate future.

"Naw, I've got something stronger in my drawer to fit the occasion," said Ward with a conspiratorial guffaw. He ushered Jeremiah through the door and closed it to the sound of a judgemental "Hmm!" following on their heels.

Ward's office looked as though he had simply transferred his old desk and all of his belongings into an enclosed room, only this time he had a window. In fact, he was certain it was the same desk, as several scars on the side and on the small portions of the top not covered in paperwork were familiar to him. Ward's blunderbuss hung on the wall as one of the few decorations, the only other being a framed commendation and a map of the city. Jeremiah watched a canal barge slowly crawl up the Tarsain as Ward settled into his chair behind the desk and opened the bottom drawer, pulling out a bottle and two glasses.

"You've come up in the world," said Jeremiah, pointing out over the city.

Ward snorted. "Hardly. The stuffed shirts needed a patsy to do their bidding and they finally settled on me." He handed Jeremiah the glass half filled with brown, pungent liquid.

"Couldn't happen to a better man," said Jeremiah, raising the glass and taking a sip. He settled into the chair across the desk and regarded his friend. "Although it does seem like this particular 'patsy' isn't as acquiescent as they would have hoped."

"It's that new Superintendent Cavil upstairs. Always finding fault with everything. Always wanting more. I keep telling him to just get out of my way and let me solve the crimes but he wants things done his way. Irritating little shit to say the least," grumbled Ward. He tossed back his glass and smiled as he felt it go down. "I can't have much of this or Slater will be on my case. Good thing you're here to provide an excuse."

Jeremiah chuckled. "Indeed. Happy to help."

Ward steepled his hands in front of his face and studied him. "You didn't come here to catch up, though, did you? You need something."

Jeremiah mocked shock. "Can't a man just stop by and visit an old friend?"

"Well, my friend, it has been over a year, so it would seem no."

"Apologies," answered Jeremiah, nodding. "I am guilty as charged. I can only offer in my defense that I have been preoccupied with a new partner of sorts and she—"

"Oh, a woman, I should have known," laughed Ward. "Leave it to a woman to turn Jeremiah Mountweazel's eye and keep him locked down for a year."

Jeremiah shook his head. "No, no, not like that. When I say 'partner' I mean it in the purely business sense. She helps me with cases, that's all."

"Mmm-hmm, and I'm your dancing Aunt Myra," said Ward, his laugh now taking over his entire body. "So what, is the woman in trouble or something?"

He had forgotten how impossible Ward could be when he got in this sort of mood. Too many nights in bars had been spent with him carefully explaining to women, or oftentimes spouses of women, that his intentions were not as his boisterous friend had exclaimed. It was usually only the bulk of Ward or the flash of his badge that kept such exchanges from turning violent.

He leaned back and opened the door to the other room. "Miss Slater, has Inspector Ward ever told you what the Countess of Philodox called him as a pet name?"

The woman appeared at the door. "Why, no, Mr. Mountweazel, he has not. Perhaps you could enlighten me?"

Ward's jovial nature vanished and was replaced with playful irritation. "Thank you, Miss Slater, that will be all," he said and he waited until the smiling woman closed the door to look at his friend again. "Ass."

"Why, as I recall, that was almost the very pet name," chuckled Jeremiah.

Ward returned to studying him but was still grinning. "As much as I'd just love for you to stay around embarrassing me in front of my underlings, I suspect you have something you actually want from me."

"I need an audience with Commander Rantallion of the Authority. I was hoping you could pull some strings," answered Jeremiah.

Ward squinted and drummed his fingers together, a sign that Jeremiah knew meant he was deep in thought, and he knew it would soon be followed by the man standing and pacing.

The burly man stood and began to pace. "That pompous windbag is no friend of mine, I'm sure you suspect, but I can get you an audience if you have a good enough reason. If I do, though, I'm going to need you to do something for me."

"A recruit on the way from Fleis to Tamarind disappeared. His parents are not sure where he disappeared exactly, and they've gotten little information from the man. I was hoping to question him myself," offered Jeremiah.

"Hmm, this might work. An investigator hired by the family, working in cooperation with the Constabulary." He slapped his hand down on the desk. "By jove, it's perfect!" He walked around the desk and flung open the door. "Miss Slater, I think my friend here has given me the ideal way to keep Cavil off my back and get one over on Rantallion. I need you to take a letter."

The woman, giving every indication that she was fully aware of the instructions that would inevitably come her way, already sat at the typewriter with the paper loaded.

"And to whom are we writing?" she said.

Chapter Four

Millie Mondegreen sat in the middle of a pile of clothing that covered what was very likely a chair in the corner of her simple flat in the south end of Tamarind. In direct contrast to Jeremiah's pristine office and quarters, hers gave the impression to the observer that she had either recently been robbed, been the victim of an unfortunate explosion, or very likely a tragic combination of the two. Not a surface in the place existed without some object or collection of objects hiding it from view.

Despite the clutter, she sat in perfect peace, cross-legged and erect with her eyes closed and her breathing shallow. The letter that she had recently composed to the Sudworths sat in its envelope on the small table next to her along with a jar of grease paint, several bread rolls hardened by time to near indestructible density, a peacock feather, and a cat that had at some point been inexplicably named Lady Tuppence Marmalade Amberjack but who typically answered to Tipsy.

The purring of Tipsy provided a relaxing backdrop to Millie's meditation, within which she pondered a multitude of current events, but focused especially on trying to sort out why she had lied to Jeremiah.

Her familiarity with the Sudworths was far greater than she had made out. In the grand scheme of society it could easily be said that they more often than not qualified as family friends to the Mondegreens. In fact, young Tomason, the missing person in question, had even been a childhood playmate of her youngest sister Lallie.

It was commonly said that Tommy and Lallie would one day be wed, paired off like sheep on the farm to breed and produce the necessary amount of children to satisfy expectations. Millie hadn't heard anything about the boy in years, so he must not have done anything remarkable enough to maintain his status as appropriate breeding stock to her mother.

And now he was missing. Had her mother had some influence in the Sudworths contacting Jeremiah? As far as Millie knew, her mother had no idea that she was working with the man. In fact, unless some unknown source had informed her mother otherwise, the story she and Jeremiah had concocted should still be held as fact by her family—that she was now a sister of the White Nettle, called Sister Lelani Xayr, and eschewed the world and everything in it.

No, it had to be coincidence, or at the very least, just a recommendation passed on by her mother after the 'success' Jeremiah had at finding her.

"So why did I lie?" she asked out loud.

Tipsy took the vocalization as all the invitation necessary to interrupt with a pounce into her lap and an immediate and vocal call for attention. Millie obliged by scratching the cat's ears as she let out a huge sigh.

"You don't know either, do you, Tipsy?" she said and she stood, much to the dismay of the feline, and grabbed her coat and the letter.

Millie did know, she just didn't want to admit it. If Jeremiah knew her family could be personally invested in the case he would have given it a pass for her sake, despite the fact that the fee he would collect would be lucrative enough to chase off his financial worries. He would pass on it because it would invite possible scrutiny by Lady Mondegreen and could very well ruin the narrative they had concocted. It was charming how protective he was of her, but also tiresome. He had a lot to learn about the capabilities of his partner.

She left her rooms and her momentarily satisfied cat and glided down the staircase to the alley behind the theater over which she rented space. Jeremiah had offered to find her a space near him, even to clear out a room for her in his apartment, but she liked to have her own space and the ability to get away when she needed. Plus, living in this part of the city gave her familiarity with more of Tamarind and living over a theater gave her access to the supplies needed for her many identities.

Today, she was simply Millie, and her red hair bounced with wild abandon as she made her way down the street to the post office. Her letter to the Sudworths, written in Jeremiah's name and, it should be said, his handwriting, let them know that they would take the job immediately and would communicate any findings forthwith by way of telegram. She knew the Sudworths would deem the use of telegrams vulgar but she also knew that they would prefer it if it meant they got information sooner than waiting on the post.

Millie loved her part of the Tamarind, unfavorably called The Bottoms by most of the city in a base recognition of geography. Life in The Bottoms was lively, with a bustling marketplace one block over from the theater and shops that stayed open most hours, along with carts that moved in an almost fluid flow up and down the streets with inexplicable predictability.

Millie saw the florist's cart coming and happily waved to the proprietor.

"Good day, Mr. Yonic, what would you recommend today?"

The man's smile lit up his face as he saw her and he pulled from a bundle a single white flower. "I think this petunia should suit you nice, my lovely," he said, handing it to her.

She took it with a curtsy and slipped it into the mass of tangles to rest above her ear. "My thanks to you, as always, for making me presentable to the world," she said, holding out her hand.

The man bowed and took her hand, placing a light kiss upon her knuckle. "One cannot improve upon perfection, my dear," he said, and he moved along without another word.

The casual observer would no doubt have found the exchange pleasant, even genteel, but then the casual observer would not have been looking for the correct clues, nor would they have been properly informed of the actual meaning of the language being used. And this was as it should be, as said observer would have left the encounter unaware of the coin that had been slipped to Mr. Yonic or the new set of lockpicks slipped into Millie's hand in exchange.

Not all transactions of questionable nature needed to be conducted in a dark alleyway, especially if one was properly informed.

The Post Office held no excitement inside for Millie as she went through the tedious process of mailing the letter with the appropriate safeguards to ensure its arrival. The postal service could be unreliable at best, but for the correct fee the chances of your letter arriving were drastically improved. It was while leaving the building that Millie noticed a woman standing across the street staring at her.

She recognized the woman immediately, of course, as it had only been that morning that she had met her. Mrs. Baader-Meinhoff was watching her with the determined air of a person trying to appear as though they were not watching but failing miserably at the task. Once the older woman realized her efforts were both ineffective and observed she shuffled off down the street without so much as a wave.

"How peculiar," said Millie to herself, making a mental note to mention it to Jeremiah, and then, noticing the time, she began the walk to his office.

She could hail a carriage, but Millie enjoyed the walk. On a good day, one where her journey faced no interruptions or saw no one she knew, she could make it from her place to Jeremiah's in half an hour. Crossing the Tarsain was usually the tricky part as the Temir Bridge, the only crossing between the railyard and The Centre, could sometimes be backed up for quite a way under the wrong circumstances and travelers would have to make the decision of either waiting or heading to the main cross. They could also swim across if they so chose, but the waters of the Tarsain were freezing cold even on the sunniest of days, so few made this choice.

This day Millie faced no impediment. She left The Bottoms and crossed the bridge north of the railyard, admiring the efficiency of the trains coming and going, unloading people and materials onto wagons and barges to either make their way up the river into or beyond the city, or down the river to towns further south. She enjoyed riding the train well enough, but not nearly as much as Jeremiah. If he had his way it would be his main means of transport.

A shadow passed over the street and she looked up to see an airship lazily glide across the sky. Now that was the way to travel! Millie loved experiencing the world from above, being able to see the small towns that dotted the landscape across the land. She enjoyed comparing the haphazard layout of Tamarind to the strict, efficient block structure of Fleis. The two cities, each resting on either end of the rail, could not be more different, and it was on this end of things that she found her comfort.

The beauty of seeing things from the air was lost on Jeremiah. The poor man was so undone by heights that, when forced to travel by air, he would sit in a seat and stare at his feet or at a newspaper, muttering to himself the entire trip that he was safely at ground level and the sway of the gondola was simply the wind on the river or the subtle rise and fall of the rails.

As the airship moved along, taking its shadow with it, she heard her name shouted by the familiar voice of Jeremiah as a steam carriage trundled up alongside her.

"Thought I might pick you up before you had to do too much of the walk," he said through the open window. "Hop in. I have something utterly peculiar to show you."

Chapter Five

The carriage dropped them off in front of the massive wood and steel gate that stood as the only visible entryway into the walled portion of the city claimed by the Authority. The property had once been the shipyard at the opposite end of the Tarsain from the railway, accepting supplies off the barges for the mines to the north, but had fallen into disuse and disrepair since the mines closed. When the Authority had asked for property, they were offered this spot almost as an intended affront by the city council.

The city council had regretted the decision once the walls had been erected and all knowledge of the interior workings of the area had been blocked.

As Millie handed Ward's letter to the guard through the small window, Jeremiah ran his thumb along the smooth surface of the device in his pocket he had been given by an almost ecstatic Ward. As much as he had wanted to toy with it in the carriage he had been given strict instructions to only activate it once he was inside.

"He was a friendly sort," said Millie after the slot had slammed shut. "Practically radiating sunshine."

Jeremiah laughed. "It's something about the uniform. Perhaps too snug in places."

"I'd like to see them refuse us an audience after what they've done," said Millie. "I mean, how do you lose a recruit?"

Before Jeremiah could answer, a loud metallic clang sounded from the other side of the gate. A small, door-sized section, which hadn't previously been obvious, opened and a young man in the crisp white uniform stepped out.

"Mr. Mountweazel, if you would kindly follow me," he said.

"And my companion," responded Jeremiah.

The man looked Millie over as if he was assessing something he had stepped in, trying to decide whether to wipe it off his shoe or throw the shoe away.

"Inspector Ward's letter only vouched for you, sir," he stated plainly.

"And I vouch for Mrs. Mondegreen, so that's all sorted. Now lead the way. There's a good man," said Jeremiah.

Millie flashed her most pleasant smile and waited to see what the young man would do.

If he had any inner conflict or even any thoughts at all they were not evident upon his face. He simply stared without expression for a full half minute before turning and stepping through the doorway with a curt, "Very well," over his shoulder.

They walked quickly to keep pace with their escort, though both made an effort to see as much as they could. Curiosity more than actual espionage fueled their inspection. Once the walls had gone up the endless speculation that came from the unknown had taken over the city. It was a rare occurrence to actually see some of the truth.

Groups of young men, likely recruits like Tomason Sudworth had intended to be, marched in unison around a large courtyard in step with the commands shouted by a man with a megaphone. It didn't escape either of their notice that the recruits were all uniform in not only their attire, but their appearance as well: clean-shaven, tall, thin, with eyes full of determination and near zealous obedience. Their escort looked to have been cut from the same cloth, almost as if the lot of them had been copied from one fanatically dedicated boy.

The buildings were all in good repair, though some were still under reconstruction. The old warehouses had been converted to what looked like barracks and the administrative buildings, which had previously been filthy with the comings and goings of miners, almost glistened in the late afternoon sun—all wood siding and cloudy windows replaced by white clapboards and clear glass.

The main building, to which they found themselves unceremoniously and silently led, was a three-story structure which also served as the only part of the property visible from the outside. A mast jutted up from the center to allow the anchoring of the airships which came and went regularly. It currently stood empty, a sharp spire stabbing up into the heavens.

Their escort saluted a guard who stood by the entryway to the building and passed through the open doorway without looking back. They followed, with only the briefest pause as Millie stopped to compliment the guard on the severity of his face.

Commander Rantallion greeted them as they entered his office like they were old friends, which threw both of them. They had expected a harsh man barking orders and refusing to cooperate but instead found this grandfatherly man who shook Jeremiah's hand with enthusiasm and seemed pleasantly surprised that Millie was also there.

"Please, come in and have a seat," he said, gesturing to the two wooden chairs set squarely in front of the desk in his immaculate office. "That will be all, Kevin," he added to the escort who still stood at attention in the doorway.

"Sir!" shouted the young man who then turned and marched away.

Rantallion chuckled as he made his way around the desk to his chair. He moved slowly, even clutching the edge of the desk once to steady himself, and as he sank down into the chair he let out a sigh of relief.

"I'll ask you to forgive my men. They are young and have something to prove. I am old and have been put out to pasture, though they are kind enough to let me pretend to still be in charge."

"Not at all, Commander. I have come to expect such… efficiency of words and movement from Authority men," said Jeremiah. Millie cut him a sharp glance.

Rantallion chuckled. "Do not worry, young lady, your companion's words will not rankle me in the slightest. I am well aware of the attitude in Tamarind toward my men, as I am also sadly aware that for the most part, it is fully merited. But that is not what brings you both here." He picked up Ward's letter from his desk and studied it thoughtfully.

"We were hoping you could assist us in locating this boy," said Jeremiah.

"Yes, yes," said Rantallion, his brow creased as he tapped his chin with a long, bony finger. "A sad affair, I'm sure. Promising lad. I recall seeing his file on my desk when he applied and I couldn't wait to stamp the approval."

Millie smiled. Tommy had always been a promising boy, even if her mother hadn't seen it. She could see him thriving in this environment, because though he was full of promise, he was also easily led and readily did what he was told. It was one of the things Lallie had liked about him.

"Undoubtedly," said Jeremiah. "And you can imagine that his parents were in full expectation of him arriving here, going through your program, and returning to Fleis with high honors suited up as an Authority man. Instead—"

"Instead they hear no word that he even arrived," finished Millie. "You can also imagine that their thoughts went to their greatest fear, that he had washed out and opted to disappear instead of bringing shame on his family."

Jeremiah flashed her a curious look. She gave him a brief, flickering smile before continuing.

"The Sudworths hold the Authority in high regard, as you know. It seems only fitting that they be treated with the same respect in regards to the fate of their son." She sat back and nodded to Jeremiah, her point made and done.

Rantallion nodded. "Young lady, I assure you that the rumors you may have heard about our methods of dealing with our less... successful recruits are egregious and categorically untrue. There is no 'vanishing down the mines' or 'exile to the Cistern' in our process. If a young man fails to meet our criteria he is simply sent home with a discharge and a suggestion of how he could better suit humanity, like through trade or accountancy."

"So he didn't—" she started to ask.

"I assure you, as I assured his parents in my letter of response, that he never arrived here. He and his fellow recruit were due to be collected at the station and when that train arrived they were not on it. I am told there was a conflict of some sort upon the train but we were not allowed to investigate further as it did not fall in our jurisdiction once the train arrived in Tamarind." There was a sternness to his eyes that hadn't been present before that quickly faded away.

"A conflict?" asked Jeremiah.

"You know how things go out in the world. Sometimes people get it into their heads that they deserve something that isn't due to them. It's one of the multitude of reasons why the Authority is trying to spread its reach—to make things safer for everyone. If that had been an Authority train I am certain nothing untoward would have been allowed to occur. As it was, it was not, and so the gods only know what befell young Sudworth and his companion, a lad named," he shuffled through the paperwork on his desk, his eyes finally finding what they sought, "Derek Fairburn."

Millie was happy she was seated. She had known Derek just as well as she had known Tommy. He was a troublemaker, but not in any sort of actual dangerous way. His antics were more like pranks than actual crimes. "You seem to know something of what happened," she managed to say, giving nothing away of the thoughts racing through her head.

Rantallion smiled at her and placed his hands upon the desk, pushing himself up to his feet. "I know very little, and it is mostly hearsay and none of my concern. I suggest, if you want facts instead of speculation, that you consult with the people who run the trains. Perhaps you will have better luck than I did."

Jeremiah slipped his hand into his pocket as he stood and palmed the device Ward had given him. Millie stood and, as they had planned, faked a swoon, falling into the approaching Rantallion who swiftly caught her. In the ensuing confusion Jeremiah had the opportunity to activate the device and drop it to the floor unnoticed.

"I'm terribly sorry and even more embarrassed, Commander," said Millie with feigned sincerity. "I don't know what came over me."

He tutted and patted her shoulder. "Think nothing of it, dear. It is in the nature of the female to experience moments of weakness."

Jeremiah watched the disc spring open, sprouting several spindly, articulated legs that lifted the device from the floor and scurried under a nearby cabinet. He turned just in time to catch the look on Millie's face as she fought the urge to respond to the man's comment.

"Are you okay, Millie?" he asked, taking her arm and retrieving her from the overly attentive Rantallion. "Perhaps we should go. I wouldn't want you to have another weak spell." He knew he would pay for the comment later, hopefully not too dearly.

"I am okay, gentlemen. I thank you both. Yes, perhaps it is time we took our leave and let Commander Rantallion return to his important work." The stress on the word 'important' left room for question of its legitimacy.

"If I can be of further service, please do contact me directly," said Rantallion, slowly escorting them to the door. "While I certainly appreciate your association with Inspector Ward or anyone else in the Constabulary, I find it is not always beneficial for anyone to involve them in affairs. They are somewhat irritatingly inquisitive regarding our processes."

Jeremiah glanced over at the cabinet but saw no sign of the device he had dropped. Ward had assured him it was simply a listening device, but he had suspicions it could be more.

"In fact," added Rantallion, "I would appreciate it if you would report anything you discover to me alone."

Jeremiah shook the man's hand. He pictured the look on Ward's face if he relayed that last line to the man and could already hear the slew of obscenities that would come. "I will be certain to keep you apprised of any discovery we make in our investigation, Commander. Thank you for your help."

The same young man escorted them through the grounds as had taken them in, and once they were through the gate it slammed shut without so much as a farewell.

They were a block away when Millie punched him hard in the shoulder.

"Another weak spell? I tell you, Jeremiah, one of these days—"

"You know it pays to play the part," laughed Jeremiah as he rubbed his arm. "And you also know that you are far stronger than I am."

"Speaking of people being stronger than they appear, that Rantallion sure is a bucket of beans with his whole doddering old man act," said Millie.

"What makes you say that?"

"The arms that caught me were not weak, old arms. That man is more than he lets on," she said.

"I could have told you that from his uniform," said Jeremiah. "That silver bar on his lapel? You only get that by personally killing over 100 enemy combatants. Personally."

"It would seem our Commander Rantallion is far more than he lets on," said Millie.

"Indeed, so you'll forgive me if I don't exactly believe that Tomason Sudworth never made it to the station."

Chapter Six

The next morning, Jeremiah met Millie at the railyard just after the sun came up. He had expected to have some difficulty in getting the full story out of the station master, but when he arrived it was to find that Millie already had the man wrapped around her finger.

"Ah, Jeremiah, so dear of you to join us," she said as he approached. The station master had been leaning over the counter toward her in a conspiratorial whisper but he straightened up quickly as the man approached. "I was just talking to Trevor here about that ghastly incident we read about in the paper."

"Um, yeah, as I was saying, Miss, I don't know what paper you read it in but they didn't say much about it to anybody. Awful business, though. Just awful." He started shuffling papers on the desk in front of him, shaking his head.

"Indeed. Perhaps you can elaborate as I'm only just joining you," said Jeremiah.

"Train came in, all sorts of hubbub about a shootout. Seems some robbers shot up one of the cars and must have done some real damage because there was blood everywh—" he stopped himself and glanced at Millie. "Begging your pardon, Miss."

She reached across the counter and patted his arm. "I assure you, Trevor, that nothing you can tell me can even hold a candle to the absolute horrors that this man exposes me to daily, so rest easy and speak freely."

Trevor shot Jeremiah a look and cleared his throat. "Yes, well, as I said there was blood everywhere. And... other bits of things."

"Which train was this?" asked Jeremiah.

"Ah, yes sir, that was on the 209. It came from Fleis that morning doing the full run of the rail."

"Do you have a notion as to where the incident occurred?" asked Jeremiah.

Trevor shuffled through the papers and pulled up a register. "Says here that it was just outside of Strode on the way to Peyze. It was about halfway between the two."

"And I trust the bodies of the fallen were taken to the medical examiner?" asked Jeremiah.

"Well, that's the thing, sir. There weren't none."

"No bodies?" asked Millie with shock.

"No, Miss. From what Miss Devyn told us the robbers threw all the bodies off the train, even a few survivors. She was lucky to survive at all, as she tells it."

"Miss Devyn?" asked Jeremiah and Millie in unison.

"Young lady, picked up by the 307 a couple of hours after the shootout on the 209. She and a soldier boy flagged them down asking for help. We don't normally stop and pick people up, mind you, because of marauders, but as it was a young lady and a soldier they stopped for them. I tell you, things were a right mess here until she came in and filled us in on what happened, but even she couldn't say much on account of being traumatized and all. Poor girl."

"She told you what happened?" asked Millie. "What did the soldier say happened? Was it the same story?"

"That's the other thing, Miss. He was picked up, but as far as we know he disappeared before the train got to Tamarind. Maybe he got off on an earlier stop, although it wouldn't seem likely as he was pretty banged up and all. Still, when the 307 got here, he wasn't on board. Poor Miss Devyn was beside herself with worry as the boy had apparently saved her life."

"I think it may benefit us to speak with Miss Devyn, if you think that's possible," said Jeremiah. Millie nodded.

"I wish you the best with making that happen, sir. We've been unable to get anything further out of her since her fiancé told us to take a walk. Seems he doesn't want her being fussed about the whole thing anymore. Trouble is, we don't know where to send the effects."

"Her fiancé? Who might that be?" asked Jeremiah.

"And what effects? Maybe we can help with that," added Millie.

"It's a sweet story if you think about it. Poor girl goes through all that then meets her future husband on the same day. The man's name is Lord Edmund Mingent and I have to tell you, I've never seen a man more smitten in my life. It's good though. That poor girl deserves something good to happen after all that."

"As it would happen I know Lord Mingent very well," said Jeremiah.

"Good, then maybe you can find out where we should send these," said Trevor, pulling a worn cardboard box out from under the counter. Inside were some random objects: a pocket watch, a rabbit's foot, and a wallet.

Millie opened the wallet to see two things that shook her, namely Tommy Sudworth's recruit ID badge and a picture of a girl. She snapped it shut before Jeremiah noticed and scooped up the other items, slipping them all into her bag.

"We will find out, Trevor, don't you worry your handsome head about it," she said, tapping the man on the nose.

He blushed and shuffled his feet, making Jeremiah fight the urge to bark a laugh.

"I appreciate it, Miss. Sure will be nice to have that off my plate."

They left the man and hailed a carriage.

"How do you know Lord Mingent?" asked Millie, once they were inside and trundling along.

"Nice man, smells a bit odd. I did some work for him in the past, while his wife was still alive. Some missing jewelry needed to be found. Pretty cut and dried, as the maid was a notorious thief but managed to convince him and his wife she was someone else. I suppose that means he owes me, though I'm not sure he would see it that way."

"Well, can't hurt to ask," she said.

"We have the Sudworth boy's ID card, right? That should legitimize our inquiry a little more with the man. What was the picture?"

Millie shrugged. "A girl."

"Let me see," he said, holding out his hand.

Millie handed him the wallet and waited. Jeremiah was nothing if not observant.

He studied the picture for a few seconds before handing it back to her. He didn't say anything, but she could tell by the look in his eyes he had already pieced together the connection.

"Her name is Lallie, short for Eleanor, and for all I knew she was through with him years ago," she said. "And as you've no doubt deduced, she is my sister."

⚜

Chapter Seven

It was rare that a person who didn't spend most of their time working in The Centre found themselves visiting all four quadrants of the city in a single day. There were plenty enough distractions in any one of them—business dealings and proper theater in the West, trading and supply runs in the North, or even gambling and prostitution in The Bottoms—that most found little reason to journey into the eastern portion, and the people who lived there preferred it that way.

Looking out the correct windows in The Centre, a person could see that the houses were of a much finer quality in the Tamarind Gardens, as that portion of the city was pompously named—less concrete and wood and more brick and granite. The roads were better, too, with more effort being put into maintaining them providing that maintenance did not occur during times of day that inconvenienced the inhabitants. Put simply, the eastern quadrant of Tamarind was where the 'well-to-do' lived, and they would thank you for remembering it.

Lord Edmund Mingent lived in a portion of The Gardens where the stately homes took the shape of brownstones—elegant, multi-story structures sandwiched together, their shared walls reinforced to prevent the passage of sound and anything remotely resembling neighborliness. The homes were remarkable in that they were not remarkable, all sharing identical facades differentiated only by tiny gold numbers situated on the columns in front of each entryway.

Jeremiah had the carriage drop them directly in front of Number 14, The Green, which sat directly in the center of a seemingly endless row of such homes. He had been quiet since Millie's revelation, and chose the moment when the both of them were standing at the door to finally broach his concerns.

"Did you petition for this job out of sympathy for me?"

Millie shook her head. "No, Jeremiah. You know I'm not in touch with my family anymore."

"Why didn't you tell me you knew the missing man? Why did you pretend you barely knew them? If the young man had a picture of your sister in his wallet—"

"Then it would stand to reason that he was a close friend of the family," finished Millie. "And if you knew I was associated with him then you would have turned down the case."

"To keep you from having to deal with your family," he said. He was staring at the door, his hand halfway out to push the bell. Millie wondered if they would have the whole conversation on the stoop.

"First of all, I don't need protecting," she said, a little testier than she meant.

Jeremiah sighed. "I know, I just—"

"I didn't know this was coming your way. I had no involvement in it at all. For all I know my mother recommended you because you were the only name she had in Tamarind."

Jeremiah pushed the button causing a loud gong sound to come from within.

"I didn't think of that," he said.

"Of course you didn't," responded Millie. "Because you're an idiot."

Jeremiah laughed as the door opened revealing a severe man in a suit who looked at him like his laughter was an affront to good taste, an attitude that he no doubt applied to all joviality.

"Jeremiah Mountweazel and Millie Mondegreen to see Lord Mingent," said Jeremiah. He handed the man a card that was snatched from his hand with impatience and placed on a tray.

"Please wait in the hall," said the man, and he turned and left without further ceremony.

"Charming man," muttered Jeremiah.

"Compared to my mother's butler this man is practically a ray of sunshine," said Millie with a shrug. She looked around the hall, taking in the decor. Lord Mingent's taste was as identical to every other bachelor's as his front door was to the next seven. Weapons of various sizes and uses hung alongside the taxidermied heads of numerous animals from the leonine to the vulpine, and the prize of the collection, an enormous elephant head with one broken tusk, hung over the stairs.

"Your man is a hunter?" Millie asked.

"Was. Not as much anymore," he said.

"Jeremiah," said a loud voice from the top of the stairs, "what a pleasure to see you again."

The speaker was an older man, hair long gone ghostly white to match his pale complexion, and he slowly descended the staircase with the help of a cane on one side and the rail on the other. Millie could see how hunting was no longer an option for someone who had such trouble with mobility.

"Lord Mingent, the pleasure is mine," answered Jeremiah.

"Oh, away with that Lord nonsense, my boy," said Mingent.

He got to the bottom of the stairs and made his way across the marble floor to them. It was only when he was a few feet away that Jeremiah moved forward to meet him, and Millie was pleased that her companion had at least remembered that bit of what she taught him.

"Teddy, you old rascal, you're looking good," said Jeremiah, shaking the man's free hand. He turned and gestured to her. "My colleague, Millie Mondegreen."

Lord Mingent graced her with a lethargic smile. "Jeremiah did always have a knack for finding beauty in the world," he said.

Millie took his outstretched hand and caught wind of the odd smell that Jeremiah had warned her about. She was happy she had been warned so she was able to control her reaction. "Lord Mingent, you flatter me."

"I have to get it in while I can so my dear Posie doesn't catch me," he said with a conspiratorial wink. "She doesn't like to share me."

Jeremiah cleared his throat. "Actually, Teddy, it was your fiancée we came to speak with, if that is at all possible. It's about that awful business on the train."

Mingent's smile faded. "My poor girl suffered quite the fright on that day. I'd rather you didn't ask her to relive it if it's all the same to you, my friend." He released Millie's hand and stood as straight as his bent spine would allow, an old man's attempt at posturing.

"I assure you we have no wish to upset your beloved, but I've been asked to look for someone who was on the train with her, and she's our only potential source for real, useful information," said Jeremiah.

Mingent frowned. He tapped his cane on the floor as he spoke, adding emphasis. "I will not have her bothered, Jeremiah. She is too dear to me."

When the echo of the cane died down a pleasant voice descended from the top of the staircase. "What will you not have me bothered with, my love?"

Jeremiah and Millie looked upwards, and Mingent turned to look along with them as the young lady came down the stairs. By best estimation she had been in the world a quarter of the years that Mingent had, and so the adoring gaze with which she graced the old man seemed more belonging to a granddaughter for her grandfather, not a bride for a groom. One only had to look at Mingent's face to see that he thought otherwise.

"It's alright, my dear, go back to your rooms. My friend Jeremiah was just leaving," said Mingent.

"Don't be rude, Teddy. If they are here to see me I should be seen. I so rarely get company from outside of the house." She was sweet in everything she did, from her tone to the gentle way she placed her hand on her betrothed's arm. There was no doubt in anyone's mind that Mingent would do anything and everything to make her happy.

"I am sorry to intrude," said Jeremiah.

"Nonsense. No friend of Teddy's could ever be an intrusion in my life," said Posie. "What is it you would like to ask me?"

"It's about the unfortunate train journey you took recently," said Jeremiah.

No one had the presence of mind or ability to catch her when she fainted to the floor.

Chapter Eight

"It all happened so quickly, it's hard to tell it," Posie said quietly. She was propped up on a chaise lounge in a large study with a pillow behind her back and a doting Lord Mingent standing behind her shaking his head.

"You don't have to go through this, my dear," he pleaded with her.

She looked back and smiled at him, placing her hand on his and squeezing it gently. "I know, thank you, Teddy," she said, "but if it will help these people find that poor boy, then I'll do what I can. He was such a helpful gentleman. Truly an honor to his uniform."

"Why don't you tell us what you remember? Don't rush yourself," said Jeremiah. He and Millie were sitting in front of her in chairs that they had dragged over from the other side of the room to be close enough to hear her quiet words. Millie kept silent and studied the girl.

Posie closed her eyes for a moment and took a deep breath.

"I was sitting in the car along with a bunch of other people— the two soldier boys, a couple of spinsters, two rough looking men, several gentlemen of no note. It was a pleasant day. A good day for a journey. I was excited to be seeing Tamarind for the first time. Gosh, I was excited by everything."

She twisted a handkerchief in her hand as she spoke and occasionally dabbed at her eyes with it.

"Why were you on the train?" asked Millie, in a harsher tone than Jeremiah thought warranted.

"It was my big adventure. I had always heard how grand life in Tamarind was, how diverse and unique. How a person could start a new life there. I wanted to do that," said Posie. She stared off in the distance as she spoke. "I was done with the small town life. I wanted to see more of the world."

"What town are you from, Miss Devyn?"

"A little two horse town called Tohester. It's a ways north of Tippoli, but still this side of the Chetans. Have you heard of it?"

Jeremiah shook his head.

"It's lovely this time of year, I'll admit. There's nothing better than sitting on the porch in the evening listening to the crickets sing to each other. It's a magical kind of music," said Posie.

Millie seemed to soften a bit, but only a little. "So you hopped on a train and headed out? What was the plan? Did you have someone here you were in contact with?"

"What my friend means, Miss Devyn, is surely it was already unsafe for you to be travelling alone. It must have been very upsetting indeed when things transpired," added Jeremiah. Millie shot him a look and he returned it.

"I know it sounds crazy, but I had no plan. There was nothing for me back home. No work, no real family to speak of save an abusive aunt and several slow-witted cousins. It was a dead end and I wanted out. So yes, Miss Mondegreen, I made a foolish choice and bought a ticket out of there, and then it became obvious how very foolish I had been."

She began to cry, quietly, into her handkerchief. Mingent tutted and squeezed her shoulder, casting a stern look at the two inquisitors.

"What happened?" asked Jeremiah gently.

Posie took a deep breath, let it out slowly, and looked up at him through red eyes. "I heard a shot ring out and there was... well... someone was hit. It was everywhere. And then there were screams. The two men, the rough-looking ones I mentioned, were waving guns around. They had killed one of the soldier boys and another boy and were threatening to do the same to anyone else who didn't do what they said."

As she recounted the tale she stared directly into Jeremiah's eyes.

"I thought they were going to kill me and the others. They took our valuables. I had little to offer so I thought that would be the end of me. They were so awful. The bald one pointed his gun right in my face and—"

She broke down into tears again, sobbing uncontrollably this time. Mingent wrapped his arms around her shoulders and let her cry into his sleeve, glaring at the two of them the entire time. Jeremiah shrugged and mouthed "sorry" to the man.

Millie moved over to sit next to the girl and gently took her hand. "Posie, I know this is hard, but if you can get through it you will be doing us a great service.

Posie looked up and suddenly threw her arms around her, crying onto her shoulder. Millie rubbed her back and shushed her. After a few moments Posie regained her composure and sat back up.

"I'm ever so sorry. It was a difficult experience to say the least," she said.

"You have no need to apologize," said Jeremiah. He looked to Millie.

"What happened next, Posie? You can do it. I'm here with you," she said, rubbing the girl's hand.

"The brutes threw open the side door and threw some people from the train. Both of the soldiers and a few other—" she drew a rasping breath "—bodies went out, and then they grabbed me. I just didn't know what they intended to do with me and before I knew what was happening I was in the air and the ground came up so quickly."

She was staring out the window, her eyes filled with fear.

"I don't remember landing. The next thing I knew I was waking up and everything hurt. My shoulder still pains me." Mingent began to massage her shoulder until she shooed him off. "I found the boy you are looking for and he was banged up pretty bad too. He couldn't see because of hitting the rocks or something. I don't know. There was a lot of blood. He had a hurt foot, too, so I helped him up and we made our way back up to the tracks and waved down the next train we saw. Honestly, I thought we would die out there, but I kept my spirits up and tried to keep Tommy's up as well."

Millie thought back to the young Tomason Sudworth and how his enthusiasm always lit up the room. On top of that, unlike most of the suitors who circled her home like vultures, Tommy was always polite and respectful, even once her mother had left

the room. She imagined it was one of the things that drew Lallie
to the boy.

"So you got on the next train, the 307?" said Jeremiah.

Mingent cleared his throat. "And that's where fortune smiled
on us both, because that's when my beautiful fiancée came into
my life," said the man with pride.

Posie smiled. "That dark day turned sunny the moment I met
my dear Teddy."

Jeremiah made an appreciative noise but Millie steered
them back.

"Tommy. What happened to Tommy?" she asked.

"I don't know, Millie. Honestly, I don't. When they took us on
board, we were both in bad shape. They took him off to fix him
up and they did the same with me. I was able to walk though, and
once they were done I made my way to a seater car and that's
when I met Teddy. I never saw Tommy again." She shook her
head sadly. "I wish I could tell you more, but that's all there is to
it. Teddy took me into his care and he showed me such loving
attention that I was delighted when he proposed we make the
temporary living situation permanent."

"So you live here?" asked Jeremiah.

Mingent blustered. "Now see here, my boy, there's nothing
untoward happening here. Posie has her own rooms and—"

"I never meant to suggest otherwise," laughed Jeremiah,
holding his hands up. "I merely wanted to make sure of where we
could find the young lady if we needed anything more from her."

Mingent stood. "I don't think that will be necessary, do you,
Jeremiah? Surely you've troubled her enough."

Posie reached out and took Mingent's hand. "Teddy, don't be
rude on my behalf. If there is anything more I can do please don't
hesitate to ask. Isn't that right, my dear?" She looked up into the
disapproving eyes of her fiancé and his face changed to absolute
compliance.

"As you wish, my love," he said. "Jeremiah, I think it's time you
left for now. Posie needs her rest."

As if on cue she laid her head back and closed her eyes. The
three left the room quietly and Mingent walked them to
the door.

"I will do anything she asks, Jeremiah, but I won't have you
bothering her unnecessarily. As you can see, she has been through
a lot," he said sternly as he shook his hand.

"I understand, Teddy. Believe me, I do," said Jeremiah. "One more question, if you don't mind. Whereabouts on the line was she picked up?"

"Is that important?" asked Mingent.

"There may be clues there," suggested Millie. "We're looking for anything."

"As I recall, it was between Stode and Peyze, although closer to Stode," said Mingent.

"Thank you, Teddy. You've both been very helpful."

Mingent shrugged. "Always happy to help an old friend, Jeremiah. I hope you find the boy, although it doesn't sound like the chances are in your favor."

As they walked down the steps neither said a word. They continued down the street in silence, both lost in thought. Finally, it was Millie who spoke.

"I'm sorry I lied."

"Water under the bridge, my friend. But you can make it up to me if you'd like," he said.

Millie groaned. "Don't make me work that case for the Hyphen Ladies."

Jeremiah laughed. "No, nothing that harsh. I would just like it if you would pay another visit to Miss Devyn and Teddy. Maybe take the girl out to lunch. She's been through a lot and he's clearly bothered by it all and on top of that completely smitten. I need to make sure he's alright."

"And you want me to make sure she's not taking advantage of an old man's generosity," added Millie.

He laughed again. "That too. Can you do that for me?"

"Will do," she said.

"Also, if you could make contact with your boyfriend at the railyard and see if you can find out anything more about what became of Tommy after they were picked up. Maybe he knows who looked after each of them."

Millie nodded. "And what will you be doing in the meantime?"

"I'm going to take a little ride down the rails. Maybe if I can find where they were ejected I can find something. Anything."

"So, you have to take a long ride and a long, sweaty walk down some tracks and I get to go out to a nice place for lunch. I'm okay with that," said Millie.

"I had a feeling you would be," he laughed.

Chapter Nine

Jeremiah had a decision to make. He could wait until the following day to head west or he could head out immediately. Train journeys were far more enjoyable if they started in the early morning, as the cars were generally sparsely filled and it was possible to get some privacy to think. However, every moment he left it made the trail go that much more cold, and as it had already been two weeks since the events on the 209 train, he was loath to leave it.

He was still mulling over the decision as he climbed the stairs to his rooms and noticed the entry door was ajar.

His profession meant that he often came in contact with ne'er-do-wells and ruffians, but it was a rarity that they invaded his home. Usually their forms of intimidation used dark alleys or deserted streets as their stage. A man knew what to do in a dark alley. There were rules. Home invasion, in contrast, is infinitely more unsettling. Who knows how many drawers the person has riffled through or how much of the whisky they had consumed?

He briefly entertained the notion that it may be Millie inside, but he ruled that out for two reasons: he had only just left her and, slovenly though she was in her personal habits, she was never one to leave a door open as a matter of rule.

He released the catch on his cane to make pulling the sword free a quicker endeavor and cautiously toed the door open. Inside he saw the thoroughly irritating image of the rude young man from the Authority compound casually reading a book by the window.

"I don't recall arranging a visit, soldier," he said, pushing the door all the way open and surveying the room. He was relieved to see there was not a platoon of soldiers waiting in the shadowy corners.

"You'll pardon the intrusion, I'm sure, Mr. Mountweazel, but it wouldn't do for me to have to wait for you in that disgusting restaurant downstairs or even worse, in the street," said the young man as he closed the book and slipped it back onto the shelf.

"I think you'll find I will not pardon the intrusion at all, Mr.—" He realized he didn't know the boy's name and left the pause in the air as a question.

"Cross. Corporal Cross," said the intruder in response. He took another book off of the shelf and began to thumb through it. "You read strange things, Mr. Mountweazel."

Jeremiah closed the door and walked around to sit behind his desk.

"As I was saying, Cross, you'll find I will not pardon the intrusion at all and would thank you to either take a seat or leave. As an option, making yourself at home is off the table." He gestured to a chair, noticing as he did so a wooden box sitting in the middle of his desk. "What's this?"

Cross shelved the book and sat in the offered chair, upright and stiff as though he was sitting on a baton. "We will get to that," he said with a forced smile. "First, I would like to ask that you forgo any further investigation into the matter of the disappearance of Recruit Sudworth. It is drawing unwelcome attention to our efforts here."

Jeremiah knew Ward wouldn't let this situation sit unmentioned. He could picture his friend now, triumphantly charging into Cavil's office with proof that they had the Authority louts 'by the short hairs', as he liked to say.

"I'm afraid I can't do that, Cross. I've been hired to discover the truth and that is what I will do," said Jeremiah simply as he steepled his fingers under his chin. "No amount of intimidation on your part will change that fact."

Cross laughed. "My good man, I am not here to try and intimidate you in the slightest, only to pass on the request. We in the Authority try to maintain a healthy, helpful working relationship with the locals in any place we occupy."

Jeremiah stared at the man and received an icy stare back. All kindness in the words were tainted by the soldier's expression, like he was talking to a dog that had just wet the flooring.

"You've delivered your message. Good day to you," he said finally.

Cross put up his hands in supplication. "We seem to have gotten off on the wrong foot here, Mr. Mountweazel."

"Breaking into a man's home will do that."

Cross sighed. "Indeed. I do apologize. I wonder if you might be swayed by the offer of a larger fee than you would achieve with whatever limited completion of this investigation you can manage. Say, double?"

Jeremiah shook his head.

"Triple then. You're a man of means by appearance but your quarters tell a different story. Surely you could benefit from such a healthy paycheck."

Though Jeremiah's thoughts briefly danced with the prospect of being that financially settled, he continued to shake his head. "I will not be threatened or bought off, soldier. Will there be anything else?"

Cross stood, barely containing his irritation. "I will pass on your response to my Commander, Mr. Mountweazel, though I'm certain he will be displeased."

"What does the Authority have to hide that you're making this play, Cross? What have you done with the boy?" asked Jeremiah.

Cross turned and walked to the door. "I will not validate that ludicrous question with any sort of answer, Mr. Mountweazel. The only thing I will say before I leave this squalid hole you call a home is that the next time, if there ever is one, that you have the chance to be graced with permission to step one foot onto our property, you will be thoroughly searched, as will anyone who accompanies you." He glanced down at the box on the desk then back up. "Good day to you."

He was gracious enough to close the door as he left. Jeremiah reached out and lifted the lid on the box, unsurprised to see the crushed remains of the surveillance crawler he had left in Rantallion's office.

Spurred on by the incident, he packed a small bag and headed to the train station. Nothing would delay him now.

Chapter Ten

Millie decided to walk home from the railyard after she had spoken to Trevor again. The man was overjoyed to once again be receiving her attention, and while she outwardly rewarded his reactions with giggles and blushes, inwardly she bristled at the man being called her 'boyfriend' by Jeremiah. She knew he meant it as a playful jab, but comments like that made her wonder if he took her seriously at all.

She was happy that Posie had been so receptive to having lunch with her the next day. Mingent hadn't been too pleased to see her on his doorstep again so shortly after being shooed away, but his young fiancée had eagerly jumped at the chance to have some time with her. It was likely having her elderly fiancé and the surly butler as companions left her wanting a little more.

Millie could tell that the girl was out of her depth in that big house. Posie came from a small town and had no idea how to conduct herself, a failure that went overlooked by Mingent but would not be so easily dismissed by the members of the man's social circle. It was like meeting Jeremiah all over again. Both were hopeless when it came to high society.

She would help Posie learn to at least fake it, she decided. She would take the poor girl under her wing and teach her the important things, like when to curtsy and which fork to use for her salad. It wasn't a world Millie had any use for anymore, but at least she could help Posie elevate to where she wanted to be, just like Millie had been able to descend to where she was more comfortable.

That was if the girl could handle it. The way she had fainted didn't speak well to her endurance. Still, most women from the upper crust only remained upright due to their corsets in Millie's experience.

Her conversation with Trevor reminded her that women on this level of society were regarded less as decorative showpieces and more as potential playthings. He had been very revealing with information while he thought he was in with a chance, but once she began to rebuff his advances she found him to be less agreeable. Once she felt his hand on her bottom she was left with little option but to twist his fingers in directions they were not meant to go, and while he got the message that she wasn't interested in that sort of conversation, he refused to cooperate afterwards.

He had given her enough, though. There had been a doctor on board who patched up both Posie and Tommy. Posie had been put into a private room to relax until the train arrived in Tamarind, and Tommy had been set up in the crew car on a cot to rest. This arrangement had little to do with gender and more to do with the fact that Tommy needed to be readily accessible and watchable, his state was so poor.

When the 307 arrived in Tamarind a search had been conducted, but there was no sign of Tommy. Posie was easily found blushing under the attention of Lord Mingent, but the soldier was missing. Various theories had been bandied about regarding his absence, ranging from him hiding from the shame of his failure to protect the people on the 209, to a darker theory that the Authority had spirited him away before he could be collected. They were certainly present at the station on that day.

Millie wasn't sure what to believe. She crossed the bridge back into The Bottoms and stopped to ponder the options. Either the boy had been taken by the Authority and they were lying about that fact, or he had abandoned the train before it reached Tamarind. Surely it would benefit the Authority to produce proof of his existence to remove any doubt of wrongdoing. The rumors of failed recruits being shipped off to mines, or worse, made such a public statement almost a necessity if for no other reason than to quell the rumors before they got more strength. On the other hand, from what she was told by the overly-amorous Trevor, the boy was in no shape to take himself anywhere, and even if he

could, why not wait until he was in the city where it was easier
to disappear?

Her musings were interrupted by movement from the other
end of the bridge. At this time of the evening the traffic on the
bridge was minimal, most having already arrived home from their
work or not yet risen to get to it, depending on how they made
their way in the world. The remarkable thing about the
movement was that it was a person, and not just any person but
none other than Mrs. Baader-Meinhoff who, upon spotting
Millie, quickly turned and walked in the other direction,
pretending for all the world that she had heard a friend
calling her.

Millie chuckled. She wasn't sure why she kept seeing the lady,
but it did serve to remind her that at some point, the Pansophic
Order of the Belletrist would be calling to demand answers, and
finding them was the farthest thing from her mind.

She found herself wishing she was on the train with Jeremiah,
assuming he had already headed down the tracks. She had joked
with him that she had it easy with the cush jobs of having lunch
and flirting, but the truth was she was happiest while actively on
the trail of the truth alongside the man. Besides, someone had to
keep him from making an ass of himself.

She continued across the bridge toward her home and noticed
almost immediately that someone was tailing her. One glance
revealed it was not the cherubic Mrs. Baader-Meinhoff as she
had hoped, but a tall figure in a black cloak.

"Subtle," she muttered, walking along as if she hadn't noticed.
The street became more populated as she moved into The
Bottoms, the inhabitants here being more inclined to nighttime
work than anything reputable that happened in the day. She
wasn't sure if it was one of those lurking individuals who was
following her or someone new, but either way, she wasn't going to
tolerate it.

Someone skilled at following a person would have been able
to spot certain clues that told them that the game was up—
stuttered movement, repeated glances over the shoulder, breaking
into a run. Millie gave the person none of those clues, but she did
make a show of being seen turning down an alleyway before
slipping off the leather belt she wore around her waist and
leaping into the air to grab onto the lower rung of a fire ladder.

She pulled herself up and looped her legs over to allow herself to hang upside down and waited. It wasn't long before the person, obvious by their mannerism not to be of the local variety of assailants, turned down the alley and began a seemingly desperate scan for her whereabouts. As she suspected, the hood kept them from being able to see up.

She slipped the looped belt around the person's neck and pulled up sharply, pulling herself up in the process to climb up the ladder. The choking and flailing from below let her know her trap was a success.

"Who, I have to ask myself, is stupid enough to follow a seemingly defenseless young lady into a dark alley, aside from someone too incredibly idiotic to realize she surely couldn't be as defenseless as she seems?" she asked aloud.

The person clutched at the belt but was unable to pull free. She kept it just taut enough to keep them on their tiptoes.

"Now, if you want to regain the ability to breathe, you're going to drop your hood and show yourself. Understood?"

Unable to answer, the person yanked the hood down as quickly as they could, revealing a young man with a severe haircut who was at that moment turning a bright shade of crimson.

Millie laughed. "Now what would a wet-behind-the-ears lackbeard of an ass-kissing Authority boy want with little old me?" she asked. She swung down and landed in front of him as he gasped for breath and pulled the belt off of his head. When he looked up it was to see a small pistol in her hand pointed at him.

"I was—" he choked. "I was told to watch you and wait for orders, is all, ma'am."

Millie swung the belt over her head and brought it down on his shoulder, eliciting a cry from the boy. She struck him again for good measure.

"Somebody should tell you ladies don't like strange men following them around, and I guess that someone just has to be me," she hissed, striking him a few more times.

He cowered and covered his head. "Please, I was just doing what I was told."

Millie stopped hitting him and knelt down to look him in the eyes. As she spoke she pointed her pistol back and forth from one eye to the other. "If I see you again, boy, I will kill you. Go home and tell your masters that they are messing with the wrong lady if they think they can intimidate me. Got it?" She could see that several of her blows had hit him across the cheek, leaving a deep red welt.

He nodded and began to back away. She lashed out one more time with the belt and brought a yelp from him as he bolted back into the street.

She waited until he had disappeared from sight before she braced herself against the wall, her heart racing. She had learned long ago that to survive in this world, in this area of town especially, it paid to make people think you were a force to be reckoned with. Make them fear you a little and they'll think twice about misjudging you. She forced her breathing to steady and allowed the relief to wash over her. He had practically been a kid. It could have been much worse.

Millie slid her pistol back into the hidden holster and slipped the belt back around her waist before continuing home, her eyes watching the shadows as always.

Chapter Eleven

Things rarely work out so perfectly as they did when Jeremiah purchased his ticket and found himself riding on the 209 train to Fleis, although he was mildly irked to discover that the passenger car in question was still at the station, having been replaced by a spare car while the other was being cleaned. Still, he was assured that the passenger car that he found himself in was identical in every way save for the lack of blood stains and broken door latch.

It was a busy car he found himself in, but that didn't stop him from wandering as he inspected the layout. The car was completely open, with four seating areas on each side, benches facing shared tables so that each section would allow for six passengers. As it was, there wasn't a section that contained fewer than four people. By Posie's description the car she was in wasn't even half as full.

He tried to imagine what he would do if an altercation broke out on this train. Would he try to hide beneath the table? Would he stand and fight? He was certain he wouldn't do anything to invite harm to himself, and he could only imagine what it would be like were he a young woman like Posie.

As the train rumbled into Thorpeworth, he moved to the door and stood there, as out of the way as he could manage, while people filed in and out. The distance to the ground between the train and the platform wasn't too high, but he knew in between towns it could be higher. Add to that the speed at which the train would be moving at full tilt, and it truly was a miracle Posie had survived the fall. He suspected the Sudworth boy would have been made of sturdier stuff, but judging by the injuries Posie reported that the boy had sustained it may not have mattered.

They passed through Peyze with an even shorter stop and Jeremiah began to watch, realizing as he did that the likelihood of him spotting anything while moving at this speed was fairly slim. Still, he watched, taking in every odd feature as a possible clue. The fact that there was little in the way of civilization between the towns did not escape his notice, and he wondered how Tommy and Posie would have fared if they hadn't managed to flag down the next train.

As the train pulled into Stode, Jeremiah gathered his things and deboarded. He still had a few hours of daylight left, and he didn't want them to go to waste. He made haste to the stables and rented a horse off a man named Hobson who assured him that he could either return the beast there in Stode or at the stables either in Tippoli to the west or Peyze to the east.

He found himself regretting not bringing Millie along as he rode east, and tried to look for signs of the aftermath Posie had described. An extra set of eyes would have been helpful, as well as someone to talk to while he looked.

"Just you and me out here, old girl," he said, patting the horse's neck. The horse snorted in response and carried on walking alongside the tracks. Judging from Posie's description of the area, he knew that the ground fell away some ways from the track near where they had flagged down the second train, because she had talked about the trouble they had climbing up.

It was an hour outside of Stode that the ground started falling away, and it wasn't long after that before Jeremiah realized it wasn't just his eyes that would help him find his quarry. The smell of decay became stronger and stronger as he walked along, enough that his horse began to balk at going further.

"Easy there, Buttercup," he said, stroking the agitated horse's neck. He pulled her to a halt and dropped off, wrapping the reins around a scrub of a tree. There were boulders throughout this part that made it hard to see very far, and he made his way around these carefully, looking for anything aside from the stench to show him what happened.

He saw the recruit's body first up ahead, and then almost immediately noticed the stains up against one boulder. As he approached the body he pulled a handkerchief out of his pocket and tied it around his head to cover his mouth and nose.

The remains had been set upon by wild birds, judging by the missing eyeballs, and more than a few other animals based on the empty abdominal cavity. Through the blood stains Jeremiah could still tell that the uniform was from the Authority, and he searched through the pockets until he came up satisfied with the boy's wallet.

It was difficult to judge only by the face in the picture, the damage was so extensive. The identification card named him as Derek Fairburn, and there were enough similarities between the remains and the picture to make Jeremiah think they were very likely one and the same. He found himself relieved that it wasn't the Sudworth boy, but also sad at the waste of life.

The screech of a vulture pulled his attention further up, and he saw another body. As he approached and shooed away the bird he realized the clothes were more common, not a uniform like Fairburn wore. The state of it was even worse than Fairburn's, so he couldn't make out any identifying features.

"You must be one of the other unfortunate souls," said Jeremiah as he searched the remains, but found nothing of value or note. "When I send them for Fairburn I'll send them for you as well, rest assured."

He surveyed the area thinking about the two survivors of the encounter, broken and bloodied and afraid for their lives. The events had clearly taken a toll on Posie, and while he hoped that Tommy was made of stronger stuff, something obviously went wrong for him to disappear like that.

He pulled a branch free from a dead tree and ripped away some of the white cloth from Fairburn's uniform to fashion a sort of flag, which he drove into the earth next to the tracks after making the difficult climb. That would tell them where to retrieve the bodies.

"Come on, girl, let's get you home," he said as he pulled the reins free and climbed up onto Buttercup. Heading back, he didn't need to be nearly as meticulous, and he got back in half the time.

As he rode, he thought more about everything the girl had gone through out there in the wild, and it occurred to him that her family may be worried about her.

Hobson was surprised to see him.

"I thought for sure you'd go straight on through to Peyze," he said, rubbing a dirty cloth across his forehead to wipe away the sweat.

"Well, I'm not sure I'm ready to give her back yet," said Jeremiah. "Tell me, how far of a ride is it from here to Tohester?"

"Why in the hells would you want to go to Tohester?" laughed Hobson. "There's nothing there but cows and midges."

"I'm told I have family there," said Jeremiah, not sure why he was bothering to lie. "Thought I might pay them a visit."

"Well, it's a two hour ride if you stick with it, so if you have a place to stay then you could head out now and almost get there before dark. But if you don't, I would suggest going that way in the morning. Folks in those parts aren't too kindly to strangers wandering around their towns at night, if you know what I mean."

Jeremiah nodded, handing the man the reins to Buttercup. "Can I get her back in the morning?"

"If she's here," said Hobson. "If not, you'll take what I have. That's how it works."

Jeremiah left the man and his horse and headed to the inn for a good night's sleep.

Chapter Twelve

"**B**y the gods, it feels so good to get out of that house!" said Posie as they sat down at the table. "I mean, I really appreciate all of the care and adoration, but sometimes a girl has to get out and stretch her legs, if you know what I mean."

Millie laughed and waved to the waiter. She had decided against taking Posie to something as complicated as High Tea on their first outing together. Best to ease the girl into things instead of overwhelming her with too much at once.

"Lord Mingent does seem to dote on you," she said. "One would almost wonder what you have done to capture his heart so absolutely." She waggled her eyebrows and laughed again as the other girl blushed.

"Oh no, nothing like that, Millie. He's a perfect gentleman. He won't even come onto my side of the house without invitation, and he hasn't set foot inside my bedroom since moving me in. It's his house and he is freely giving it over to me so I can heal."

"Must be quite a change coming from a small town to suddenly living in a fancy home with a butler," said Millie.

Posie nodded emphatically. "It's a whole new world. You have no idea what it's like to be waited on hand and foot."

And there it was. Either Millie had been living the normal life for so long that she had lost the inherent air of pomposity that came with her name, or this girl was so clueless that she thought Millie was also out of her element.

"Posie, I may not have mentioned, and believe me I do not mention it now to gain any sort of awe or adoration, but I come from this world." She waved her hand around. "I chose to leave it behind because it didn't suit me, but this was my world for the first two decades of my life."

"Oooh, I had no idea I was dining with the hoity-toity. Should I curtsy?" teased Posie.

"Yes," laughed Millie, "You most certainly should. But only every time I enter or leave a room."

Both women laughed, and Millie realized how much she missed having someone to talk to who was, if not similar to her, at least similarly out of place.

"Teddy keeps telling me not to worry. Once we're married, he will get me all the help I need with the house and with any social obligations. Honestly, it's terrifying. I'm just a simple girl. I keep telling him I'm not up to the task, but he won't hear it."

"Men can be stubborn when they see something they want. Or someone," said Millie, pointing at the girl. "Don't be afraid to put your foot down. If that old man wants what he wants out of you, it's to be expected that he should give you some of what you want as well. And if you need help with any of the fancy things," Millie said, reaching across and taking Posie's hand. "I'm here to help."

Posie smiled. "The past few weeks have been such a whirlwind of terror and happiness that I don't know if I'm coming or going."

Millie nodded solemnly. "I went through just such a period of time. Then I met Jeremiah."

"So what's the story with you two?" asked Posie, the teasing tone returning to her voice. "How long have you been together?"

Millie barked a short laugh. "We're not at all together in that notion, my friend. Our relationship is purely professional. Although, some time when we have access to wine, remind me to tell you how we met and you may think otherwise."

Posie raised a finger and said, 'Wine, please." She meant it as a joke, but within a minute a waiter was at their table pouring two glasses of white wine. The two exchanged a look that went from wanting to point out the mistake to rapidly accepting that the mistake had somewhat changed their plan for the afternoon.

"So you find things for people?" asked Posie as she sipped from her glass.

"People, things, information, whatever. People come to Jeremiah with something needing to be found or found out and he makes it happen," said Millie.

"How does he do it?"

Millie stared out the window and then laughed again. She pointed to a person walking by. "He's very good at noticing patterns, or the lack of patterns, and putting together what that means. Take for instance that woman there."

Posie looked out and saw the grey-haired Mrs. Baader-Meinhoff walking by across the street.

"I met her just the other day, and now I've seen her everywhere. Not while I'm looking for her, just passing by in the background. Is that significant? Maybe. Or maybe it's just that once you've seen a person you're more likely to see them again in a crowd."

"She's looking at you," giggled Posie. "Do you think she heard you?"

Millie looked out and saw that her friend was right. The pudgy face of Mrs. Baader-Meinhoff was facing in her direction, and the woman's eyes were filled with what could either be intense curiosity or fear. It was hard to tell from this distance. After a moment of the two staring at each other, Millie waved and the older lady quickly walked away.

"How utterly peculiar," muttered Millie.

"So you see patterns in things and those patterns lead you to what you need to find?"

Millie snapped her attention back to Posie. "No, that's what Jeremiah does. My methods are more, shall we say, discrete."

Posie leaned forward, chin resting on her upturned hands and her eyebrows raised. "That sounds interesting. Tell me more, please."

Millie laughed and took a swig of the wine, feeling the buzz in her head that reminded her she hardly ever touched the stuff. "Now, now. A girl doesn't give away all of her secrets on the first date. Let's just say if I need to be unseen, I have my ways of making that happen."

Posie leaned back in her chair and took a drink of her wine. Millie could see the same apprehension on her face about its effects.

"Well then, we'll just have to do this again so I can pry all of your secrets from you," she said with a pleasant smile.

Millie nodded. "I'd like that. I'd like that a lot."

They spent the afternoon sitting at that table nursing their accidental glasses of wine. Posie opened up about her fears, how the incident on the train made it hard to trust anyone she didn't know. She adored the attention Mingent gave her but didn't think she deserved it. She was afraid of the future and her place in this foreign world.

Millie told her about her family, how she left them all behind—her controlling mother and her catty sisters—and made her own way. She told her about how working with Jeremiah helped her find purpose and direction that she had been lacking before.

They walked back to Mingent's place arm in arm, sisters where once they had been strangers, and Millie finally felt like she had found someone who she could relate to, although moving in the opposite direction. Where Posie was moving upwards, Millie was sauntering downwards, and the two seemed to meet in the middle and find a fast friendship.

As she said goodbye to her slightly tipsy new friend, and her confused and mildly cross fiancé, Millie wondered if Jeremiah had made it back yet and what he had found. She wanted this case to be over to settle the disquiet in her soul, but she hoped it wouldn't be too soon so that this new friend didn't slip from her grasp while it was too new to preserve.

In her current state, she was wholly unprepared for what she saw next as she walked past the grand entryway to the Gramercy Arms Hotel, the most expensive place to stay in all of Tamarind. Maximilian and Norina Sudworth stood on the front steps studying a map with none other than her younger sister Lallie.

Chapter Thirteen

When Posie had referred to her hometown as a 'two-horse town', she hadn't been lying, although it's possible she was exaggerating by one horse. Tohester was essentially a single dirt road defined by a line of buildings on either side, most of which were boarded up. A nearby swamp rendered the air especially humid, and Jeremiah had to once again pull his kerchief up to cover his nose and mouth to keep the swarms of midges from entering either opening.

In the center of the left-hand side of the road sat a shop labeled only by a simple sign that read 'Store', and it was into this part of the building that Jeremiah retreated, both to get away from the bugs, and to inquire about the location of Posie's family.

A tiny bell rang as he entered, causing the old man behind the counter to snap awake.

"Eh? What? What do you want?" demanded the man. He was thin and bent like a willow, with a bush of white hair that exploded out of his head with nearly as much enthusiasm as it escaped his face. The only coloration in the mass was a brown line down the front, caused by the wad of tobacco bulging in his cheek.

Jeremiah brushed a few errant midges out of his hair and pulled his kerchief down to smile at the man. "Sorry to disturb you, my good man, but I was hoping you could point me in the direction of the Devyn place."

The man squinted at him and spat a stream of tobacco into a nearby spitoon. "What do you want to know that for?"

"I was just in the area and thought they might want to know about an incident involving young Posie," Jeremiah said. One glance around the store told him that the idea of a new item was unknown in Tohester. Anything on the shelf that was intact was bordering on ancient. He decided against making any sort of purchase.

The old man grunted. "Pretty girl, their Posie. Glad she got out of here. Hope she's not in too much trouble."

"Not at all. When I last spoke with her she intimated that her family may be in a state of worry about her situation. I only want to put their minds at ease."

The old man grunted as he stood up and limped around the counter to the door, but stopped short of opening it. He pointed up the road. "You want to head that way until the trees start, then it'll be the first house you see. Place used to be white, but now it's in a bad way. Still, you can't miss it."

"Thank you, sir," said Jeremiah. "Now if you can just let me know how I'm supposed to deal with those bugs out there."

The old man laughed. "The midges? That's easy. Stay inside."

Jeremiah pulled the kerchief back up and rushed through the swarm to his horse, which stood shaking its head back and forth and whinnying with agitation. He saddled up and led the horse up through town, hoping that maybe once they entered the trees the situation would change.

The house was just where the old man had said, but the description was in no way accurate. It wasn't just in a bad way. In fact, it was in such a dilapidated state that Jeremiah was certain a stiff wind would push it over. Clapboards hung from the walls, some held up only by the twisted vines that climbed all the way to the roof, which was sunken in the middle as though a giant had stepped on it. The few windows that were not shuttered were intact, though more than a few of them were cracked. Jeremiah dismounted and climbed the steps carefully, fearful of falling through with every step.

"That's far enough, mister," said a woman's voice and he heard the unmistakable sound of a hammer being pulled back on a revolver.

Jeremiah held his hands up and looked around, but saw no one. "Please pardon the intrusion, my good lady, but I was looking for the family of Posie Devyn."

"She dead?" came the curt reply.

"No, no, nothing like that at all. There was an incident on the train during which she was injured, but I wanted to let you know that she has fully recovered and is currently being looked after by a gentleman in Tamarind," said Jeremiah. He scanned the windows but still could see no sign of anyone watching him.

"Well ain't that something. Last I heard she had done run off with some boy called Elmer, but now you're saying she's up and gone to the big city."

Jeremiah shrugged. "The impulsiveness of youth, I suppose, allows for a change in direction at a whim."

There was a long pause, during which Jeremiah wondered if he should put his hands down. The midges were just as bad here as they had been in town, and he desperately wanted to swat them away but didn't want to provoke the person with the gun.

"So what do you want with me?" the woman finally asked.

He wasn't sure where to go from there. "I suppose I just thought I would do you the kindness of letting you know she was safe and looked after."

"Alright then," said the voice.

When no other conversation was offered, he backed down the steps slowly. "Good day to you," he said, and he slipped up onto the horse and rode away as quickly as he could, fearful the entire time of a bullet in the back. He couldn't wait to get out of this town. He could imagine what it was like for a young lady, especially one with an aunt as indifferent as that.

Once he was back in Stode and free of the irritating insects, he returned the horse and bought a ticket back to Tamarind. He longed for his chair and a glass of whisky, and he wanted to compare notes with Millie to find out what she had discovered. Nothing about this case was sitting right with him and it bothered him that he couldn't quite put his finger on what it was.

It was just outside of Thorpeworth as the train pulled away that he heard the buzzing sound in his ear and pulled an errant midge out before it could get too far in. He held the thing up to look at it closely. "Awful little bugger, aren't you. Just like a pest to try and hitch a free ride from a gentleman."

And at that moment one of the pieces fell into place.

Chapter Fourteen

Millie sat in her apartment, staring at herself in the mirror as she applied glue to the bridge of her nose. Of course the Sudworths had contacted Lallie. And if Lallie was there, her mother wouldn't be far behind, and the year of peace she and Jeremiah had achieved through their deception would come to a crashing end. There was no way she could work on this case with Jeremiah and also stay out of sight.

Still, it didn't mean she had to give herself away immediately. As much as she had wanted to run over and hug her sister, Millie knew that once she did she would have to answer questions from Tommy's parents, and, as she had no answers, she decided to avoid the situation. Hopefully she would get a chance to have a moment alone with her sister before things wrapped up.

She applied the prosthetic nose and shifted the wig so that it was in place. It took a lot to wrangle her mass of hair under a wig cap, and done improperly things could easily spring free at the wrong moment. Nothing was as jarring for a person as to see the man they were talking to suddenly sprout a head of ginger locks.

She had to be a man, of course. It was easier to hide in plain sight that way, plus it gave her plenty of time free from that cursed corset that society still expected her to wear when she wore a dress. With a properly done chest binding, which was nearly as bad as a corset but more bearable, and the right combination of false hair and extremities, she could pass as a man well enough.

Also, since Lallie had no notion of her talents in the arena of disguise, it would be easier to fool her if needed.

She had gotten close enough to the touring trio to hear their plans to pay a visit to Jeremiah's office in the morning. Leave it to the impulsiveness of the entitled to simply show up and expect results.

"Hmmm. I'm thinking 'Tristan'," she said into the mirror as she blended the makeup covering the false nose into her own skin tone. She deepened her voice. "Hello, my name is Tristan. So nice to meet you."

Satisfied, she was dressed and out the door before her cat Tipsy had a moment to complain about being abandoned yet again. She made short work of the journey by hailing a carriage, paying for it out of her own funds.

She found the Sudworths and her sister in the park across from the Gramercy Arms. Mr. Sudworth was sitting on a bench engrossed in the newspaper while his wife and Lallie sat on blankets on the grass. A picnic large enough to feed an orphanage was laid out around them, no doubt a benefit of staying at the hotel. Millie, in gentleman's clothes with a hat and umbrella, passed by them without arousing even a hint of curiosity.

"What if he knows nothing?" asked Tommy's mother in a pleading voice. She was an elegant woman, with olive skin and long, brown hair that she kept arranged in an elaborate braid on top of her head, giving her the appearance of a woman wearing a large, decorative helmet. Her dress and her manner were all impeccable.

Lallie was a beautiful girl, and in contrast to her sister's red, tangled mane, she had long, brown hair that she wore down. A passing observer might easily decide they were mother and daughter save for the fact that, like Millie in this one way, Lallie's skin was decidedly pale. Her blue eyes shone with that sort of complacent innocence that failed to represent how cunning the girl could be.

"Mother was very praising of his talents, and you know what a remarkable thing it is to achieve praise from Mother," said the girl.

Both women laughed at that, a shared joke at the expense of Lady Mondegreen.

Millie fought the urge to snicker along with them and found a bench within hearing distance. She pulled a journal out of her pocket and began to feign writing.

"Yes, I recall when she came back. She was rather displeased with the results of her interaction with him, so I was surprised when she recommended him," said Mrs. Sudworth.

Lallie blushed a little. "Ah, about that. I hope you will not be too cross with me, Norina, but I fear I must admit to you that Mother had nothing to do with steering you in his direction. I'm afraid I may have misled you a small amount in that regard."

Millie sighed with relief. It was now increasingly possible that her mother was not in Tamarind after all.

Norina laughed a low, throaty laugh. "I had my suspicions, my dear."

"You're not angry with me?"

Norina reached out and stroked the young woman's cheek, showing her more affection in that single moment than Lady Mondegreen had shown any of her daughters their entire lives. "My lovely girl, nothing you could do would ever make me cross. You've given us hope where all hope was lost. I just pray that hope bears fruit."

"I pray the same, Norina. I honestly do."

Things crystallized for Millie. Her mother hadn't sent them to Jeremiah. Lallie had, probably based on the fact that he had managed to find Millie herself over a year ago. She suddenly was desperate to find the boy, if for no other reason than to give her sister a happy moment in her miserable life. Perhaps Lallie wanted to escape just like Millie had, but her methods were less direct.

She almost rose to leave but the conversation went in a direction that caused her to pause.

"Have you heard from her at all?" asked Norina softly.

Millie heard her sister sniffle. Their mother had always chastised Lallie for sniffling.

"Nothing since she left. If what Mother says is true, she's one of those nuns now. She's not even my sister anymore. She has a new name and a new life and cast aside everything that made her who she was before, including me," answered Lallie.

"We can ask him if you'd like. I'm sure he will help you make contact. If he requires a fee we will be happy to pay it. It's the least we can do," said Norina, stroking the young woman's hand.

Millie felt a lump in her throat. She had been so desperate to get away she hadn't even considered how her three sisters felt about it. They had all seemed so content in that life that she imagined they would be happy just to not have to share that bit of attention. Whoever was Mother's favorite at a given time benefited greatly. Remove a player and things could only look up.

"Perhaps," answered Lallie after a pause. "I do not want to get distracted from why we have journeyed all this way. First let's find Tommy, then I'll worry about my sister."

Tommy's father cleared his throat. "Ladies, I have had enough of what this city deems 'fresh air' and will now retire to the club room at the hotel. Can I have them send you out anything?" He stood and folded the paper, tucking it under his arm.

Norina held up an arm. "Help me to my feet, Maximilian, and I'll retire to our rooms while you have your fun. Eleanor, would you like to go in as well? I can have them bring you a lounge chair if you would like."

Lallie smiled up as Norina rose to her feet. "I think I would like to stay here a while, if that is alright. It's a lovely enough day, and I have a letter to write that I want to give some thought to before I write it."

Norina nodded, a knowing glint in her eye, and she took her husband's arm and walked away. Lallie lay back on the blanket and stared up into the sky.

"A teapot. A penny farthing. Uncle Walter's corgi," she said to no one.

Millie fought back tears. She was torn between revealing herself to her sister and maintaining the ruse. The decision was made all the more difficult by the fact that Lallie was playing the game that Millie herself had taught her. She took a deep breath.

"I'm afraid that one looks more like a hippopotamus than a teapot, young lady," she said aloud. She continued to face away from the girl, but spoke loudly enough to be heard in the huskiest voice she could muster.

Behind her, Lallie giggled. "That is patently absurd, sir. That is clearly a handle, and the other side looks like a—wait, I retract my argument. That is most certainly a hippopotamus. Well spotted, sir."

"Likely the wind reshaped it, I'll grant," said Millie. "Shall we call it a draw?"

Millie could feel her sister's eyes boring into the back of her head.

"A draw it is, sir. I appreciate your clemency," she said.

Millie wanted to turn around and rip off the nose and wig. She wanted to run to her sister and hug her like her life depended on it. It was like an itch that she was desperate to scratch.

"Not at all," she managed to say. "You were spot on with the other two, although I'm not familiar with your Uncle Walter so I'll have to concede you may be more of an expert, doglike though the cloud is."

There was a long pause. Millie fought the urge to turn around. She was confident that her disguise would fool the casual observer, but her sister was far more familiar with her.

"I feel it is inappropriate for me to be conversing with you in this manner without at least having the pleasure of an introduction, sir," said Lallie. "My name is Eleanor Mondegreen. To whom do I have the pleasure of speaking?"

Panic filled Millie. As much as she wanted to talk to her sister, she didn't want her new world, her life in Tamarind, and her partnership with Jeremiah to be put into jeopardy because she was feeling nostalgic.

"Sorry to intrude on your private moment, Miss Mondegreen. I bid you good day," she said, and she was on her feet and walking swiftly away before she could second guess her decision.

Chapter Fifteen

That evening, Jeremiah, Millie, and Ward sat at their table at Cobbler's Rest. Jeremiah nibbled on a large salad, his appetite always at its lowest when he was deep in thought. Millie once again had the soup, although even if you paid her a handsome fee she could not tell you what it contained, only that it was delicious. Ward, much in his way, took up half a table and devoured a rare steak.

"Remember when this place was a steakhouse, Jeremiah?" asked the big man.

"Yes, of course," answered Jeremiah distractedly. "Called 'The Deep Cut' or some nonsense like that." He twirled his fork in front of him, watching the piece of lettuce as though it were a marionette show.

After a long pause, during which Ward stared at his friend waiting for more, Millie broke the standoff. "So, Inspector, Jeremiah tells me the two of you go back quite a ways."

"Years and years, my good lady. I could tell you stories about this man that would curl your hair. That is, if it wasn't already so curly."

Millie was back to being herself, the Tristan disguise being discarded upstairs the moment she had arrived. While she enjoyed playing parts, being herself was the most comfortable. "I'm sure I've seen a few things of that sort. Ask Jeremiah about Norris Levon and the statuette sometime," she said.

Ward stared at her looking for jest and finding none, broke into a resounding guffaw that drew stares from the other patrons. Jeremiah remained unphased, still fascinated by the lettuce.

"Well I can see you are a fair match for my boy Jeremiah, Miss Mondegreen," Ward said, slapping his knee.

"Please, sir, call me Millie. I won't stand on ceremony with a friend of my friend," she said.

Ward nodded. "Then if you're to be Millie, I must insist on being Radclyffe. You can even be so bold as to call me Clyffe, as Jeremiah does when he's paying attention at all." At that he reached over, snatched the fork out of Jeremiah's hand, and hurled it over the bushes into the river.

Jeremiah's head snapped around as if he had been sleeping. After a moment of focusing, he was back with them. "Apologies. There are several aspects of this case that don't want to add up, and they're vexing me quite considerably."

"Such as?" prompted Ward.

"The second train picked up Posie and Tommy on the tracks, after which they were both treated and Posie joined the other people on the train while Tommy rested. Somewhere between the place where they were picked up," he said, placing a crouton on the table, "just before Peyze, there were only two stops where he could have departed, Thorpeworth and Kevin." He marked both in a line before adding a salt shaker at the end to represent Tamarind.

"So maybe he got off at either place," suggested Ward.

"I don't think so," said Millie. "First of all, he was terribly injured. To hear Posie tell it he could barely walk, much less manage to sneak away."

"And, on my return trip I asked the station masters at both towns if an injured man was offloaded at either stop and both said they had no memory of it," added Jeremiah.

"Memories can be faulty," offered Ward.

"True, but a bloodied Authority man may draw more attention than anyone else, especially this close to Tamarind," said Jeremiah.

"But he wouldn't have looked like an Authority man," said Millie, snapping her fingers. "Posie said they changed him out of his uniform into fresh clothes. She said they didn't want to upset any other passengers should he decide to move around."

Jeremiah tapped his chin and scowled. "Still, a bandaged man would draw attention. Both station masters swore they had no knowledge, and since it happened during the day—"

"They would have seen. Yes," said Ward. He, too, began to tap his chin and the sight of the two of them doing the same motion made Millie laugh. When they both looked at her she cast her gaze between them to pretend she wasn't laughing at them and that's when she saw the man walking towards the door leading to Jeremiah's offices.

"Gentlemen, we have a visitor," she said, pointing. Both men turned to look. The three of them were mostly hidden from view due to the garish plants that surrounded Mr. Panglossian's deck, so they were able to watch without being seen.

The figure, wearing a black cloak with the hood raised, glanced around before slipping a device from within the folds of the cloak and sliding it into the lock. The audible click let the observers know that short work had been made of the lock. Without another look the figure moved inside the building and shut the door behind him.

"By the cloak it's one of those Authority lads," said Millie. "I had a run in with one the other night who was dressed similarly."

"And by the audacity, I think I know which one it is," said Jeremiah.

"Well, isn't this our lucky day, because it just so happens that whoever that is, he just illegally entered a residence in front of an officer of the Constabulary," growled Ward. "What do you say we go up and greet him?"

A quick wave to Mr. Panglossian with a promise to settle up later freed them from their obligations and they slipped, as quietly as they could, through the door and up the stairs. Millie stayed at the bottom of the stairs in case the man made it past both of them. They could see light coming from above which meant the entry door into Jeremiah's office was ajar, and as they reached it, Ward put a hand on his friend's shoulder and pulled him back.

"Allow me," he said, and without waiting for an answer he pushed open the door and stomped inside.

Corporal Cross stood frozen over by the book case where Jeremiah had last found him. He held the same book in his hand that he had before, and it became obvious to Jeremiah that the purpose of his previous visit was, in addition to returning the listening device they had planted in Rantallion's office, to place one of his own in Jeremiah's.

"Well isn't this a fine how do you do?" said Ward loudly. "Might I prevail upon you, *laddie*, to tell me why you have invaded this man's home?"

Cross's eyes narrowed as he weighed his options. Jeremiah pushed the door closed.

"There are no other exits aside from this door," he said, locking it with a key from his pocket. "Unless, that is, you plan to leap from the window, which is not something I would suggest as the restaurant below has a great number of posts spread throughout the courtyard for lanterns. I would hate for you to impale yourself in a desperate attempt to explain why you have intruded upon my hospitality again."

Cross sighed and dropped the book on the table next to him. "You're a clever man. I'm certain you've already sussed what my intentions are."

"It's obvious what you're doing. What I want to know is why," said Jeremiah.

Cross picked the book up and flipped through the pages, showing both men that it held nothing but words. "All fixed, so you have nothing to complain about. Now if you'll excuse me, I'll see myself out." He walked toward the door and almost made it past Ward before he found himself on his back, the wind knocked out of him.

"I don't think you're going anywhere, *laddie*, not for a while now," said the big man as he loomed over him.

"How dare you! I am a representative of the Authority!" shouted Cross through gasps for air.

Ward laughed. "No, you are a criminal, caught in the act of breaking into the home of an upstanding citizen of Tamarind, and I hereby arrest you on the authority of the Constabulary." He reached down and lifted Cross up by the front of his cloak. With one quick movement he tore the garment from the young man and began searching his pockets, tossing everything he found onto Jeremiah's desk.

"This is outrageous! You can't do this!" shouted Cross.

Ward grabbed him by the face and squeezed, making the young man look a parody of a fish. Fear flashed in Cross's eyes.

"Listen here, soldier boy. That sort of talk may fly in Fleis or wherever you crawled here from, but you're in my city, and I am the law. I decide what is allowed and what is not, and as I see it, you are caught dead to rights. Now the next thing I want to hear out of your mouth is an explanation, told with respect for me and Jeremiah here. I'm talking 'yes, sir' and 'no, sir' instead of this pompous peacocking thing you're trying to do. And I'm warning you. Do not test me on this. Bigger men than you have learned to fly for crossing me. Do you understand?"

Ward's face was less than an inch from Cross's as he hissed the words. Cross gave a brief nod.

"I don't think I heard that response," growled Ward.

"Yes, sir," said Cross sullenly.

"Good, now sit down," ordered Ward. He shoved the young man into the other chair.

Jeremiah moved to sit behind his desk. As he sat down and began to look through the confiscated items Ward stood behind Cross, his hands on the young man's shoulders. It didn't take a great imagination to picture them easily wrapped around the soldier's neck.

"Once again you insult me by invading my home," said Jeremiah. "Why?"

"Surveillance. We wanted to know what you know," Cross answered sharply.

"Is this because you are afraid of what I've discovered or because you are clueless as to the facts and think this is the only way to ascertain them?"

"I was given my orders and I followed them," said Cross.

Ward slapped him on the side of the head. "Answer the question you are asked, boy."

Cross glared at Jeremiah, cleverly choosing not to point such a look at his large captor.

"Commander Rantallion thought if we could discover what happened to Sudworth, we could approach the family and regain the favor we lost in losing him."

"So you don't have him?" asked Jeremiah.

"What do you think?"

This earned him another slap. He growled, then thought better of escalating his reaction.

"No, we don't have him. We never saw him. He wasn't on the train when it arrived in Tamarind. Neither of the recruits was. We don't know where either of them is. Happy?"

Jeremiah smiled. "Well I knew that. I just wondered how long it would take one of you to admit it."

Ward chuckled. Cross's glare deepened.

"As it happens, I know what became of Derek Fairburn. I'm afraid he is quite dead."

Cross's expression changed to shock. "How do you know this? Where did he—"

"No, I think I've given you enough for free. I cannot possibly respond to your poor behavior by giving you rewards you didn't earn. But taking your statement as truth, which I am inclined to do because despite how clever you think you are, you are simply terrible at lying, I am left with a conclusion that unsettles me greatly."

"Which is?" asked Ward.

"Tell me, Inspector, what do you intend to do with our invader here?" asked Jeremiah.

"This little lackbeard is spending the night below the river," said Ward.

"What? You can't possibly be serious! This is an outrage!" shouted Cross, earning himself another slap to the head.

"Keep at it and I'll make sure you spend the night sharing a cell with one of our many regulars who has what you might call a low opinion of you soldier boys," hissed Ward.

Cross stopped shouting and returned to glaring.

Jeremiah nodded. "If you'll allow our prisoner to answer another question, Ward, I have to ask. What will the Commander's reaction be to his man landing under the river?"

A push from Ward made Cross answer. "He will come and demand my release, of course."

"Well then, I'm sorry to cut the night short, but I have some things to organize. Ward, if you could try to arrange it so that Rantallion collects him at the railyard around noon tomorrow I will be sure to meet you there with all of the answers I am able to gather. Sound fair?"

Ward sighed. "Whatever you say, old friend."

"Splendid. Do take care in transporting the Corporal to The Centre. I would hate it if he came to any further harm," said Jeremiah with a grin.

"What about my property?" asked Cross, staring at the items on Jeremiah's desk that Ward had confiscated.

Jeremiah pulled open the drawer and swept the items into it. "I'm not sure I know what you mean," he said, sliding it closed.

Cross sputtered but said nothing as Jeremiah unlocked the door and he was roughly led downstairs. As they passed Millie she smiled at Cross.

"Say hello to your friend for me when you see him," she said. "You'll know which one. He's the boy with red welts on his face and back."

Ward laughed. "I see why he keeps you around, but as for why you put up with Jeremiah, I'll never know." His laughter trailed down the street as he dragged the simpering Cross alongside him.

Millie found Jeremiah sitting at his desk studying the items he had confiscated. The listening device was obvious enough—small and flat so that it could be slipped into a narrow space—but the purpose of the other items was unclear.

"You've got that look on your face," she said, dropping into a chair.

Jeremiah smiled sadly. "Do I? I wonder if you know how dreadfully sorry I will be if my theory turns out to be true."

"What is it?" she asked, worried.

"I'm afraid I have to tell you some things, Millie, and at least one of them may break your heart."

Chapter Sixteen

Jeremiah stood on the platform next to two cars, a passenger car and a caboose. His face betrayed nothing of what he was thinking, much like Millie who stood next to him.

"Are you ready for this?" he asked quietly.

"As I'll ever be," she said. "I hope you're wrong, though, just so you're aware."

Jeremiah nodded sadly. "I know."

Ward was the first to arrive with Cross in tow. The poor Authority man looked like he hadn't slept a wink, which made Jeremiah wonder if his friend had made good on his promise to house him with an undesirable roommate. It was more likely that a night sleeping under the river did a sufficient job of inducing insomnia, with the din of barges passing by and other sounds, which no doubt came across as unworldly when translated through metal, glass, and water.

Rantallion appeared shortly after accompanied by seven Authority men, all marching in unison as the old man walked slowly down the stairs, putting on his decrepit act for the masses. When he spotted Ward and the cuffed Cross he stiffened, but said nothing, instead nodding to Jeremiah and then Ward in greeting.

Lord Mingent arrived with Posie a few moments later. When the young woman saw Millie she smiled and waved. Millie waved back and returned the smile.

"What is the meaning of this, Mountweazel?" asked Mingent. "Hasn't my fiancée suffered enough because of this missing boy?"

Rantallion looked at the man, then over to Jeremiah. "What is this man talking about? What does Sudworth have to do with this girl?" He gestured as though he was trying to shake something undesirable from his hand.

"Look here, sir, I'll not have you talk to her like that," barked Mingent, stepping forward. Posie patted him on the arm and pulled him back.

"Gentlemen. Ladies. Please do pardon my insistence that you all join me here today, but I thought it would be best to inform everyone at once so that there would be no further need for us to spy on each other," said Jeremiah.

Ward and Rantallion both looked at each other as if the other was the only guilty party.

"There has been concern over the fate of Tomason Sudworth, and shockingly little concern over the fate of his companion, Derek Fairburn, but I can now tell you all that I have located both young men." Jeremiah watched the faces of all gathered without expression.

There were murmurs from all assembled, but no one interrupted, so he continued.

"It is my sad duty to report to you that Derek Fairburn is deceased. I located his body myself and reported it to the authorities in Stode. It is my understanding that his family will collect his remains and will likely plan a funeral within the week," said Jeremiah.

"And Sudworth?" asked Rantallion.

"Well, in contrast to the other I am happy to report that he is very much alive," said Jeremiah simply.

"What?" said Ward. "You found him?"

"This is incredible!" said Rantallion. "Where?"

Everyone showed their shock, but Jeremiah was only watching one of them.

"I did," said Jeremiah with a satisfied smile. "You see it occurred to me that if a man could fall off a train once, he could just as easily fall off it a second time. All that remained was for me to find where he fell."

Posie's eyes fluttered and she leaned on Mingent. "I'm not sure I'm feeling up to this," she said quietly. "That train car is bringing back so much."

"It should," said Jeremiah. "This," he said, gesturing to the passenger car, "is the car where the altercation took place. And this," he gestured to the caboose, "is from the same train. It's amazing, really, that the railyard hasn't fixed either one yet but they have so many trains in and out there must not be time."

"Honestly, Jeremiah, what has gotten into you?" asked Mingent. "You torment my dear Posie with your callousness." He draped his arm protectively around the girl.

"I do apologize, Lord Mingent. Sometimes I get so caught up in the truth that I forget the social niceties. Speaking of which, when I made my trip down the rails I paid a visit to your home town, Posie. My intention was to render a kindness by letting them know of your situation. I've dealt with a lot of runaways in my profession, so I know how families tend to fret."

"How did you know where my family—" started Posie.

"A little two-horse town called Tohester, where the crickets sing this time of year making beautiful music," said Millie, reciting the description without inflection.

"Only there are no crickets in Tohester. Not this time of year. There are, I found, thousands of irritating insects. The kind that would keep a person from spending more than a moment on their porch unless they were being held at gunpoint. Trust me, I know from experience," added Jeremiah.

"I would like to go home. Please," begged Posie to Mingent.

"Of course, my dear, of course. Jeremiah, we are through here. Honestly, I expected more out of you, sir," said Mingent with a scowl.

"Ask yourself a question, Teddy. How could a girl who faints at the very mention of a bad memory, who is so weak that she needs a man of your advanced age to keep her upright. How could she manage to be thrown from a train and still be able to drag herself and a man larger than her up a steep incline?" asked Jeremiah.

Ward had released Cross and moved to stand next to him. "Where are you going with this, Jeremiah? What does this have to do with Sudworth?"

"Tommy Sudworth was a man in love, Inspector Ward," said Millie. "He once had the hand of a girl, but that girl's family found him unproven and therefore unworthy. To prove himself he did the only thing he could think of and joined up with the Authority. Maybe once he made his name they would allow him to ask for her hand again."

"That's a lovely story, Millie, but what does it have to do with any of this?" asked Ward.

"There is no way he would throw his life away. There is no way he would jump from a train, especially not after he had already suffered being thrown from one. He had too much to live for. He had something to prove," said Millie. She stared into Posie's eyes, willing any argument to come from the girl.

"Which means, if he didn't jump and yet he ended up taking a second tumble, that someone had to have helped him do so. This is verified by the broken chain on the caboose over there," said Jeremiah, gesturing to the car.

"You can't possibly be suggesting my Posie had anything to do with that?" demanded Mingent. Posie was crying into his chest as he held her up.

"I'm afraid I am. As to why, we'll have to ask Tommy. He should be here in just a few moments," said Jeremiah.

Posie stiffened, then stood up straighter.

"Well, fuck," she said, and she shoved Mingent to the ground and bolted down the tracks.

All of the men moved to give chase, but Millie held an arm out.

"She's mine."

While the rail platforms were somewhat crowded, the path the fleeing girl took down the tracks was unblocked by pedestrians or buildings. Millie watched Posie, or the person claiming to be Posie, struggle to run in the skirts she wore. Millie, in trousers, was confident she would catch up until she saw the fleeing girl tear away the skirt and toss it aside, revealing trousers underneath.

It seemed Posie had been prepared to flee at a moment's notice after all.

Her legs unencumbered, she was able to gain speed and, much in contrast with the weak, helpless show of herself that she had been maintaining, this version of the girl was more athletic. Millie, also in trousers, struggled to keep up but fell behind.

She heard a triumphant laugh and saw what prompted it. A train was slowly pulling out of the station, and she saw Posie leap onto the back of the caboose and slip into the door without a glance backward.

"Oh no you don't, you fraud," growled Millie. She channeled her anger into energy and ran faster, her legs burning, her chest aching as the train gained speed. Pouring everything she had into the effort, she closed the gap and grabbed hold of the ladder just as she tripped on a slightly raised railroad tie.

Her legs flew up into the air but she managed to hold on, waving for a moment behind the train like an enthusiastic flag before gravity reasserted itself and brought her crashing down. Fortunately, she managed to catch her foot on the very bottom rung of the ladder and she launched herself upwards to land, gasping, on the tiny platform at the back of the caboose.

Everything ached, but adrenaline drove her upward. She found that Posie had been confident in her escape and not latched the door to the small car, even leaving the door that exited the other end open in her flight. Millie pushed through, determined to find her, when she felt her world turned upside down as her legs were swept out from beneath her.

"Damn, that was impressive," said Posie as she straddled the recumbent Millie and pressed a knife to her throat. "I honestly thought I would get to watch you tumble."

Millie started to rise but felt the blade press deeper so she instead concentrated on catching her breath. She glared up at her captor, whose entire persona had changed. Millie was accustomed to being other people, taking on identities other than her own, but she had never been confronted with someone whose skill topped her own. Where there had once been an innocent, fragile girl there was now a heartless, cold-blooded killer.

"Oh, that look on your face," said Posie with a sneer. "Is that disappointment, Millie my dear? Did you think you would save this poor, wretched girl? Take her under your wing?"

"Who are you? What did anyone do to deserve this?" asked Millie.

"Oh, are you still hoping I'm poor, little Posie? Ha! That stupid bint couldn't hold a candle to me. I guess I should have found out more about her before pretending to be her, but it didn't matter until you and your boss came along," said Posie. She looked around the car while still holding the knife to Millie's neck.

"I don't understand. Was this all just to get Mingent's money? What did that have to do with Tommy?" asked Millie. She saw a toolbox sitting partially off a shelf, probably knocked forward during the scuffle. A broom handle was leaning against it. She inched her foot over as she stared into Posie's eyes.

"My word you are an idiot. Tommy and his soldier friend were supposed to die first. I told Jared to take them out first, but he was too slow. Popped the one's head, but then the other people on the train got involved," said Posie. The scowl on her face matched the anger in her eyes, and Millie was amazed she hadn't been able to see it before.

Things clicked into place in Millie's head. "The robbery. You weren't a victim."

Posie laughed. "Hells no, we were the robbers. Only Jared didn't have the balls. Once he saw the one guy's head explode he panicked. If he had just kept shooting, those other people would have kept in place. Instead, he caught a bullet himself."

"And then they threw you off the train," finished Millie.

"Bastards. Threw us all off. If I wasn't so hurt by the fall I would have been laughing about the fact that the soldiers got tossed out with the rest of us. But I was hurt, and then I found that whining shit of an Authority boy all banged up and blinded, and all it took was pretending to be sweet little Posie Devyn to get him to help me."

"So why kill him? Once you were picked up you were saved. You could have disappeared." Millie hooked the broom handle with her foot and waited for the perfect moment. Luckily for her, Posie seemed content to gloat.

"Well I met my man, didn't I? Money bags fell head over heels for poor, wounded Posie. I couldn't have soldier boy spilling the beans on me. Sure there was a chance he wouldn't get his sight back, but I couldn't risk it. So I went and found him, took him out back to get some air, and stuck a knife in his gut." She was grinning as she retold the tale, and the anger in Millie rose to the surface.

"You're sick," Millie hissed.

"You should have seen him tumble. It was like a porcelain doll falling down a staircase," laughed the girl.

Millie pulled on the broom handle, sending it crashing into the toolbox, which left the shelf and fell to the floor. Posie twisted around to look, giving Millie the moment she needed to shove the girl back off of her.

"You're going to rot under the river," said Millie, springing to her feet. She grabbed the broom handle from where it fell and struck out, landing a solid blow to Posie's hand. Posie screamed in rage as she dropped the knife, then lurched forward, shoving Millie toward the open back door.

Millie didn't fall as the girl had expected, but she did stumble into the open door, throwing her off balance. Posie turned and ran toward the front of the car, racing through the door as Millie regained her feet.

A storage car was next, filled almost completely with crates that left only a narrow path. Millie slipped through and stepped over the expanse into the next car, a passenger car with private rooms.

"There's no point hiding," Millie shouted. "I will find you and you will go to jail." She hoped that anyone present in the cars would stick their head out, keeping her from having to search each compartment. The door at the other end of the car stood closed, and Posie hadn't had enough time to reach it.

No one responded. No heads appeared, ruling out rooms. Millie sighed, rubbed her aching shoulder, and tried the first one. It opened easily to an empty cabin. The one across the hall was the same. She stepped quietly down the hallway to the next two, trying the one on the left and finding no one. A thump sounded from the one on the right and she froze. She cursed the fact that she had failed to bring her pistol and tightened her grip on the broom handle. All of her muscles tensed as she reached out and turned the handle, pushing the door open suddenly and pointing inside with the handle.

An older woman was cowering, holding a bulging carpet bag in front of her face. After a moment's pause, a cherubic face peeked over the plaid container.

Millie shook her head and looked again. "Mrs. Baader-Meinhoff?"

"Please, don't turn me in. I'm sorry. I'll give it back," said the woman, tears running down her round cheeks. "I just wanted to stick it to that horrible woman and get away from it all."

On any other day Millie would have had the presence of mind to process what had been said, but every bit of her focus was on finding Posie.

"Yes, well, don't do it again," she said, and she shut the door and turned to head to the next set of rooms.

The distraction had been sufficient, and she saw the door at the end of the train sliding closed. She could see through the window that Posie was unable to open the next door, and she saw the girl begin to climb the ladder to the top of the train.

"Oh no, you don't," she said, racing down the hall. She threw open the door and looked up just in time to see Posie's shoes disappear over the top.

In the back of her mind, Millie knew that Jeremiah would be grateful she was the one giving chase. She imagined him struggling to climb even that short ladder, the world below looming further and further away in his mind. For her part, she was hardly confident in her situation. Looking down she could see the ground moving by at a dangerous speed. The very idea of falling filled her with terror.

But the anger drove her on. She could not let the imposter get away. She climbed, cautiously glancing over to make sure no strike would come, and then pulled herself over the top.

She quickly spotted the retreating form of Posie who struggled against the wind to walk forward.

"You won't get away," Millie shouted. "We'll be in Thorpeworth soon, and it will be easy to rouse the constables. Give yourself up."

Posie turned and glared at her. "I had it made, Millie. Sure, the old man smelled of piss all the time and probably couldn't satisfy a woman to save his life, but I could have had him die of natural causes in a month or two. It was perfect until you lot butted in."

"Tommy survived. You would have been found out," shouted Millie. She stepped forward slowly, closing the distance.

"In a big city like that? Ha!" yelled Posie. "Never would have seen him. And even if I did, I could have gutted him again without a thought."

Millie's mind kept trying to see Posie Devyn, her new friend, and everything in her person wanted to help her still, but that girl was gone, replaced with evil glee by the murderous fiend that stood mere feet from her, tensed and ready to spring.

"Is there nothing of my friend in you?" she asked sadly.

The laughter that came as a response bore into her soul. There was nothing redeeming in this person, no hint of the friend she had thought she was making.

"You rubes are so easy, it's almost not even a challenge."

Millie saw the bridge and quickly turned her attention back to the shouting girl. She gave no indication of what she had seen.

Posie lurched forward and pushed Millie, and she let herself fall onto her back.

"How would you like to feel what I felt when those assholes threw me over the side?" she snarled. She loomed over Millie, stepping slowly toward her.

"Goodbye," said Millie softly.

"What?" demanded the girl. "Was that you begging for your—"

The bridge hit the girl, or rather the girl hit the bridge, with a sickening crunch. Her head, no doubt filled with evil thoughts and horrific plans, crumpled with the impact and her body landed on the top of the train in front of Millie with a loud thud that she would always remember.

Posie's lifeless eyes stared at her over a sneer that somehow remained.

Millie began sobbing, pouring out all the sadness and loss she felt onto the metal roof. She looked away from the horrific stare of the girl she had hoped would be a friend, unable to take the gaze. When the train pulled into Thorpeworth, she calmly climbed down, notified the station master of what had occurred, and bought a ticket back to Tamarind.

Chapter Seventeen

Lallie looked beautiful in the light of the hallway overlooking the medical ward of St. Dismus. She stood on the balcony, the beds below barely separated from each other by flimsy curtains held up by metal frames. She was crying. Millie wasn't sure if that was a good sign or not.

Millie hesitated. Revealing herself to her sister meant that her life, which had been unfettered by her mother's influence, would be over. Once Lady Mondegreen discovered that she hadn't joined the Sisters of the White Nettle, the woman would fully expect her daughter to return home and do as she was told. Millie would sooner die.

But her sister was crying, and as the oldest of four it was Millie's duty to comfort them when they were sad, even if it meant nothing good came to her as a result of the action.

She stood behind her sister and placed her hand on the girl's shoulder.

"He's broken, Lallie. He'll never be the same as he was before," she said. It was best to lay the cards out on the table. She needed to know what sort of person her sister was growing up to be. Were her tears driven by grief for Tommy's sake or for her own?

Lallie turned and hugged her, giving no indication that she was surprised by her sister's presence. Millie returned the hug, recalling all the times they had hugged before—those nights when one of them would return from their mother's attention, devastated or filled with self-loathing, and they would hold each other tightly, wishing things were better.

"What happened to him?" cried Lallie. "What did they do to my Tommy?"

So he was her Tommy still. Millie was glad to know that. She thought about all that the boy had been through—rejection by her mother, choosing this hard life path and then not even being allowed to go through with it before he was beaten, thrown from a train, stabbed, and discarded. Jeremiah had been the one to finally check if any unknowns had come into the injury ward at St. Dismus. He surmised, correctly as it happened, that the crews that kept the rails clear near Tamarind would certainly talk about finding a body. As it was, they talked about finding someone near death and, despite his injuries, there was enough left of him to match the photo on the identification card Jeremiah had kept.

But Millie didn't want to tell her sister all of that. Not yet.

"He's been through a lot, and none of it good since he left Fleis," she said.

"He was supposed to be a soldier. He was going to make a name for himself and come back for me. Mother couldn't refuse him then," whimpered Lallie.

"What are you going to do?" Millie asked.

Lallie turned from her and looked down again at the heavily bandaged man on the bed. The Sudworths sat on either side of their son, each holding a hand as he slept.

"You mean, will I follow Mother's wishes and be done with him? He's of no use now, she would say. He's not even fit to bring to a dinner party. All of the talk would be about how horrendous his scars are, or how he needed help cutting his meat." The vitriol with which Lallie spoke about her mother surprised Millie. She had always suspected the youngest sister to be the most compliant. It seems her big sister rubbed off on her after all.

"He will need help. But I know he loves you," said Millie.

"And I loved him," cried Lallie, turning and crying into her shoulder again.

"Loved? So will you leave, or stay with him?" asked the older sister calmly. It had been roughly two years since they had last spoken—one year of which Millie had made her own way, and the last year finding the right path as Jeremiah's partner. How had her sister changed in that time without her there to influence her?

"I suspect Norina expects me to flee. She told me I could return home if I wanted. It wasn't a dismissal as much as permission, I think. She expects me to turn away from him now that he's hurt."

Millie nodded. "You are your mother's daughter. As much as she obviously loves you she's likely preparing herself for the worst."

"Isn't this the worst? Isn't losing your son, and then finding him so injured, the absolute worst?" pleaded Lallie, turning and gesturing below. "What could be worse than losing a son?"

Millie leaned against the railing. "Losing a future daughter at the same time, I suppose."

Lallie nodded, staring. "I love him, Millie. I love him with all my heart."

The guilt that had been building in Millie's chest melted away. Lallie had turned out to be a good person all on her own. "Then go to him. Help him."

"Mother will be furious," said Lallie.

"I suspect once you tell Mother what you've discovered about me, all of your faults will be forgiven in the wake of her fury," said Millie softly.

Lallie smiled. "She doesn't know I'm here. She doesn't know I've kept in touch with Tommy and his parents. And she most certainly will not know I saw you at all."

Millie kissed her sister on the forehead. "Go see your fiancé. Come see me before you depart. Jeremiah will know where I am."

Lallie nodded. "It's good to see you, sister."

"You as well," said Millie.

Lallie held up an object between them. Millie recognized it as her journal.

"You make an ugly man, by the way," said Lallie with an enormous grin, and she slipped out the door and down the stairs.

Millie watched as her sister joined the Sudworths. She saw Lallie lean down and kiss Tommy on the forehead, and she knew the girl would be alright.

"Are you okay?" asked Jeremiah. He had entered as Lallie left.

He had wrapped up the loose ends. Both Commander Rantallion and Inspector Ward had parted ways amicably, the former relieved that the Authority was not to blame and the latter content that he had gotten one over on the irksome group by jailing Cross. Mingent, devastated by the betrayal and embarrassed by his naivete, had retreated after muttering a few words of apology to everyone present. He would likely be more careful in the future with who he trusted. And the Sudworths had found their son, and now they had found that they still had a future daughter-in-law.

Millie nodded. "All is well, my friend. And I suspect you got your payment?"

Jeremiah smiled. "We'll be dining well for quite some time yet."

A memory snapped forward into Millie's mind. "Oh, right. Speaking of payment, you'll never guess who I bumped into on the train."

Chapter Eighteen

"So you see, Mrs. Dunning-Kruger, the money was there all along. It's just that your accounting practices were a bit, shall we say, inefficient."

The three women sat and stood in the exact same arrangement as they had the week before. Mrs. Baader-Meinhoff's face was an expression of gratitude that increased with every word Jeremiah uttered.

"That's nonsense. I looked at the books myself. Money was missing," spat the leader of the group. She was flipping through the pages of the journal to find the offending entries but was finding little success. That was largely in part to the doctoring of said book by Millie and Mrs. Baader-Meinhoff to cover the tracks of the elder lady's shenanigans.

"I am loath to disagree with a woman of your stature, Mrs. Dunning-Kruger, but I think you'll find I am correct," said Jeremiah calmly. Millie stood behind him, her face betraying none of the joy she found at the woman's confusion.

"I guess it's possible I messed it up," said Mrs. Weber-Fechner with a shrill laugh. "I told you not to make me be the accounts keeper."

Undone by her apparent mistake, Mrs. Dunning-Kruger stood and handed the book to her companion. "I suppose I should apologize for wasting your time, Jeremiah, but I'm sure you will forgive an old friend of your mother's this small oversight. While I'm sure there are reasons it took you a week to reach your conclusions—conclusions I still argue are patently false, though I will not waste my time proving it to you or anyone—you must understand that we have important business to attend to, so I must bid you a good day."

"But Pris, what about the man's fee?" asked Mrs. Weber-Fechner, earning a glare from the other woman.

"Fee for what? He found nothing!" spat the woman.

Jeremiah smiled broadly. "There will be no need to pay any sort of fee. As Mrs. Dunning has said—"

"Dunning-Kruger!" shouted the woman.

Jeremiah nodded, secretly enjoying her irritation. "As Mrs. Dunning-Kruger said, there was no money missing, so no money to be found. We'll call it a wash."

Mrs. Dunning-Kruger turned and left with a simple "Hmm!" by way of farewell.

"Awfully nice of you," said Mrs. Weber-Fechner as she stood and followed the angry woman. "Good day."

Mrs. Baader-Meinhoff remained, holding her carpet bag, now emptied of the stolen money, in front of her. "Thank you both. I don't know what came over me."

"Not at all," said Jeremiah.

"Agnes, now!" came a shout from the stairs.

Mrs. Baader-Meinhoff, now a new person, walked over to the top of the stairs and looked downward. "Keep your wig on, Priscilla. I'll come when I'm ready."

Outraged sputtering came from below.

With a satisfied smile the woman gave a little wave to Jeremiah and Millie and, with a bounce in her step that hadn't been there before, walked down the stairs.

The Ghost of Gilgungate

The cool waters of the Tarsain River cut through the landscape, dividing forest land like a wandering knife. A widebeam canal boat, its sides painted in bright blues, reds, and yellows, glided along with the current with all the rush of a languid swan. Jeremiah and Millie sat in lounge chairs at the bow, glasses of sparkling wine in their hands.

"Cheers, Millie," said Jeremiah, raising his glass.

"Well, this certainly is a different experience than what I've grown accustomed to working with you, Jeremiah," said Millie, as she sipped the glass of wine that had been delivered to her by a laconic waiter. She enjoyed the gentle roll of the river as they glided down toward their destination. Much to her annoyance, she was dressed properly in full corset and dress. One had to fit in where one was going.

Jeremiah laughed, his spirits high since financial security was once again reality. He swirled the wine in his glass and watched the leaves waving lazily in the air above them from the drooping arms of outstretched trees. Windfall aside, he hadn't sprung for this casual and comfortable means of transportation.

"It's great of Lord Neumany to treat us to such an elegant means of arrival," he said. "We could easily have taken a carriage, but this is far better."

Millie raised her glass. "As I've told you before, my friend, there are some benefits to having a ludicrous amount of money, such as having the option to splash out. Although I would trade it in a heartbeat to take this damnable corset off." She shifted until she managed to find a more comfortable position in the lounge chair.

The boat that carried them down the river was remarkably different than when it had been used to move supplies up and down the waterway. At some point in the vessel's past, an enterprising person had taken a mind to converting it into a luxury boat, complete with deck seating and a single servant whose entire purpose was to make certain the occupants were never without what they wanted, while at the same time, using as few words as possible so as to not be intrusive.

The servant, a tall man who tended to forget he no longer had to stoop when he was above decks, was so skilled at his profession that the only thing the two passengers knew about him was that his name was Kelner and it was, in fact, a good day. Otherwise, he was invisible.

"So, we're ghost hunters now?" teased Millie.

Jeremiah groaned. "No, we most certainly are not, because there is no such thing."

"Oh, I don't know. My parent's home in Fleis is said to be haunted by all of the servants who died there waiting on my mother to be pleased with anything they did." She laughed at her own joke. "But seriously, when I was a girl we used to hear moans late at night coming from all over the house. Sometimes even shrieks."

"Mmm-hmm," said Jeremiah as he watched another boat float by.

"I told my sisters that there were ghosts roaming the halls so they wouldn't ask questions. You should have seen their faces."

"And did you ever see one of the 'ghosts' which brought such terror to those impressionable young girls?" asked Jeremiah.

"No, but I did see something far worse. One night, after getting them to sleep, I went to investigate, creeping down the hallway with no light to guide me lest it give me away, and I reached a door down the servants' hall, behind which the ghosts were most certainly hiding. I reached for the handle…"

Millie sat upright with her eyes wide and her arm outstretched in front of her, mimicking the event. Jeremiah watched her with amusement.

"I'm guessing two people?" he said.

Millie shot him an annoyed look then, her reveal thwarted. "Indeed. In fact, it was my father and the head maid. Seems they grabbed every opportunity they could to have a rendezvous, in whatever location was most convenient. I'm sure Mother was aware and simply didn't care, but once he was discovered, Father dismissed the maid and moved away within the month."

Jeremiah studied her face. "I'm never sure if a story from your childhood is going to be a happy story or a sad one. In this case, I'm still not sure."

"The old man got away. A few years later I did the same. It's happy for both of us," she said simply, sitting back and sipping her wine.

"Well, I think it's likely that Lord Neumany's ghost will be of a similar ilk, though to hear him tell it in his letter, the entire estate of Gilgungate is overrun with spectres." Jeremiah held the letter up. "Come at once my good man, and deliver us from these evil manifestations that have corrupted our beautiful property."

"Hasn't it only been his 'beautiful property' for a short time?" asked Millie.

"Right you are. Neumany bought Gilgungate a little over a year ago once the previous tenant, Lord Gilgungate himself, passed away. It is my understanding that the deceased's children were not pleased to lose their home, but as I hear it, they were all looked after in the will, so none of them have true cause to complain."

Millie laughed. "Oh, Jeremiah, people of this level of society will embrace any small wrong as a mortal wound and vow vengeance. Taking their home from them, that's no small wrong."

Jeremiah sipped his wine. "You may be right. You can already imagine the direction my mind is moving. All that remains is to gather the facts to make it clear, and it seems that time is shortly upon us."

The endless stretch of the river was interrupted downstream by a building that seemed to float on the water itself. It looked ancient compared to the newer structures they were accustomed to seeing. It leaned slightly to one side and appeared to be held together by several dozen layers of paint, which gave it a mottled appearance despite the fact that the latest layer looked relatively new. The glass in the windows was thicker at the bottom in some cases and not in others, showing evidence of recent repairs.

The dock to which the building was attached sat just over the water line, so close that the decking disappeared to the eye unless you stared directly at it. It jutted out from a rocky shore that was distinct from the surrounding areas where the ground simply fell away to the water with occasional trees that looked prepared to follow suit.

The boat steered toward the dock, upon which stood a man bedecked with a checklist of items that declared him to be a gentleman: cane, top hat, monocle, and overly waxed moustache so thin it could have been drawn on. As they approached, he raised his hand in greeting and smiled, showing two rows of perfect teeth.

"Mr. Mountweazel, I presume?" said the man, as if he hadn't been the one to send the boat to retrieve them.

"The same," said Jeremiah. "May I present my colleague, Miss Mondegreen."

Lord Neumany bowed stiffly and held out a hand to help Millie disembark. She took it with an amused smile and stepped over. "I hope you will forgive me greeting you myself. I wanted a chance to speak to you before we were inside the house where we could be overheard."

Jeremiah climbed off the boat and accepted his and Millie's bags from Kelner, who simply nodded and disappeared below deck when thanked. The boat drifted away as languorously as it had arrived.

"Not at all, Lord Neumany. This is your home. Please do not stand on ceremony with us," said Millie. "We are here to help."

"Indeed," said the man. "And it is my hope that your help will put an end to this nonsense. Shall we walk? It is only a short distance, but it will give me the time needed to hopefully provide some clarity as to what I expect from you."

Neumany waved his hand and servants appeared as if from nowhere to gather up the visitors' belongings and spirit them up to the house. The three walked slowly, unconsciously matching the pace of the barge that had delivered them.

After cresting the incline from the water, they passed a large, ornate fountain. It stood dry, seahorse and water nymph gargoyles standing useless, their mouths permanently open in silent song. A man stood in wading boots in the stagnant pool in the basin, hammering on a pipe inside an open compartment. He did not look happy.

"What a beautiful fountain," said Millie.

Their host harrumphed and continued walking, irritation flickering on his face. It was quickly replaced with his previous genial look.

Millie raised an eyebrow to Jeremiah, who shrugged, but she could see him filing it away as something of interest.

"First of all, I would like to clarify that I do not believe for a second that my home is haunted," said Neumany, as he moved past the fountain without acknowledging the man.

"Your letter—" started Jeremiah.

"I know what I said in the letter, and I suspect that you, a man of reason, were quick to decide that I must be perfectly insane in the writing of it. But I assure you, I did so simply to mollify my wife who was composing it, and entreating me to take it down word for word. You see she is the one who sees spectres in simple things. I do not."

"Thus the reason for this walk," prompted Millie.

"Indeed," said Neumany. He had a tendency to speak directly to Jeremiah even when answering Millie, a fact that irritated her no end. "I do not want to alarm her with what I believe to be the true haunt of our home, the irksome insistence of the Gilgungate brood that they have any right to the place. I believe with all my being that one of them is responsible for the sounds we've been hearing."

"So there have, in fact, been sounds?" asked Jeremiah.

"Oh, yes. Long, drawn out moans. Screeching sounds. Banging. It's dreadful."

Millie snickered, then, realizing it was out loud, transformed it into a feigned sneeze.

"My dear, is the outdoors too overwhelming for you? I could have a servant come and bring you a cart," said Neumany.

The tone of his concern betrayed his condescension in deeming her weak because of one sneeze. She began to wonder what sort of frail being his wife was.

"I will be just fine, Lord Neumany, I assure you," she said.

"So you were talking about the noises?" prompted Jeremiah.

"Oh yes, there's no doubt that the noises are real, as you will hear for yourself. I just ask that you do not condemn my wife's conclusions too harshly, wrong though they are. She is a sensitive soul and should be treated accordingly."

After following the drive around Gilgungate Manor, they arrived at the front door of the enormous house and were greeted by servants. They were ushered into the hall and were relieved of all accoutrements—hats, canes, handbags—then guided into a sitting room, within which waited their hostess sitting wide-eyed and eager for their arrival.

"Basil, my dear, is this the man you were telling me about?" she asked, though she knew the answer.

"It is, my love. Allow me to present Jeremiah Mountweazel and Miss Mondegreen," said Neumany.

"Millie," said Millie.

Lady Neumany clapped her hands with glee. "Oh, I just know you'll rid us of these terrible spirits," she said breathlessly. "You'll see. Nighttime is when they come to this side of the veil, and you'll hear them. You'll see."

"They will, my love. Don't over excite yourself," said Lord Neumany.

She settled down a bit at that, smiled brightly, and clapped two sharp claps. "Anyone for refreshments?"

Dinner that night was an elaborate affair, with more courses in that one meal than Jeremiah or Millie usually ate in a day. The fare would be considered exotic by most—squid, rare beef, whole fish with their eyes beaming up from the plate—and the guests showed suitable appreciation for the bizarre variety. An uncountable number of meals at Mr. Panglossian's restaurant beneath Jeremiah's office had prepared them for the joining of culinarily disparate foods.

It was clear that the Neumanys were giving every effort to let their guests know that not only were they absurdly rich, they were also generous with their riches.

"Please, if I may be so bold as to broach the purpose of our visit, could you tell me about your experience with the phantom that torments your home?" asked Jeremiah as the dessert course was being laid in front of them. He was uncomfortably full, but knew it would be rude to refuse the slice of sponge topped with what was likely a fruit he had never encountered before.

"It's not just at night, but that's when it is most active," said Lady Neumany. Whenever she had a chance to speak she did so emphatically, with eyes bulging and hands waving like an orchestra conductor plagued by bees. "You can hear it in all parts of the house, but it's the wine cellar where it makes its home."

"The cellar?" asked Millie. "Can we go there after dinner?" She didn't look nearly as uncomfortable as Jeremiah felt. Millie had years of experience pretending to eat meals of this sort that Jeremiah lacked. She knew just how much she had to eat to not give insult.

"Oh, I won't go down there, my dear, and I suggest you avoid it, too. Best leave that for the men to sort out. It's far too scary," said Lady Neumany.

"Right you are, my dear. I'll take Mr. Mountweazel down after our port and he can apply his investigative talents. Miss Mondegreen, the servants will make certain you are comfortable," said Lord Neumany loudly. He snapped his fingers and two young women appeared behind her.

"If you'll follow us, Miss," said one. The other simply smiled.

Inwardly bristling, but knowing to show it would be to give insult, she followed the maids out of the room, casting a brief glare at Jeremiah who shrugged, powerless in the face of propriety.

After Lady Neumany wished her husband a good evening and was also escorted out, the two men retired to the study where they lit cigars and sipped from small glasses. The room was massive and every wall, save one, was filled with books, the other being solid windows, which were currently curtained. The books looked new for the most part with pristine, unblemished bindings. They may just as well be filled with blank pages, for as much use as they were likely to get beyond decoration. Jeremiah couldn't help but feel that whatever luxurious accommodations were currently being offered to Millie, she would certainly rather be in this room, having a glass of port the same as he was.

"It's a rum business, Mountweazel. I need you to find out how the Gilgungate brats are doing this and put an end to it. I'm so sick of hearing about poltergeists and demons," said Neumany.

"Well, if you would like to show me the cellar, I would be happy to, as you say, apply my investigative talents," said Jeremiah. "Miss Mondegreen would also be of great use, as her eyes sometimes see things that mine overlook."

Neumany looked perplexed. "I am sure we needn't bother her with these things. You know how women are. Too excitable."

At that moment Jeremiah was grateful that Millie was not in the room. He was sure how poorly that would have gone for the man. Every bone in his body wanted to argue with Neumany, but he was under strict instructions from Millie to play along with whatever social structure was in place here, so he bit his tongue.

He settled on a curt nod and the immediate draining of the small glass in his hand.

They made their way down the hall and down a set of stairs, into what was the largest cellar Jeremiah had ever seen. The entirety of his office and apartments could fit inside, with room left for the same again. Racks were arranged in rows, each heavily laden with bottles of all shapes and sizes, most covered with a fine layer of dust.

Jeremiah walked the perimeter of the large room, looking for vents or any sort of doorway or porthole. The walls all felt solid with no visible cracks or scrapes on the floor that would betray a secret room. There were newer shelves on one end of the room, but they felt solid and an examination of them provided no satisfaction.

"Did you install these shelves?" asked Jeremiah.

"No, they were here when we arrived," said Neumany. He joined Jeremiah in studying them and also found nothing. "Do you think that is important?"

Jeremiah shook his head. "Not sure, but likely not. It's best to not leave any detail undiscovered, though. You understand."

Neumany nodded as if he did.

"The doorway we came through is the only path into this cellar?" Jeremiah asked.

"Oh yes. Well, that I know of. If you find out otherwise I expect to be told," answered Neumany, eyeing the shelves again. He tapped a few then stepped away content. "I just can't sort out how they are doing this."

"So you suspect one of the Gilgungate children? Which one?"

Neumany scowled. "I've only met two of the three, Gavin and Gabriella. They were at the auction when I landed the winning bid. Both of them tried to argue with the authorities against my legitimacy as the new owner, but lost. Honestly, it's not my fault that their father hated them so much as to leave in his will that if their older brother wasn't around to claim the property, the estate would be sold off. They got a monetary inheritance of their own out of it, so I have no clue why they're so angry."

"And the third child?" asked Jeremiah. "The oldest?"

"From what I understand, he left years ago and hasn't been heard from since. He didn't turn up at the funeral and wasn't at the auction. They said he already had everything he needed out of the old man. Must have been a big falling out, if you ask me. So this all has to be down to the other two trying to scare us away."

Jeremiah nodded. He had yet to hear any haunting noises or anything similar to what the Neumanys had reported, but that meant little. Just because he hadn't witnessed it, did not make it untrue, though he had begun to suspect they were overstating the events when they did occur. The way Lord Neumany spoke about the Gilgungate children showed not only an indifference to their loss, but also a strong contempt for their very existence. Perhaps the haunting sounds were just the ghosts of guilt taunting the Neumanys.

It began then. A long, screeching wail.

"There! Do you hear it?" hissed Neumany in a loud whisper.

Jeremiah held his hand up to silence the man. The sound continued, eerie and unpredictable, reverberating around the room. It began low, then rose in timbre, a cacophonous keening that hurt his ears. Then, just as suddenly as it had started, it stopped.

"Enough to make you believe it's otherworldly, isn't it?" said Neumany. He had a terrified look in his eye that made it clear his capacity for reason ended when actually confronted with the inexplicable.

Fortunately, Jeremiah was less swayed by the apparent supernatural. "Not at all. I've found there is a simple explanation for most things, once the facts are discovered."

The wail began again, this time accompanied by a pounding sound. Neumany took two steps backwards, clearly fighting the urge to flee.

"The house is singular on the property, yes?" asked Jeremiah. "No outbuildings, cottages, guest houses?"

"None, aside from the boathouse you saw. Lord Gilgungate liked to keep everything under his thumb, so I'm told. It works out for us, because my Penelope has an immense dislike of long walks."

Jeremiah turned and regarded his host. "Shall we retire upstairs? I doubt any new information will reveal itself to us from here."

Neumany practically raced to the stairs. Jeremiah did his best to keep up.

"I trust I can leave you with it," said Neumany quickly as they reached the top of the stairs. "I must check on my lovely wife."

Jeremiah smiled. It would be easier without the man under foot anyway. "Of course, Lord Neumany. I trust I have leave of the property to investigate?"

"Whatever you like, just sort it out, Mountweazel," said the man, who then beat a hasty retreat down the hall.

Jeremiah decided it was time to go for a walk.

Millie allowed the maids to coddle her just enough that they could report back to their employers that she had been appropriately compliant. They had both been lovely girls, offering her a bath and to help her get dressed for bed, and both had been shocked when Millie not only asked their names, but also asked whether or not they were happy to be employed at Gilgungate.

The younger of the two, Tibby, swore up and down that it was the best job she had ever had. Millie got a feeling that the poor girl suspected any answer she gave would be reported back to the lady of the house. Mona, the other, had a more sarcastic demeanor and merely described the place as "remarkably bearable."

"It's not like they ask too much," continued Mona. "I've worked jobs where the lady of the house is constantly snapping her fingers and shouting demands. Lady Neumany shouts at Lord Neumany more than at us. With us she's almost apologetic."

"That's what being new to riches will get you," said Tibby, who then slapped her hand across her mouth and teared up. "Begging your pardon, Miss Mondegreen. I didn't mean to speak out of turn."

Millie hugged the girl, which surprised Tibby, then held her out at arms length. "You say whatever you like to me, Tibby my girl. I'm no more likely to rat you out to your employers as I am to strip naked and race through the dining room singing 'Who's Your Aunt Fanny Now', alright?"

The change that came over both maids was immediate and remarkable. They laughed with shock and relaxed considerably. Once the giggling died down, Millie asked them about the supposed ghost.

"I've heard it sometimes when I walk past the cellar," said Mona.

"Maybe someone was killed down there," suggested Tibby in a conspiratorial whisper.

"Walled up when they built the place and cursed to roam the cellar," added Mona teasingly. "Forced to stare at uncountable bottles of wine with no way of having even a single sip."

Tibby shuddered and Millie chuckled.

"That would be a torment," Millie said. "What about the Gilgungate children? What were they like?"

The maids both looked at her strangely. "We wouldn't know, Miss. We were hired by the Neumanys," said Tibby.

"We all were," added Mona. "All the staff."

Millie's eyebrows raised at that. She had never heard of new owners of a home clearing out all the old staff. It was usually proper to keep them on. Sure, you would rout out a few who didn't measure up to standards, but you needed people who knew how to run the house.

"So you all had to learn everything new, like where things were stored, how to source food, where to order supplies?" Millie asked.

"It did take a bit of feeling around, but we know what we're doing," said Tibby.

"Of course you do. I didn't mean to imply otherwise," said Millie.

"Poor Mr. Holde doesn't seem to, though," said Mona. "For us it's simple. There are closets you expect to find, rooms with purposes, that sort of thing. But that poor man is having a time and a half with that fountain, and Lord Neumany is getting more and more frustrated about it."

"The fountain?" asked Millie. "I saw it on the walk up. It's pretty, but I'm guessing the fact that it wasn't actually fountaining anything is why the man I saw working on it looked so vexed."

"I heard him grumbling to the cook that it stops working whenever it feels like. He goes and makes a show of working on it to make Lord Neumany happy, but he confessed to her that just as suddenly as it stops working it starts, no thanks to his efforts," said Tibby with a frown. "I wonder if that's the work of the ghost as well."

Mona snorted. "More likely him just not knowing what he's doing."

The maids stood as if some internal clock let them know they had lingered in one space for too long.

"If there's anything you need, Miss, don't hesitate to ask," said Tibby.

"Pull the bell by your bed and one of us will come running," added Mona. "Don't worry about bothering us. We're often grateful for something to do."

Millie thanked the girls and feigned going to bed. Then she stood by the window and admired the river. It was a full moon, and the dance of its reflection off the softly rippling waters of the Tarsain made it look like a circular stage lit by footlights. She imagined actors stepping onto the boards, the words of geniuses uttered with deliberate certainty from their lips as the crowd held its collective breath, the often inoperative fountain the centerpiece of their drama.

Her imaginings were interrupted by the sight of a figure walking across the edge of the yard by the river. In the moonlight she could only make out that whoever it was, they had a large amount of unkempt hair and wore clothes that did not suit the surroundings. The figure was moving away from the dock and into the surrounding woods.

Millie dove into her bag and pulled out a tunic and trousers, which she quickly slipped into. If she hurried, she might just be able to catch up with the person well enough to find out more.

Silently she moved through the house, wary of running into any servants or worse, her hosts, and having to explain what she was doing. It bristled her that Jeremiah would likely have leave to move freely but she was relegated to pampering and simply being seen.

Her internal grumblings distracted her just enough to turn the corner without looking, sending her headlong into a waiting figure.

"Gods, Millie, what cannon were you shot from?" whispered Jeremiah as he pulled himself up from his back and pushed the woman off of him. She had hit him with such force that the two of them had lost their footing, creating quite a clamor as they fell into a side table.

Both waited for the staff to come running but no one came.

"I suppose they're used to odd sounds in the night at this point," said Jeremiah. He stood and helped her to her feet. "Now where were you off to at such a tilt?"

"There is a person skulking around outside. I want to see who it is," said Millie as she pulled him to the door.

Jeremiah knew that though the standard response to a woman wanting to rush out into the night after a dark figure was to caution against it for fear of her safety, those words should never be uttered to Millie, especially when she had a purpose in mind. He was beyond confident that she would be able to handle herself in any altercation with far more success than he could manage.

So, in light of this knowledge, the only sensible path to take was to follow her lead without question.

Their journey was cut short by the sounds of loud singing and the unmistakable crash of broken glass.

"What in the hells?" hissed Millie.

This time the house did stir, as lights began to be turned up and the sounds of staff began to travel down the hallway.

"You're not exactly dressed for bumping into our hosts," said Jeremiah. "Follow your lead, and I'll investigate this ruckus."

Millie nodded and disappeared. Jeremiah made his way down the hall as two male servants rushed past him and out the front door. He followed and saw a visibly drunk young man standing in the gravelled drive, shaking his fist at the house and the two men who approached him.

"A rum business," said a voice behind him, and Jeremiah turned to see a bleary-eyed Lord Neumany staring over his shoulder out the door. "That damnable Gilgungate boy comes around whenever he has too many cups and thinks he can shout the house back into his family. I apologize for you having to see this, but I think it only reinforces what I've said, that the children are the culprits." Jeremiah walked forward with him to stand in the doorway.

"It hardly seems sensible for him to be so subtle as to sneakily haunt your home and then announce himself with such vulgarity, though, Lord Neumany," answered Jeremiah. "In my mind, this puts him out of the suspect list almost entirely." He watched as the two men subdued the drunken miscreant, a task made none too difficult by his inability to stand or even point in the right direction. Jeremiah looked down and saw the shattered remnants of a wine bottle just outside the door.

Neumany frowned, then shrugged. "I leave it to you to sort out, just as I leave it to my servants to clean up the mess." He looked down at the bottle fragments, sniffed loudly, and retreated back inside and up the stairs.

Jeremiah considered trying to talk to the Gilgungate son, but saw that consciousness had left the man as he was bundled into his carriage and removed from the premises. He knelt and looked at the bottle shards, seeing from the label that it was not an older vintage, but something new and inexpensive, so it most certainly did not come from the cellar.

He slipped back inside and made his way through the house to hopefully catch up with Millie. She was waiting by one of the back doors, her face a scowl.

"Blasted servants made it impossible to get away. I kept having to hide. I considered beginning to howl like a ghost but thought it might cause more problems than it helped." She grinned and motioned for him to follow as she slipped outside.

Millie cut a straight line across the lawn to where she had seen the person last. Even in the light of the moon, Millie was hard to see in her dark clothes, so Jeremiah had to follow the line of trampled grass until he caught up with her.

"He was here, heading that way," she said, pointing. "So the question is, where was he going?"

"And from where did he come?" added Jeremiah. "Let's see if we can determine that and go from there."

They followed the path down to the dock, looking around with more intent than when they had arrived. As they made their way, Millie filled Jeremiah in on what the maids had told her. She couldn't see him well, but she knew the look on his face, and knew what he would say next.

"Interesting."

In the low light Millie grinned.

The small boat house was locked, a barrier Millie quickly overcame with some tools from her pocket. Its contents revealed nothing remarkable outside of their lack of use. It seemed the Neumanys were not boat people.

"What now?" asked Jeremiah. "Do you want to head in the direction the person went? There may not even be a trail."

Millie started to answer then looked over his shoulder, grabbed him and pulled him into the shadows. She pointed up the hill.

The man looked even more unkempt up close, his hair a tangle of unbrushed locks, his clothes worn and fraying in places. He walked with an almost casual gait as if unconcerned with moving in secret at all.

They watched as he walked to the side of the dock and stepped down on the rocks, picking his way across them for a few dozen yards before reaching into some brush and twisting something.

A doorway opened, casting a faint light into the night for a few seconds before he disappeared within, pulling it shut so that it disappeared without an obvious trace.

"Bet you didn't expect this turn of events," whispered Millie.

"I had a notion," said Jeremiah with a satisfied smile.

The two made their way over to the hidden portal. The entire thing was obscured from view, cleverly disguised with underbrush and stones, which had been attached to the outside to help it blend. It was a solid wood door, reinforced with steel bands, with a wheel in the center that Millie turned.

The corridor beyond was long, and lit by a series of dim bulbs set into the ceiling, half of which were blown. They could see that it went for a while then ended.

"Shall we?" said Millie, and she headed down the corridor, Jeremiah close behind her.

Partway down, they encountered a small alcove in which a confusing mass of pipes and valves were housed. Jeremiah pointed out one knob that showed more use than the others.

"The fountain? But why?" whispered Millie.

He nodded and pointed down the path that they continued to follow.

The hallway ended and turned left abruptly, the light spilling out almost blinding after their journey through the dark.

The room was large, about the size of the sitting room in the house, and opulently decorated. Some effort had been made to section the room into separate parts, though without walls, and it was in the section that could only be described as a makeshift music room that the man stood, violin to his chin and bow in hand.

"Mr. Gilgungate, I presume," said Jeremiah loudly, bringing a start from the man and a curious glance from Millie.

The man looked at them and sagged. His face, which had previously been blank, now showed sadness.

"The same," said the man. "Though I'm called Gideon by my friends. Will you call me Gideon?"

The question hung in the air. Were they friends or foes? They had entered what he clearly deemed his home uninvited. What was the purpose of such an intrusion?

"Hello Gideon, I'm Jeremiah and this is Millie."

The man relaxed and set the violin down. "Can I offer you something to drink?"

Millie looked back and forth between Gideon and Jeremiah. "You both seem well versed in what is going on here and yet I stand here uninformed. Kindly inform me," she insisted.

Jeremiah stepped in and accepted the tumbler of whiskey the man offered him. "Millie, meet Gideon Gilgungate, eldest son of Lord Gilgungate and rightful heir to the Gilgungate estate."

"But they sold the estate," she said.

"Because I let them," responded Gideon. "My brother and sister, insufferable cretins that they are, wanted the house. As soon as father fell ill, they both started trying to work their machinations on me. I wanted naught to do with it."

"So you let the estate be sold off unchallenged?" asked Millie.

Gideon let out a deep-throated laugh. "You should have seen their faces."

"And you're responsible for the awful sounds they are hearing in the house?" asked Millie.

Gideon looked from her to Jeremiah in confusion. "Awful sounds? They shouldn't be able to hear anything. I made sure the wall was thick enough."

Jeremiah gestured to the violin. "You play?"

"I'm self taught," said the man proudly. "I also play the bodhrán and didgeridoo," he said, holding up the drum and the long tube.

"I'm afraid the walls aren't nearly thick enough," laughed Jeremiah.

"So this vagabond has been squatting on my land this whole time?" shouted Lord Neumany. "This is an outrage! I will have him thrown off the property at once!"

Jeremiah held his hands up in a placating manner. "I would suggest you quell that urge long enough to fully grasp the situation, sir."

"What is there to grasp? He is a trespasser!"

They had explained the situation to the Neumanys over breakfast. They told them how Gideon, fed up with the antics of his siblings, had taken residence in the shelter that had been fashioned a decade earlier. He had closed up the door that led to the wine cellar, once providing a path to the dock from inside, and made it his home. The only reason they had any clue he was there was when he redirected the water from the fountain to have a bath or when he felt inspired by the musical muses. He had opted not to resurface at his father's funeral, already having made his peace with the old man before his departure, and then chose not to appear and stake his claim.

"But he cannot live on our land, surely," whimpered Lady Neumany.

"I would advise you to allow it to continue. It would only take his appearance in front of a magistrate to nullify your claim on the home and make it his again. As it is, he is content with his life and has no wish to change his situation."

"So we're trapped. We have to let him stay," muttered Lord Neumany.

"You know, I've heard it said that in Fleis, it's very on trend to have a hermit living on your property," said Millie.

Lady Neumany perked up. "Is that right?" she said, staring wistfully at the ceiling.

"It is. Much like having a garden or a tennis court, having a hermit gives the estate character. Everybody who is anybody has one," said Millie.

"And what do you do with them?" asked Lord Neumany, suddenly curious.

"You just let them go about their business," said Millie.

"It's like having a pet," whispered Lady Neumany.

Jeremiah watched the exchange with great amusement. "So it's settled, then. You will allow him to stay and in return he won't challenge your claim to the home."

"I wonder what you feed them," said Lady Neumany, suddenly engrossed in the idea.

They saw him at the dock as they were waiting for their passage back up the Tarsain to arrive. The Neumanys had been hospitable, but suddenly finding out they had another inhabitant in their home with little choice in the matter was hardly a favorable outcome, so Jeremiah and Millie had excused themselves to wait on the dock for their transportation. Lady Neumany, when they left, was still talking with eager fascination about the hermit and how envious the neighbors would be that they had one, so Lord Neumany seemed at least a little content that the spirits had been dispelled.

Gideon stood on the stones by the water and gave them a lazy wave.

"If you're ever in Tamarind, look us up. I know a lot of musicians," shouted Millie.

The man smiled and nodded, then disappeared through the hidden door.

"You know, it's never a dull moment with you, Jeremiah."

"Says the woman who charged fearlessly down a poorly-lit corridor in the middle of the night," he said with a chuckle.

The boat pulled up to the dock and Kelner wordlessly took their bags and helped them aboard. As they settled into the chairs once again, and took the offered glasses of wine, Jeremiah began to laugh.

"What's so funny?"

"It's amazing that you convinced them they wanted to have a pet hermit. Who ever heard of such a ludicrous thing?" he said.

Millie joined his laugh. "I wish I could say it wasn't true," she said.

"What?"

Millie nodded.

"Ye gods, I will never understand your people," Jeremiah said and the two toasted the end of another case.

The Body Beneath the Boards

Jeremiah stepped out of the carriage into the busy, cacophonous street and looked up at the colorful facade of the theater over which Millie rented a modest room. He had been to this part of The Bottoms many times to pick her up, but had somehow neglected to see the inside of the theater, or for that part, inside Millie's apartment.

As for the latter, he imagined that this day was not the right day to change that. Millie's private life was hers to lead. She had made that clear when he had offered her accommodations in his apartment and she had refused. The separation of their lives undoubtedly helped their working relationship.

As for the inside of the theater, he was delighted that his ignorance of it was due to change that evening. Millie had insisted that he join her for the variety showcase that was due to open that night and would feature a friend of hers.

Jeremiah looked up and chuckled at the name of the place written in large, multi-colored letters across the overhang: The Callipygian Theatre. The Bottoms was a dangerous neighborhood that his partner chose to call home, full of thieves and cutthroats, but he was happy to see that at least some parts of it maintained a good sense of humor.

Millie's apartment, he knew, could only be reached from the alley off to the left of the theater. She often regaled him with stories about the performers she met as she went to and fro, and how frequently after parties spilled out into the alley, giving her a free show and celebrations to join. He looked up the metal staircase that climbed the side of the building to a small landing and took a deep breath. He was no fan of heights, and even less so when the only thing keeping him from hurtling to the ground looked as though one heavy step could tear it from the wall. Still, if Millie went up and down those stairs without fear of impending death he had to concede that they were likely safe enough.

As he grabbed the railing and mounted the stairs he heard the unmistakable voice of Millie coming from further down the alley.

"It will be alright, Pashsha, you'll see. My friend will be here soon and I'm sure he will help," she said.

Jeremiah thanked any gods that may be listening and hopped down, walking around to find Millie and a woman standing just outside the backstage door. Millie, in defiance of her upbringing and embracing comfort, was dressed in her usual blouse and trousers, a fact which raised fewer eyebrows here in The Bottoms than it did on The Strand where he kept his rooms. Her companion wore a diaphanous robe over a sequined leotard.

Jeremiah cleared his throat as he approached.

"Good afternoon, ladies," he said, with a short bow.

"This day is not so good any more," said the strange woman with a lyrical Borovian accent. She stared at him with large, brown eyes puffy from excessive crying. She began to cry again, earning her a hug and further soothing from Millie.

"What has happened?" he asked.

"Pashsha was just telling me the showcase might be canceled because someone has stolen all of the equipment," said Millie, frowning.

"My silks, the dummy, the brothers' pins, even some of Nandi's props. Gone!" wept Pashsha into Millie's shoulder.

Jeremiah had no idea who most of the people were that she had mentioned, but she could mean none other than The Great Nandi with the last, the headlining act of the show and the one he was most excited to see perform. Posters featuring the magician waggling his fingers and peering at the viewer over a sparkling top hat began to appear as soon as Jeremiah's carriage had entered The Bottoms and became more frequent the closer to the theater he moved until he found the front of the building itself papered with the things. The drawing was so realistic that one could almost see his long, curled mustache twitch as you watched it.

Millie gave him a look and raised her eyebrows, a silent 'can we help them?'

Jeremiah nodded. "Please tell me more," he said. "Perhaps inside, where we can be heard better over the noise of the street?"

Pashsha managed a smile and gestured to the door, which stood propped open. The three entered the room and found almost as much movement as outside. She grabbed the sleeve of a passing stagehand, a tall and lean man just out of boyhood, and spun him to face her.

"Have you found them yet?" she demanded.

"No, sorry Miss Pashsha. Not yet," he said. He moved to go and she held tight to his arm. "If you'll pardon me, Miss, I can't look while I'm standing here with you," he said.

"You're a good boy, Simon," she said as she released his sleeve and smoothed it down. "I know you'll find them."

The young man raced into the next room, joining several others who stood shrugging before moving off to look further.

"So you came to the theater today and your supplies were missing?" asked Jeremiah. "How many people have access to the theater?" He glanced over at the open door and could picture people coming and going as they pleased—until a large man, easily a head taller than Jeremiah and nearly twice as broad across his shoulders, came from the next room and took up residence in the chair next to the door.

"Thanks for watching, Miss Pashsha," he said. "Mr. Maffick told me to ask you to join him on the stage for a palaver."

"Thank you, Bert," she said and, grabbing Jeremiah and Millie by the sleeves, said, 'Come, come, we go," before pulling them along with her up the stairs.

On the stage stood a collection of people, all gathered around a small man with thick spectacles and a bald pate poorly covered with a comb-over. He was waving his hands, trying to quiet the group, but none of them were interested in being silenced.

"I expect more professionalism out of the venues in which I perform, Mr. Maffick," said a man in a cardigan despite the heat of the theater. His hand was twitching at his side like it was meant to be doing something and was not able.

"We trusted our equipment—" said one man with shaggy, brown hair wearing orange and purple tights with the name 'REG' sewn on the front of his tunic in large letters.

"—would be looked after and kept safe," said another slightly taller man in identical tights whose bald head shone in the spotlight and whose top advertised him as 'TOM'.

"It is an outrage," added Pashsha to the riot of sound.

Simon, the stagehand who had just been accosted by Pashsha, stood in the wings along with another younger boy, both waiting to be told what to do.

Mr. Maffick looked past Pashsha to Jeremiah and Millie, his face a mixture of confusion and irritation at the intrusion amid the chaos swirling around him.

"Gentlemen, and lady, please," shouted Maffick. He mopped his forehead with a handkerchief as he continued to wave them down with the other hand. "If you'll let me get a word in, we can discuss what needs to be done."

All assembled stopped speaking at once, leaving a sudden silence that hung in the air, which seemed to surprise Maffick until he realized the fight he had been expecting was over, and he finally spoke.

"We can split hairs about who is responsible for the theft later but, at the moment, we need to either find your equipment or agree on how we want to change the show," he said. "Because as you all know, the show must go on."

"I do not fly with no silks," said Pashsha with an exaggerated pout. "You want I should stand on stage and flap my arms like a bird?"

"Without Bok I have no act," said the man in the cardigan. His hand twitched again and Jeremiah realized that the man was obviously accustomed to having his dummy on his hand. "Who would do such a thing as take a man's companion?"

"We can juggle all sorts of things, but—" said Reg the acrobat.

"—it won't be the show people want to see!" continued Tom.

"Where is Miss Vila?" asked Maffick. "And Nandi? Where are they?"

"Very suspicious," said the ventriloquist. "Perhaps they've gone for some private time."

Simon stepped forward. "I saw Tegan, um, Miss Vila in the green room just a few moments ago. She was helping look for your things, so you can stop saying such horrible lies." The young man was red in the face and stood with his fists clenched.

The ventriloquist held up his hands. "Sorry, lad. I didn't mean to upset you by suggesting the young lady who, I might add, is the only one of us who can still go on since her voice cannot be stolen, might be up to no good. I mean who am I to suggest that, innocent though she may appear, the young lady could have a nefarious streak to her that prompts her to commit a few acts of theft to promote her prospects.”

“Hey, wait—” said Reg.

“—he's right!” added Tom.

Simon stepped forward again and was stopped by Maffick's hand on his chest. “Settle down, boy. You'll not gain any girl's favor being a brute. Trust me. Please go and fetch Miss Vila and bring her up to speak with us. While Dr. Philodox and the Spanghew Brothers may have a point, they also have hit on the reality of the situation, and that is that we have to put on some sort of show tonight and right now, she's the only player who can perform.”

The four performers began shouting at Maffick again, all outraged that he would so easily toss them aside. Simon, a satisfied look on his face, retreated to the wings but only got so far as the curtain before a piercing scream stopped him in his tracks. All present stopped as if they weren't sure of what they had just heard but sprang into action as another scream followed.

The assembled broke into two groups, some going down the stairs on one side and the rest on the other, all with the goal of reaching the area below the boards from where the sound had originated. As they merged back into a single group below it was to find a young woman, white as a sheet, crying into Bert the bouncer's shoulder as Simon tried to get her to say why she had screamed.

“Dead…body…” she managed to say, pointing over her shoulder. She sobbed uncontrollably and refused to turn around.

All assembled looked in the direction she had pointed and saw what she was talking about. On the top shelf lay an old rug, bulging in the middle, and sticking out of one end was the unmistakable shape of a bloody arm.

There had been some speculation regarding what needed to be done, but all of it struck Jeremiah as needless and inappropriate. The tendency of people in The Bottoms upon being confronted with a dead body was usually to keep walking and hope it wouldn't be there on their return trip. Very seldom was the Constabulary called, usually only when the body had been seen by more than a few people who then couldn't get their stories straight.

When Maffick had ordered Bert to pull the rug down Jeremiah had stepped in and explained to all present that they were all witnesses to something that could not go unreported, and because of this fact it was best to leave things as they lie until the proper authorities could be notified and summoned. Reluctantly, everyone had agreed, and Maffick had sent a runner to the nearest call box to summon Inspector Ward at Jeremiah's prompting.

Simon, his face as white as Tegan's and fear in his eyes, had escorted her upstairs, followed closely by the acrobats and Dr. Philodox, who chose that moment to regale the retreating company with the story of how he first found his wooden companion, Bok, and how their friendship was eternal. No one had the heart to tell him how ridiculous he sounded in the wake of current events.

Jeremiah and Millie stayed below, and once the crowd had cleared he turned to her with a frown. "You know I have complete faith in your ability to take care of yourself, but I feel like now would be an appropriate time to renew my offer to take a room in my apartment."

Millie laughed. "What, and miss all this fun?" She walked over and looked up at the hand. "Gruesome business, though. Who do you think it is?"

Jeremiah frowned deeper. "Judging by the ring on his finger, I think it's fair to say it is likely our missing magician The Great Nandi, which is a terrible disappointment if I'm honest."

"Did you know him?"

He shook his head. "I knew of him. He was a much bigger deal when I was younger. I even saw him perform once or twice. But you know how things go. Trends come and go, and after a while his act wasn't of interest to anyone anymore and he faded from the spotlight."

"Poor old man," said Millie.

"He didn't deserve to end up discarded like this," agreed Jeremiah.

"So who do you think did it?" she asked.

"That's what I aim to find out," he said.

Maffick had ordered Bert to close up the theater, locking everyone in who was there when the body was found, partly to contain the knowledge that it had happened and partly to potentially trap the killer inside to be discovered.

"Assuming Mr. Maffick is correct, one of the people on the stage is a killer," said Millie. She slipped her hand down her calf and pulled out a small pistol, checking to make sure it was loaded and ready.

"Do you think it will come to that?" asked Jeremiah. He twisted the head of his cane and pulled up slightly, revealing the blade before snapping it back down.

"It never hurts to be prepared," she said. "Now let's get upstairs so you can work your magic."

They found everyone on the stage once again tormenting Mr. Maffick with demands.

"I am well aware of the reputation of this part of the city, Maffick, but I thought for certain my safety was never in question," railed Dr. Philodox. "I mean the very idea of my poor Bok being stolen by some greedy guttersnipe is appalling enough, but now I could be murdered just for the sake of someone's amusement. I may be old, Maffick, but I'm not foolish. I insist you open those doors so I can leave this cursed place and get myself to safety immediately."

Pashsha was quietly weeping, her arms around the distraught Tegan who cried along with her. As Philodox paused for a breath, she snapped her head around and glared at Maffick. "If you think I perform in this place now, you are fool, Mr. Maffick. And I will not leave young Tegan here to suffer any ills either."

Simon stepped forward. "Surely people who have already bought tickets will be expecting a show."

Maffick looked at the young man like he was insane. "There is a dead body beneath our very feet," he spat. "And you want us to open the doors!"

Simon shrugged. "It's The Bottoms, Mr. Maffick. You see dead bodies all the time in The Bottoms. If businesses shut down every time someone died, nothing would happen."

"You know who I think it was?" asked Reg.

"The magician," answered Tom. "He's the only one of us—"

"—who isn't here," finished Reg.

Jeremiah cleared his throat and stepped forward. "I'm afraid I took a closer look, and The Great Nandi's ring is on the finger of the body. Though we can't definitively say it is him, the evidence does seem to support it. We'll know once the Constabulary arrives and examines the body."

"When will that be?" demanded Maffick.

"Any time now," said Jeremiah, though he didn't know for sure.

"Well then," said Maffick, rubbing his hands together as he began to pace. "We can still salvage this. All we have to do is decide what kind of performance we can do."

"You cannot be serious," demanded Pashsha. "It's utterly vulgar to ask us to perform on top of death, and even if we wanted, Tegan here is only one whose act is unaffected, as we said earlier."

Dr. Philodox stepped forward and pointed a finger. "Maybe that was the plan all along. What did you do, missy, steal all of our gear and then lure poor old Nandi downstairs and cave his head in?"

Tegan erupted in sobs again and shook her head vigorously. "No no no! I could never!"

"Don't be absurd, Philodox. How in hell is she to have lifted the body up to where it hides. Look at her. She's tiny," said Pashsha, her irritation with the man finally bubbling to the surface. "Besides, I heard you were jealous Nandi had the top spot. In fact, I heard you yelling about that yesterday in the alley."

"Maybe she had—" said Reg.

"—help from someone," added Tom.

"Like who?" asked Maffick.

Jeremiah had been watching the exchange with great interest, and in doing so, had neglected to pay attention to everyone else. Once he realized his mistake he took inventory of the parties present and found one missing.

"That's a good question, Mr. Maffick," he said. "And if you'll excuse me for a moment, I think I may have an answer for you. Millie, can you help me please?"

He headed for one side of the stage and pointed her to the other before descending the stairs. When he reached the bottom, it was to find her looking at him from across the room before both of their attention was caught by the movement under the stage.

Simon was struggling to pull the body down from the shelf, oblivious to the fact that the two of them had walked up behind him.

"Ah, Simon, that's a good man," said Jeremiah. "Let me get the other end and we'll make quick work of it."

Simon spun around and let out a nervous laugh. "I just thought I would get it down so that the constables wouldn't have to mess with it," he said.

"You're awfully cavalier about handling a dead body," said Jeremiah.

"Right, earlier you looked terrified," said Millie, "and now you're willing to manhandle it yourself. Very strange."

"Almost as if he knows what's in there," said Jeremiah.

Simon laughed again. "Well, it's a body, isn't it? We all know what's in there."

The arm, which hung farther down than it was before due to the young man's efforts, slid free from the rug and fell to land with a solid thud on Simon's shoulder. He grabbed it and threw it to the ground behind him.

"How in the hell?" said Millie.

Jeremiah laughed. "Millie, did I ever tell you about the time I saw The Great Nandi saw off his own arm?"

Simon's face was red, though it was hard to tell if it was from anger or the horror of the situation he was in.

"No, I don't believe you did," she said.

"Amazing trick. Really stymied me as a child until I worked out how he did it," said Jeremiah. "You see, it was a prosthetic arm that he sawed through. Probably one of many he kept on hand. Then after he sawed it off, he could regrow the arm by slipping his actual arm out."

Simon moved to push past them and Jeremiah grabbed his arm.

"Why don't you help me get everyone's gear down, Simon, and we can clear this whole mess up without much more fuss?"

"**S**o there is no body?" asked Ward.

"I'm afraid you were pulled away from your comfortable office for nothing more grand than a case of stolen property that wasn't actually stolen," laughed Jeremiah.

Simon was being held in the green room by a more-surly-than-usual Bert who assured them the only way the young man would leave without permission is in pieces. Maffick hadn't decided yet what he wanted to do with him.

"That's alright. Miss Slater was being extra persnickety today and Cavil is on the warpath since the Sudworth affair, so it's good to get out. But since you've already solved the crime, why don't you fill me in?" said Ward.

"It's a love story," said Millie with a grin.

"Unrequited, though, so it hardly counts," said Jeremiah. "Simon, the young stagehand being held under threat of dismemberment in the other room, is madly in love with the young lady upstairs, Miss Tegan Vila. It seems he decided it was unfair that she didn't have top billing in the show tonight and would steal parts from every other act so that she was the only one who could perform."

Millie laughed. "In his haste to hide the things, he neglected to fully hide Nandi's fake arm, so when everyone saw it, still sticky with fake blood from its last use, and the bulging rug they concluded it was a dead body."

"We all came to that conclusion," said Jeremiah with a sheepish grin. "But then I realized Simon was acting strangely and when everyone was distracted with blaming each other he decided to move the stolen goods so when you arrived there would be nothing to investigate and the show could go on, albeit with only his love on the boards."

"But what about the missing magician? If he's not dead, where has he been?" asked Ward.

Millie laughed. "The old man was sound asleep at the back of the house. Third seat from the left in the very back, or what he likes to call the 'Snorer's Seat'. He says if he sleeps there before the show, no one will sleep during the show."

Maffick came into the room shaking his head. "Performers, eh? Never a dull moment with this lot."

Ward took out his notepad. "How would you like to proceed, Mr. Maffick? If you like I can take the lad for a stay under the river. A night or two should show him the error of his ways."

Maffick laughed. "Goodness, no. This is The Bottoms, Inspector. If you locked up every soul who was up to no good I would have no customers." He pointed across the room and they watched as Tegan quietly knocked on the green room door and entered as Bert left and stood outside. "Besides, I think some good may have come out of it after all."

"So that's it? The boy steals from you all and makes you think there's a corpse in your basement and in the end he gets the girl?" asked an incredulous Ward.

Maffick smiled the smile of an entertainer. "Love makes stories worthwhile, Inspector. As for your time, can I interest you in a ticket to tonight's show, on the house?"

Ward shrugged. "I'll never understand people, Jeremiah."

Millie laughed and took his arm. "Let's find our seats, Radclyffe, and enjoy the show. It won't make anything make sense, but at least you'll have a good time."

The Autonomous Automaton

Millie Mondegreen, in complete defiance of the rules posted at regular intervals along the viewing rail of the airship, knelt on the railing and leaned out against the glass that divided her from the safety of the gondola and several thousand feet of rapid descent to the earth below.

"Jeremiah, you just have to see this," she said over her shoulder. "I promise you it's safe."

Her companion was unimpressed with her guarantees and was more interested in reading the newspaper, which he held in his lap, than any of the sightseeing available.

"I'm quite content here, in my seat, looking at the words on the page and pretending with every ounce of creative juice in my brain that we are on a train, thank you very much. In fact, I would argue that if we had chosen that means of transport we would already be in Mellick booking a ticket up the funicular to the waystation instead of slowly creeping across the sky," said Jeremiah.

The railway that Jeremiah so desperately wanted to be riding on stretched out in an almost perfectly straight line below. Millie could make out the towns as they passed them that sat along the rails, and if she squinted she could spot the smaller towns peppered sporadically across the land, connected to each other with roads like thin veins in the brown and green expanse.

"It's so beautiful," she said, wide-eyed and smiling like a child.

"I'm sure it is, but do you know what's more beautiful?" Jeremiah said.

"What's that?"

"Not falling to my death because I fell through an airship viewing window."

A man in a transport uniform was slowly making his way toward her, ostensibly to assist her with reading the signs warning her against the very thing she was currently doing. Millie hopped down and smiled sweetly at the man as he approached. She whistled a tune while glancing around the cabin brimming with innocence. Seeing she would no longer be a problem, the man walked by as if he was simply passing through, giving her a brief nod and a "Ma'am."

"Do you have any plans for that infernal tune to leave your head any time in the near future?" grumbled Jeremiah. It had sprung to her lips dozens of times over the last week since she first heard it from a busker by The Centre, and the repetition had clearly begun to grate on her colleague.

She laughed and decided to deflect. "What is it with you and high places, anyway?" she asked, sliding into the chair next to him. They had decided to ride in relative comfort, paying the extra fee to be in the upstairs portion of the gondola, an area adorned with large, comfortable chairs and wait staff instead of the hard wooden benches and bar downstairs.

"Something in me doesn't cope well with the concept," he said, folding the paper up and giving her his attention. "While you seem to be able to walk around and foolishly climb on things as though you are on the ground, my brain cannot release the fact that I am at a far higher elevation than I have any business being, and as my brain is occupied with this knowledge, my legs are rendered useless."

Millie patted him on the arm. "Well thank you for agreeing to take the airship to get to the Chetan Waystation."

Jeremiah picked up the paper and opened it back to the page he was previously reading. "As I recall, you refused to come with me unless we were flying."

"Aren't you glad you caved, then? What would you do without me while you...what are we doing again?"

"Investigating the continuous disappearance of goods coming into and out of the waystation. A man called Buccula, in charge of the safe transport of goods, is under fire for the discrepancies from his superiors. He hired us to look into the matter to satisfy their need for action. His letter had, for lack of a better way of putting it, pessimistic undertones."

"He doesn't think we'll find anything?" Millie asked.

"It did not seem so. As I recall, the Chetan Waystation is a whirlwind of activity on its slowest days. The marketplace in the main section runs all day and night, and people come and go with such frequency, including the vendors, that investigating any person in particular is a fruitless cause at best." Jeremiah shrugged. "Still, he is required to take action, and we are to be that action. The way I see it, we get to travel and get paid to be a showpiece, and even if we don't solve the case we still come out ahead."

"Why you?" Millie asked.

Jeremiah feigned insult. "Why, whatever could you mean?"

Millie grinned. "If they just want a figurehead to come in, look around, and shrug, they could hire anyone."

A long whistle sounded, telling them that they were due to arrive soon.

"A few years back I worked a case for the head of the Waystation, Valeria Beldam, involving some missing jewels from her home. Seems she remembered me and essentially forced Buccula to hire me."

Millie's face twisted as though she smelled something awful. "So this Buccula guy?"

"Likely not to be a friend," said Jeremiah.

"Splendid," Millie said sarcastically. "And also not likely to be happy when you solve his conundrum and make him look bad to his boss."

Jeremiah smiled. "I prefer not to celebrate success until I've achieved it, but yes, he will likely be unhappy, especially if he is the culprit. Are you ready for your part?"

The grin that spread across Millie's face was both childlike and sinister. "Oh, don't you worry about me, Jeremiah. You go do your official handshaking and hobnobbing and leave me to the dark corners and alleyways."

"There aren't likely to be any alleyways in a building perched on top of a mountain," said Jeremiah, a small shudder passing through his body as he contemplated the full significance of that fact.

"Well then crawl spaces. Whatever there are, that's where you'll find me."

"Then I suggest we take leave of each other before we dock," said Jeremiah. "You will be able to locate me easier than I you, so please keep in touch."

"I will. But now, I'm going to go watch us dock before it's too late," she said, and she sprang from her chair and rushed down the stairs.

Jeremiah stood and slowly, as though a single misstep could mean his doom, walked to the viewing window. He reached out and clutched the guard rail, holding back so that he could not see down but could see out, as the airship approached the waystation.

It had been clever, all those years ago, for the people of Mallick to build the station. At the base of the mountain the town sat, larger than most on the rails because it was built around the tunnel that cut through the Chetan Mountains. A short ride up the funicular railway connected the town to the station, and this meant that trade could come by air, by rail, or by road and Mallick acted as a hub. Nowhere was that more evident than in the marketplace of the waystation, which Jeremiah was moments away from seeing again.

The structure was sound, he had been assured the first time he had traveled there, in that it was built upon a flattened portion of the mountaintop, but also held up by struts which braced any portion that hung over the edge. It was composed mostly of metal, solidly riveted together, with windows that had been installed to be blast proof, though Jeremiah wasn't certain they had ever been properly tested.

He could see people staring out at the airship through those windows as it docked, both adults and children with their faces pressed against the glass in rapt fascination. Jeremiah had to admit that if the heights didn't stymie his enthusiasm, he would be just as fascinated.

He thought about Millie, down below, likely already changed into whatever appearance she chose for this case, and wondered if he would even know it was her if they met on the floor.

Jeremiah stayed there, clutching the rail, until the final whistle sounded announcing the airship was completely docked. Only then did he walk back to his seat, gather his things, and join the crowd heading through the doorway to the gangplank.

He tried to put out of his mind the way the floor swayed to and fro. As the doorway opened, he was happy to see that the exit was fully enclosed, a far cry from the platform in Tamarind that only had the suggestion of rails and tended to slide back and forth as a person walked across.

He made it through quickly regardless and found himself confronted with a wall of sound as soon as the second door was opened.

The docks for the airships released passengers onto the upper level of the waystation. This allowed for people to gain the full vantage to see all that was available the moment they stepped through the door.

Below, covering the massive open floor, were rows and rows of booths, some permanent structures and some simply tables but all laden with wares for sale or trade. Jeremiah could see dried meat and fish hung next to perfumeries and jewelers. Book stands nestled up to tea shops and chemists. The mercurial nature of the market meant there was no rhyme or reason to the placement of any of the stalls.

A traveler's vardo selling scarves of every color—a rainbow punch in the middle of the madness—sat next to a long, enclosed portion fronted with tables laden with weapons of all sorts, from guns to blades. All of this sat under the watchful eye of a man who could only be described as a giant. If there was something you needed, it could be found at the Chetan Waystation, but guard your wallets and purses as you buy.

Jeremiah knew that though things seemed completely legitimate on the surface, in any number of those shops illicit items could be bought. A woman could buy cologne for her lover and poison for her husband in the same stall if she knew the right way to ask. One could order a first edition print of a classic novel and arrange for your employer to be killed by talking to the same people. Anything was possible.

Millie, he knew, was already a part of the crowd, and he envied her that as he saw three men in station uniforms march directly toward him, one holding a sign that irritatingly read 'MOWNTWEESELL'. Fighting the urge to pretend he hadn't seen them, Jeremiah raised his hand in greeting.

"Mr. Mountweazel?" said the man with the sign. He was a few inches shorter than Jeremiah and far more plump—a fact punctuated by his shirt, which was at least a size too small and buttoned to the top, giving him a prominent double chin. The other two men were nondescript, save that one of them had a lazy eye that seemed to be studying the wall to the left.

"The same," said Jeremiah. "I presume you are Mr. Buccula?"

With a delivery as deadpan as a priest practicing to an empty church the man said, "Gee, you're as clever as she said. Follow me," and he turned and stalked away without a glance back, followed closely by the two men.

Reluctantly, Jeremiah followed.

Millie was in her element. She had joined the throng of commoners leaving the airship and melted into the crowd, wild red hair suppressed under a brunette pageboy wig. She had changed her dress and finery for filthy work clothes that made her, after the careful application of a few smears of grease, appear to be the sort who worked on the machinery. This essentially rendered her invisible. Like the maid in a mansion, the worker in a complex like this disappeared from notice.

She slipped through the crowd and surveyed the floor. Though she could spend a considerable amount of time going stall to stall sampling, haggling, and purchasing if the mood struck her she wasn't here for that. She was here to find things out and the best way to start on that was to find the places that weren't supposed to be there: the hidden hatches and doors.

She reached into her satchel and pulled out a pair of goggles that she slipped onto her head and a small box with two dials and a meter on the front that she held out in front of her. A clicking sound emitted at random intervals from the device and she began a pattern of studying it, looking around, and stepping slowly and deliberately toward some unknown destination.

The fact that the device did little other than make the required noise was lost on all but her, and anyone observing her would have seen her adjust the dials with such severity that they would have been loath to interrupt her, much less ask what she was doing. The occasional swear while slapping the side of the box completed the idea that this was a person hard at work and someone who would not tolerate interference.

In this guise she moved freely and watched. She saw the traders hawking their wares to the people who, lured by the promise of a bargain, had taken the lift up to the waystation to shop. She saw the security detail doing their patrols with such irregularity and indifference that she knew she could pick all their pockets and they wouldn't even notice, or if they did, wouldn't care. The crowd moved through the place with an almost organic flow, wave tips showing with the raised hands of hagglers, ebbs in the movement of carts laden with exotic materials.

She watched the current and soon could pick out the irregularities. There were only a few obvious to the serious observer, but she saw them. One ducked to the side when the security patrol moved by. Another followed some people too closely and others at too great a distance. She watched one young man over the rim of her device relieve seven different people of items from their pockets or bags and though she admired the skill with which he performed the task, she quietly tutted at how clumsy he ultimately was, in that she had seen it all.

She followed him as he loped along like a newborn gazelle stretching its legs and was happy to see him duck into a corner and disappear. This was the sort of thing she had been looking for since she started her hunt.

The corner was unremarkable, and of course there was no obvious means of egress save for a vent that, with very little effort at all, swung open. Millie patted herself in several places, making certain her weapons were in place, and slipped into the tunnel hidden behind the vent.

The tunnel was just a few inches shorter than she was, so she had to duck down, but it was wide enough to be comfortable as a passage. She followed it for a few dozen yards, noting as she did that the sound of the market faded to a dull roar, and then came to a fork offering either a forward veer to the right or a sharp turn to the left.

As she paused and listened, the scrape of a boot on metal drew her left, and as she moved along she noticed that the tunnel was slowly descending. She pictured the outside of the complex as she had seen it from the airship and, based on what she had seen of the supports and ductwork, wondered whether she currently hung out over the expanse below.

As she came to a window, she realized that she was inside one of the many struts that held the complex up. It hadn't occurred to her when she saw it from outside that the supports may be hollow and, not only that, useful as storage. A doorway led off to the right and through the window set in the door she could see a room beyond, the end of which was sloped so that the ceiling was taller at the end.

She tried to continue onward but found the hatch was locked, so she tried the door, and was delighted to find the locking mechanism was busted.

So, the young man she was following was in that room, but aside from a few boxes off to one side, she could see no one inside. She pulled the hatch open and slipped inside, conscious of the loud, scraping noise it made but hoping it wouldn't be heard over the other sounds: the hissing of steam through pipes, the wind outside racing past the support, and the faint noise of the crowd far above.

Her footsteps echoed as she walked across the floor. Realizing her hopes of making a subtle approach were already out the window, she stopped in the middle of the long room and stomped a foot.

"Hello? Is there anybody in here?" she said loudly.

Over at the end of the room, where it sloped down toward her, she saw a head pop up through the narrow space between the outside wall and the floor. It was the young man, as she had expected, and he stared at her with a mixture of fear and surprise.

"Look, it's not what you think," he said. "I'm looking for my pet rat, Stuart."

Millie laughed. "Really? That's your cover story?"

The young man pulled himself up and lumbered toward her.

"I usually carry him in my pocket, you see, only he got frightened by the crowd and slipped out. I chased him down here but I still can't find him. Maybe you can help me." As he spoke he walked past her to the hatchway, gesturing for her to follow.

"Sure, I could do that," she said. "Or I could see what sort of setup you have down there." She quickly walked over and slipped through the opening, noticing as she did that he was racing over to try and stop her. Before he could catch up to her she had made it down below.

The area beneath the floor was clearly never meant to be used as it was cut through with cross beams at regular intervals and the walls were covered in pipes and wiring that the young man had tied up out of the way with leather straps. Planks had been placed across the beams, creating a sort of floor, and shelves had been rigged along the bolts on the wall. It went back a fair way, easily the distance to the hatchway up above, and Millie guessed that if she pulled up any of the floorboards she would see the strut sloping away below toward the mountain.

"Nice place you have here," she said as he slid down next to her.

"It's not mine, Miss. Like I said, I was just looking for my rat." The panicked look in his eyes made her almost feel bad for intruding into his space.

"Relax, pal. I'm not here to bust up your setup. I just want to talk to someone in the know and you seem like the kind of guy who knows where all the toilets are, as they say."

"You're not with Security?" he asked.

"Gods, no. Those buffoons wouldn't be smart enough to hire someone as good as me," she said with a grin. "I'm Millie, by the way."

The tension in the young man's shoulders seemed to melt away, and he pulled over a chair he had fashioned out of a crate and gestured for her to do the same. "I'm Jase."

"How long have you lived here, Jase?"

He eyed her with suspicion. "Not long."

Millie smiled. She looked around the makeshift apartment at his bed fashioned out of a tabletop sitting on a few crates and the shelves filled with everything from canned goods to watches to comic books. This was a place that was well lived-in. "Look, I get it. You don't know me. You have no reason to trust me, and I wouldn't expect you to. Let me tell you what I know about you, though, Jase."

"You've just met me. What can you possibly—"

"You're somewhere between the age of sixteen and twenty-two, and it's possible you don't know for certain where you fall in that range. You've lived here for a while, probably a year or two judging by the number of things you have accumulated, scraping by with what you can swipe from people in the market and then trading said items for food and supplies. You're good at taking care of yourself, but you're not greedy. Am I right so far?"

"I'm nineteen," he said sullenly.

"You're a thief, but a kind one. I saw you take a wallet out of a man's pocket, take a few bills out, and put it back. A cruel man would have just taken it outright. You're also polite, in that a woman forced her way into what is essentially your home and you have neither manhandled me or threatened me even though I clearly make you uncomfortable by being here."

Jase shrugged. "It's not like I have a proper claim to the place," he mumbled.

"So," said Millie. "Assuming I'm right in my assessment, and I'm hardly ever wrong, I think it's fair to say you're the sort of person who can be trusted, so I'm going to tell you something I probably shouldn't, and that is that I am here to do a job and could use some help. What do you say?"

Jase stared at her, unblinking, and finally seemed to come to the decision to trust her. He grinned and nodded.

"Good. Now what can you tell me about the useless prats who keep this place secure, aside from the fact that they never look in here?"

Jeremiah sat and stared at the large pile of shipping manifests and receipts that had been presented to him unceremoniously by the recalcitrant Buccula. He wanted to tell the man that looking through poorly maintained paperwork was not how he went about his business, but Buccula had left him alone shortly after placing him in this windowless room to peruse the documents.

It didn't take much of a sleuth to see that the money collected as a fee for allowing supplies to run through the place was as inconsistent as it was possible to be, and the fact that each of the documents had the security chief's initials in the top corner led Jeremiah to believe that the man was either a blatant criminal or exceptionally stupid.

Jeremiah rubbed his eyes and stood so that he could pace around the room. He was reluctant to try the door out of fear he would find himself locked in, so to put off that potential discovery, he circled the table as he thought.

He had been granted a brief tour of the warehouses where the shipments came through and been allowed to see one such transaction take place. Goods came in documented on a manifest. The warehouse workers checked off all that was present, the supervisor signed off that they had counted correctly, and everything was passed by Buccula before being allowed to leave again. The trouble was, somewhere between the corpulent man signing off on things and the items leaving, things were disappearing.

When Jeremiah had asked Buccula for theories about how this was happening, he had been ushered into this room and left to sift through the essentially meaningless documentation.

Jeremiah decided there was nothing to be gained in continuing this farce so he finally tried the door and was relieved to find that it opened. Much to his annoyance, the two men who had been following Buccula like obedient hounds were sitting outside the room, and both stood to confront him as he made to move past.

"Chief says we're to keep you here until you are through," said the wall-eyed one. The other actually moved to block the hallway.

Jeremiah fought the urge to clench his fists, instead stretching his fingers out to their extremes and then slipping them into his pockets. "I am finished with the files," he said simply, and he took a step forward, hoping the men would move.

They did not.

"Why don't you just wait in there until the Chief gets back and we'll see what he wants you to do next," said the man, one eye staring hatefully at Jeremiah and the other looking at his companion.

The sound of a throat being cleared behind them caused both men to stiffen.

"Gentlemen, I'm certain your *talents* would be better used patrolling the market instead of barring this good man from going about his business," said a woman's voice.

Both men turned around to regard the woman who showed them such an unflinching smile that they left without saying another word, giving her a wide berth as they passed.

The woman held out her arms. "Jeremiah, my boy, you look just as I remember."

She was an elderly woman, but anyone thinking that meant her frail would discover their mistake quickly after a moment of dealing with her. As she pulled Jeremiah into a hug he felt his lungs crushed with the strength of her embrace.

"You haven't aged a day, Valeria," he said, only then noticing a man standing behind her.

"Jeremiah, this is my grandson, Ubel," said the woman as she released him. "He's learning how things work so that one day he can take over for me.

Ubel smiled. "That day is years, maybe decades, in the future for sure, Grandmother," he said. He shook Jeremiah's hand. "I just do what I'm told and stay out of the way."

"A wise move, if my memory serves me," said Jeremiah. "There are not too many people left standing who stood in the way of Valeria Beldam."

Valeria slapped him on the shoulder. "You make me sound like an absolute horror, Jeremiah."

"Well, you made those two men retreat with just a look," he said.

She scowled. "I'm glad you're here. Something is rotten in this place and I don't like it. That security chief of mine is an idiot, and either he's stealing from me or his men are."

"Pretty bold making him call me in, then," said Jeremiah. "Was that your way of putting him on notice?"

She laughed. "He's had his knickers in a twist ever since you responded. Now come on. You don't need to be stuck in a dank room with nothing to eat or drink. Let's head up to my office where we can chat properly."

With Ubel leading the way they left the barren hallways and took a lift to the uppermost level where Valeria kept her office and her living quarters. The room she used as her office was a large, quarter circle room with windows along the broad, curved wall. Jeremiah tried not to think about the fact that if he walked over to them he would be able to see exactly how high up they were.

She settled into her chair behind the desk, the windows at her back, and Jeremiah took one of the chairs in front of the desk. Ubel made them all drinks and then joined them.

"What have you sussed out so far?" she asked.

"Your man Buccula is as much of an idiot as he is an ass, if you'll pardon me for saying," answered Jeremiah. "He thought he could just sling me through the place and bury me in paperwork."

"I'll bet you noticed more on the quick tour he gave you than that man noticed his entire time here," said Valeria with an enormous grin. "Ubel, did I ever tell you about when Jeremiah here got me my jewels back?"

Ubel sat forward in his chair. "Is this when the maid had them in her undergarments?"

Valeria laughed. "You should have seen the girl's face when our man Jeremiah told her a person shouldn't jingle when they walk. She was gobsmacked."

"I would hope you learned your lesson that day, Valeria," chided Jeremiah with a smile.

"Yes, yes, I always do background checks on the help now. Don't you worry about that." Her smile melted into a frown. "If only I had been able to have a choice in who the security chief was."

"I thought you were in charge," said Jeremiah. "Can't you just let him go."

"I'd like to let him go right through that window over there," she growled.

Ubel held his hand up. "Now, now, Grandmother. Remember what we discussed. Killing the help is counterproductive," he teased.

"It would make me feel better," she muttered.

"While Grandmother is indeed in charge," explained Ubel, "the decision on who fills certain positions is up to a board of directors down in Mallick, one member of which just so happens to be the father of that useless sot Buccula. That man was quick to put his son forward as the new chief when the old one retired."

"So you're stuck with him, unless you can catch him at being up to no good?" asked Jeremiah.

Valeria pointed to him and smiled again. "Give that man a cookie. Now he gets it!"

Millie and Jase sat perched over a grating that allowed them a full view of the warehouse below. The tunnel was incredibly hot, making Millie regret choosing a wig for this particular disguise because it made it even hotter. Her tattered clothes stuck to her uncomfortably, a situation made only slightly more bearable by the fact that her companion was suffering the same fate, but seemed unaffected.

"Why is it so sweltering here?" she whispered.

"We're near the steamworks that they use to power the place. If we tried to go any farther down the tunnel we would need protective gear to avoid being boiled in our skin," said Jase. "Look!"

Millie tried to shake the image of being boiled from her head and focused in the direction he had pointed. A series of carts were being pulled along by a man in a small vehicle past a man in a security uniform who barely looked at them as he ticked boxes on a clipboard. Once cleared, they were moved to the far end of the large, cluttered room and unloaded by another man and an automaton.

Millie watched the process, the man doing the unloading merely putting in a token effort while the large steam-powered man did the majority of the heavy lifting. Once the carts were unloaded the man said something to the machine, even playfully punched it on the arm, and then shrugged as the thing shut down to wait for the next load.

"That silly man thinks he's got a chum over there," said Millie.

"The warehouse guys believe the automatons are alive. They even give them names outside of their number designators. That one," he pointed at the one Millie had been watching, "is called Chunk." He pointed to two smaller metal men positioned next to a conveyor belt where they pulled things off, seemingly at random, as they passed by. "Those two are Verne and Early, and somewhere around here is a lifter called Stretch and a greaser called Squidge."

"I guess it helps to identify them," said Millie.

Jase shook his head. "No, you don't understand. They really think the machines are alive. I heard one the other day talking about how Verne was funnier than Carl, and another guy was complaining that Squidge had insulted him and was even planning on knocking him one, until his buddy reminded him that damaging the machinery was a terminating offence."

"Just goes to show you, Jase my boy, that superstitions and mythologies can spring up at the drop of a hat if the circumstances are right," said Millie. "Wait, what's that one's name?"

Jase looked to where she pointed and saw the machine in question. It looked dirtier than the others, tarnished silver where the others were a mixture of brass and tin, and was moving behind the stacks, lifting particular crates and slipping them into an opening they couldn't see.

"I don't know that one," said Jase.

If the others in the warehouse knew it was there, none of them acknowledged it. In fact, she was fairly certain they couldn't see it, and the only reason she could was that she was at such a high vantage point.

"How do we get over there through the tunnels?" she asked. She was eager to move out of the heat because she was certain there was a puddle underneath her.

Jase looked at the ceiling and moved a finger in the air, moving through the mental map he kept of the place. "It's on the other side from my squat, but we should be able to get there easily once we cross the floor."

"Well, let's go before I melt," she said. They crept along on their hands and knees until the passage became taller and, Millie was happy to find, incredibly cooler. She let Jase move ahead of her and checked her wig to make sure it was still in place. It wouldn't do to walk out on the floor with tendrils of red shooting out all over the place, although with some of the wild hairstyles she had seen on the stall keepers it would hardly be noticed.

They slipped out of the vent and rejoined the mass of civilization on the market floor. The ventilator windows were opened enough to allow a cool breeze to flow through the place, and for this Millie was grateful as she felt her body temperature returning from the boiling point to normal.

"People don't pay attention to you unless you ask them to," said Jase. It was adorable to her that he felt the need to coach her, but she allowed him to continue. "It's like, if you're unimportant to them, you're invisible, and that works for me."

She watched him lightly brush by a man and come away with a handkerchief that he used to mop his brow. Though her fingers remembered the movements, she left the belongings of everyone she passed safely in their pockets.

Up ahead through the crowd she spotted a familiar sight, that of Jeremiah's smiling face talking to an older woman and a man who walked at her elbow. She stopped for a moment, drawing a curious look from Jase, and pulled a slip of paper and pencil out of her pocket.

"Come here for a moment," she said, and she turned Jase away from her and used his back as a surface to bear down on while she wrote a short note.

"Okay, let's go," she said. As she passed by Jeremiah—who, she was amused to see, did not even acknowledge she was walking by—she bumped into him just enough to draw his attention and slipped the note into his breast pocket.

"Begging your pardon, Sir!' she said in a strange voice.

"Not at all," Jeremiah responded, and he moved along without looking back, though she was again amused to see him pat down his pockets in a cursory check he hadn't been picked.

"This way to the tunnel," prompted Jase. She sped up to join him, passing once again from the public turmoil to the private tunnels without a single person taking notice.

Or so she thought.

Jeremiah walked across the market floor with Valeria and Ubel and marvelled at how the crowd parted as they strolled along. Most people who passed greeted the woman with great respect, like they had suddenly found themselves in the presence of their grandmother who had arrived unannounced. It didn't escape Jeremiah's eye that certain aspects of the stalls disappeared as soon as she came into view, and he wondered if it was out of fear of reprisal or acknowledgement that the less she could say she saw, the better. Though he understood what sort of operation ran here, he still was not sure how deep her awareness was.

Ubel, contrary to his grandmother's seeming indifference to all of the things around them, scanned the crowd and remained silent as she spoke.

"I've been doing this job for thirty-three years now, Jeremiah, and in those years I have whipped this place into shape. You should have seen it before," she said.

"I'm told it was quite the nightmare," said Jeremiah.

"Oh, nightmare is putting it mildly. Fights were a regular occurrence, often leading to bloodshed. A day couldn't go by without a person being murdered right here on the floor, in front of everyone. There was even, for a period of about three years, a gang war of sorts between two rival factions that almost brought the place crashing down off the mountain."

Jeremiah shuddered.

"You've turned this place into a well-oiled machine Valeria, that's for sure," said Jeremiah.

She nodded. "All I need is for you to find the leaks so there will be no challenge from the board when Ubel takes over."

Ubel tutted. "That's a long way away, Grandmother."

Valeria shook her head. "I'm feeling my years, boy. We need to get our affairs in order so that when I tell those stuffed shirts down below you're taking the reins, they will have no grounds to argue. I'm authorized to appoint my replacement if I have the favor of the board."

Ubel looked panicked, then quickly shook off the expression and replaced it with one of deep caring. "Grandmother, please. I won't hear such worries."

Valeria turned from the man and looked at Jeremiah. "You see this. I offer him the wheel of a smooth sailing ship and he acts like I'm putting the weight of the world on his shoulders. If he doesn't take over, they'll send some idiot like Buccula to run things, and in no time it will be back to chaos on this floor. I won't have it."

The last few words came out louder than she intended, drawing a few curious looks from passersby who quickly found something else to hold their concern. Valeria had stopped walking and the two men had stopped with her. As she pointed forward she scowled, drawing both of their gazes to the man beside the door peacefully sleeping on a bench, a half-eaten sausage drawing a mustard smear across the leg of his wrinkled security uniform.

Ubel groaned and took a step forward, only to be stopped by Jeremiah. "Please continue your pleasant stroll with your grandmother and leave this to me," he said. Valeria nodded her approval and turned to stalk away, her grandson following closely behind.

As much as he wanted the slumbering guard to be Buccula, it unfortunately was not, nor was it either of his companions from earlier. Jeremiah approached the man and stopped in front of him, tapping his cane loudly on the floor to rouse the sleeper. When that failed, he poked the man in the chest with three sharp jabs.

The guard snapped awake and shot up, the forgotten sausage rolling across the floor. He stared at Jeremiah as his sleep-addled eyes fought for focus and, finally realizing he was no one that he recognized, adopted that superior look people try on when they want to fake authority.

"Good day to you, sir! Do you need help of some sort?" said the man in a half shout before finding control of his voice.

"Absolutely. You can escort me to wherever in this place your superior currently lurks," said Jeremiah, striking the floor with his cane in a resounding thump.

"Ah, no need for that, sir. Mr. Buccula is a busy man, you see, and shouldn't be bothered unless it's absolutely necessary."

Jeremiah scowled, secretly enjoying the man's discomfort but showing none of it. "I should say a gentleman being robbed at gunpoint in a crowded room in front of a sleeping guard is reason enough, my good man. Had you been awake and doing your duty, I would still have my valuables. Now, because of your laziness, I am poorer and in need of someone to report the crime to, and since I cannot trust you to stay awake long enough, I insist on seeing this Mr. Buccula at once!"

The guard snapped to attention, an act that caused him clear physical discomfort, and gestured down a hallway. "This way, sir, if you will follow me, sir." At that, he marched away quickly, Jeremiah following at his heels.

As they approached a door labeled 'Security', shouting could be heard from the other side.

"What do you mean more is missing? That's impossible! And with that man here, too? Dammit all to hells, man, the old bat is going to have my head for sure!"

Things clicked in Jeremiah's brain.

The guard raised his hand to knock but Jeremiah's cane was there first, striking three loud taps against the wooden door. All shouting ceased and the door was snatched open revealing Buccula sitting behind a small, metal desk and the two guards from earlier standing in front of it, one holding the door. At the sight of Jeremiah all three scowled.

"What is it, Sover?" barked the chief.

Sover, the drowsy guard, looked back and forth from Jeremiah to Buccula unable to find the words he was supposed to say next. Jeremiah thought about making him twist in the wind for a while, but he found that he was more impatient to get on with the case.

"Thank you, Sover, for showing me the way. That will be all," said Jeremiah.

Sover, realizing he was not about to be called out for sleeping in front of his boss, left quickly.

Buccula faked a smile. "What can I do for you, Mr. Mountweazel?"

"Well, first you can tell me what is missing," he said, walking in and closing the door. The three men stared at him in shock as he pulled up a chair and sat staring at the chief. "And then, I can tell you how you may just get out of this mess without losing your job."

The passageways on this side of the complex were darker and less maintained than on the other, and were equally abandoned. Millie and Jase only twice encountered a person who was actually working, and in both instances there was an equal measure of indifference to the fact that they were present, aside from a few slightly raised eyebrows.

"I don't have much cause to be in these parts," said Jase, as he had to stop for the third time to guess the direction they should go. "I have what I need. Figure it's best to leave the others to what they have."

"Are there more people like you?" asked Millie.

"Place is full of us rats. That's what they call us, you know. Helps to dismiss us as vermin so we're not anything they need to have a proper worry about. There's a guy upstairs who lives in the back of one of the restaurants, over the ceiling. He stays in until the shop closes up, then drops down and makes himself something to nosh like he's at home."

Millie shook her head. "What a mad existence!"

"Hey, it gets us by," said Jase, though if he was insulted by her comment he didn't show it. "Everybody's just trying to get by in the world."

As they moved farther along they found themselves passing rooms similar to the one under which Jase had his squat.

These, however, contained more crates. The last five before the warehouse were filled to the door, and all were locked.

"I wonder what they store over here that they don't on your side," mused Millie.

"Not a clue. These rooms aren't meant for proper storage. There's no temperature regulation and they can sometimes leak," said Jase.

"How do you stay warm and dry?" asked Millie.

Jase grinned, rubbing his knuckles on his shirt. "Skills."

Millie recalled how his floor didn't reach all the way to the walls to allow any water running down the slope to continue on unencumbered. The piping the man had run likely brought heat down from the steam system that ran through the place. She began to think her new friend might be more clever than she had initially thought.

They found the hatchway that the rogue automaton had used but found no sign of the machine. Jase explained that they were steam powered, which meant that the mobile ones needed to be connected to the main system at regular intervals to recharge.

"Verne and Early are stationary, so they have a permanent feed going to them, but the others need a coffee break, so to speak, so he's probably plugged in."

"I still wonder what they are keeping in these rooms," said Millie. She examined the padlock of the closest one and smiled. Pulling out the set of picks from her satchel, she set to work on the lock.

"You're a woman of many talents," laughed Jase.

"You have no idea," she said. She focused on the lock, slipping her tools in and smiling whenever she felt something that told her she was on the right path. "Almost there."

Jase tapped her on the shoulder as she popped the lock, pulled the door open, and glanced inside. A further tap brought her attention around to the man who stood in the passageway pointing a rather unfriendly-looking revolver at the two of them.

"Can I help you?" he demanded as he pulled back the hammer of the gun and drove away all thoughts of the brushed-metal head she had seen inside the room.

"So you're saying it's someone inside the building?" asked Buccula, his brows knitted in confusion.

"That's a sure likelihood based on the fact that people outside the building would fall to their deaths," said Jeremiah, instantly regretting his sarcasm after receiving a glare from the large man. Buccula had cleared the room of his cronies so that it was just the two of them.

"I mean an inside job. Somebody who works for the waystation," growled Buccula.

"Indeed. It would have to be someone intimately familiar with the inner workings, the comings and goings, in order to be able to coordinate such a feat without being noticed. How well do you trust your men?"

Buccula frowned. "They're all loyal to me cause I got them their jobs."

"As it should be," said Jeremiah, nodding.

"Besides, I keep them on a short leash," added Buccula.

Jeremiah remembered Sover, the sleeping guard, and thought little of the chief's leash. He opted to say nothing.

"Well someone is trying to make you look bad. Your initials are on every manifest, so when it's all said and done, you're the one who is responsible," Jeremiah told him.

Buccula slammed his fist on the desk. "I didn't do anything!"

Jeremiah smiled the smile of a patient parent dealing with a chaotic child. "That is essentially the reason you're under question, Mr. Buccula, because you are regularly seen to do very little at all." When the man began to bristle Jeremiah held his hand up. "Please do not think I say this to get a rise out of you. You must realize the general opinion of your skill as the security chief."

Buccula groaned and rubbed his face. "It's just so much to keep up with. All the paperwork, and the personnel, and old Beldam breathing down my neck all the time. It's too much. I don't know why my father insisted I take this job. He knew I wouldn't be good at it."

Jeremiah was shocked to find himself feeling bad for the man. He himself had never known his father, and his mother had been incredibly supportive until the day she died, so he couldn't relate entirely, but his conversations with Millie had educated him quite a bit on how overbearing and insistent some parents could be.

"You have two options here, Mr. Buccula. You can either help me solve this case and make yourself look better both to

Mrs. Beldam and your father, or you can give up and wait for the eventual sacking and jail time that will likely come your way should these thefts continue. What's it going to be?"

Jeremiah waited as the man continued to rub his face. Finally, Buccula looked at him and nodded. "What do I need to do?"

"Good man!" shouted Jeremiah. "Now take me to the warehouse and give me a proper tour and we'll get to the bottom of this conundrum in no time."

The sounds from the warehouse were almost completely absent, it being that time of day when shipments were not forthcoming and the machines were being greased and recharged. Millie could hear the occasional bark of laughter or shout, but there was little else to drown her out should she decide to scream. Despite this possibility, she knew that option would likely be fatal to her and Jase.

"Begging your pardon, sir," she said. "We were told to look into a leak in the steam pipes and got turned around. If you would be so kind—"

"Hold your lying tongue, woman," hissed the man. He was smaller in stature than Jase, but still slightly larger than Millie. He wore clothes similar to what they were wearing, and he too looked like he had been in the steam tunnels by the way he was drenched in sweat.

"Honest, mister," said Jase. "We're just lost. We'll be on our way."

The man struck Jase across the face with the gun, knocking the young man to the floor. Jase stared up in shock as blood began to run down his face from the gash the hit had created.

"There's some of that for you, too, if you don't tell me what the hell you're doing here," said the man as he pointed the gun back at Millie. She had been poised to jump but held back as she stared down the barrel.

"We're just lost, is all," she said. "If you doubt us, take us to the security office and turn us in. We can sort it out there."

"I saw you pick the lock," the man hissed. "I don't want them nosing around down here any more than I want you doing it.

I think a better idea would be if I put a bullet in you and your boyfriend here and toss your bodies out a hatch. What do you say to that?"

Millie heard a familiar voice along with another coming from outside on the floor. She knew she only needed to shout to draw them in, but in that action she may very well cause the man to shoot.

She opted to whistle instead, seven clear notes. The notes meant nothing to her captor or even the recumbent Jase who pressed his stolen handkerchief on the wound on his head to try and staunch the bleeding. She knew the only person the notes would mean anything to was Jeremiah, as it was the same seven notes she had been repeating for a week that never failed to irk him.

Her captor was neither impressed with her pitch-perfect rendition of the song's opening nor the fact that while he threatened her she had opted to react by whistling. He lurched forward, grabbing her by the throat and pressing the barrel of the gun to her forehead.

"You think I'm joking here," he growled. His breath smelled of vinegar and tobacco.

"I would appreciate it if you would unhand the lady, sir, lest I be forced to take action," said Jeremiah from behind him. He stood with the sword from his cane pressed against the side of the man's throat next to Buccula whose only weapon was his sneer.

The man raised the gun into the air in surrender and was quickly tackled by Buccula and locked inside the compartment with the stolen goods. "That should keep him," said the chief, his face crimson with the effort.

Jeremiah turned to Millie. "Two things: Are you okay? And will you please stop with that damned song already?"

Relief flooded Millie's face, and she drew a deep breath and forced a smile. "Thanks for the rescue," she said as Jeremiah sheathed his sword back into the cane.

"You would have found a way out of the situation," said Jeremiah. "But you're very welcome." He turned to Buccula. "I trust I can leave you for a few moments to look after…" He trailed off, looking from Jase to Millie.

"This is Jase. He helped me," she explained.

"Splendid. Mr. Buccula, perhaps you and Jase can debrief one another while I confer with my colleague? Then we can pay a visit to Valeria and put this whole matter to rest."

The look of confusion on Buccula's face, though a look that never fully went away, was out in full force at this moment. He nodded and finally took notice of Jase.

"Who the hells are you?" he asked.

Valeria sat behind her desk, her arms crossed and her face expressing every bit of irritation she felt at that moment. Ubel stood next to her desk, arms crossed similarly, but his face was completely blank. They had been in the middle of a conversation when Jeremiah had knocked and entered, followed by Millie, Buccula, and Jase.

"Ah, Jeremiah, are these the culprits?" asked Valeria, gesturing to Millie and Jase who had moved off to one side.

Jeremiah laughed. "Oh, no, not at all. In fact, please allow me to correct a previous error on my part and introduce my colleague, Millie Mondegreen."

Millie, her mind still back on the warehouse floor facing a gun, curtsied without thinking, an action which looked strange given her haggard appearance. "Pleased to meet you, Mrs. Beldam. I've heard a lot about you. This is my friend Jase."

Jase curtsied as well, completely confused not only as to how he should act, but why he was there in the first place. Seeing the grins on more than a few faces, he bowed slightly and smiled through his embarrassment. "I, um, I live here," he said, eliciting a raised eyebrow from the older lady.

"So if these aren't our thieves, am I safe in assuming you've brought Mr. Buccula forward as the perpetrator?" said Valeria with a sigh.

"Now look here—" began Buccula, but fell silent when Jeremiah raised his hand.

"If I may?" said Jeremiah, gesturing to an empty chair. When Valeria nodded he took one after guiding Millie to the other. "We have apprehended a man in a hidden area off of the warehouse, a man who has, believe it or not, been masquerading as a worker automaton for some time. In this guise he has been ultimately ignored and free to remove items at his leisure."

"That's nonsense," interjected Ubel. "The men down in the warehouse know all of the automatons. They even give them names."

Jeremiah nodded. "The purposed ones, yes. Millie?"

"Jase explained it to me. Verne and Early are the sorters and need regular maintenance. There's a loader called Chunk, a lifter called Stretch, and—" she looked over her shoulder. "Who am I forgetting?"

"Squidge the greaser," answered Jase. He tried not to make eye contact with Valeria, who had taken an interest in him.

Millie snapped her fingers. "That's it. Squidge. But those aren't the only ones, just the ones that get used constantly. There are others who move about unnoticed, and it was as one of these that our man was disguised."

"Okay, so where is he now?" asked Valeria.

"We had a bit of a fracas, so he had to be locked in one of the rooms with his stolen goods," said Jeremiah. "He'll be there when we go to collect him."

"I've put guards on him," said Buccula proudly.

"Well, you've all made a good job of it then. Thank you very much, Jeremiah. I will arrange for your payment before you leave." She stood and extended her hand. Jeremiah remained seated and gave her a sad look.

"He didn't work alone, Valeria. He had help."

"What is this nonsense?" asked Ubel. "We have our man. Let's take him down to Mallick and have him thrown in jail. I'll go collect him myself, Grandmother, and make sure he pays."

Buccula stepped in front of the door and crossed his arms. Ubel's shoulders sagged.

"You don't want to take over here, do you Ubel?" asked Jeremiah.

Valeria sat down again. She stared at her grandson. "What does he mean, Ubel?"

"You won't listen. You never listen," whispered the man.

"Ubel knew that it was only a matter of time before you stopped talking about stepping down and actually went through with it, and he knew that when that happened, the last thing he wanted was to be here to be handed the keys," said Jeremiah.

Ubel nodded. "I just wanted to save up enough to get away. That's all."

Valeria shot to her feet. "So you STOLE from me? ME?" she shouted. "I've given you everything!" Her face showed the anger and betrayal she felt as she stared daggers at him. He took a step back and began to quietly sob. He tried to offer further explanation but the words wouldn't come. She took a long, deep breath, composed herself, and turned to face the assembled group.

"Mr. Buccula, it appears I owe you an apology," she said. "I thought you an idiot and a mastermind at the same time, never sure which was your true face, but it seems I was wholly incorrect in assuming you were behind the thefts."

Buccula blushed. "Thank you, Mrs. Beldam. I appreciate it." It took him another moment to realize that the only option she had left in her assessment was that he was an idiot, but by that point she had moved on.

"Jeremiah, as always you have done your name proud. I will see you compensated in full, plus a bonus for helping me clean my house." She glared at her cowering grandson for a moment, then turned to regard Millie and Jase. "As for you two, I have no idea who you are, but if you are friends of Jeremiah's then you are friends of mine, so I thank you for any part you played in uncovering this unfortunate turn of events."

Millie merely smiled from her chair while Jase blushed and gave her a short bow.

"Now if you will all excuse me, I need a moment with my grandson. Mr. Buccula, please wait close by as I will need you to perform your duties."

"About that—" started Buccula.

"Thank you, that will be all for now," she said sharply, and everyone quietly left without further argument.

Outside her office, Buccula turned to Jase and eyed him suspiciously. "How do you know so much about the waystation?"

"I, um, like I said, I live here," said the young man.

"Any interest in a job in security? We need people who actually know the place."

"Sure, I mean, yes, I suppose that would be okay," said Jase.

"Good. As your first official act I hereby command you to do whatever it is that Mrs. Beldam expects me to do when she's through with her prat of a grandson. While you're doing that, please let her know that I resign, effective immediately."

Jase, suddenly terrified, stared at him.

Buccula turned to Jeremiah. "This isn't for me. It never was. I'm sorry I misjudged you."

"What will your father think?" asked Jeremiah.

Buccula chuckled. "I'm sure he'll be happy if he never hears another complaint from that old battleaxe in there about his idiot son."

Without another word he left.

Jase turned to Millie. "What just happened?"

"I think your living situation just improved," she said.

"Oh, okay then," was all the young man could come up with to say.

"**N**ow see this, Millie, is how a person was meant to travel." Millie looked out over the town of Mallick as the funicular slowly descended the slanted tracks. "It's still high up, Jeremiah. Come look."

Comfortably seated at the back of the car, Jeremiah fluffed the newspaper and focused on an article. "I'm fine right here, thank you very much."

They had the car to themselves, and Millie was once again standing on the railing leaning against the glass, although this time there was no one to tell her off for it. She had discarded her wig and now fluffed her hair at regular intervals, relishing how free she felt.

"So what will happen now?" she asked, as she watched the city slowly begin to fill the window.

"Ubel goes to jail, though Valeria will petition for a light sentence. His companion will go for longer due to his attack on you and Jase. And as for Jase…"

Millie pushed off the glass and dropped down off the railing, joining Jeremiah at the back. "Well?"

"That poor man has found himself in charge of security for the waystation. It seems that a few minutes of conversation with Valeria convinced her that he knew more about the secrets of the place than she did and, especially after what just happened, she wasn't going to let someone like that get away."

Millie smiled. "Good. He's one of the good ones."

"Speaking of good ones, Valeria doubled my fee. How about we get some dinner in Mallick before we head back."

"I could go for a nice, ridiculously expensive meal after all of that," said Millie with a mischievous grin.

"The sky's the limit," said Jeremiah.

The Chance for Change

The season was turning and, in a mountain town like Tamarind, that meant the bitter cold was just around the corner. The time of year was rapidly approaching when people retreated from the streets to sit indoors huddled around fires drinking hot beverages. In defiance of this impending change and, in some ways, as a means of seeing the warmer season off appropriately, the streets were full of people reveling in the fact that they could still escape outdoors without donning seven layers of clothing.

Jeremiah, Millie, and Inspector Ward sat around a table at Cobbler's Rest sharing tales of the past in that age-old effort of bringing every member of a party up to speed on the things the others had seen. Ward had just finished telling Millie about an event he called 'the Gunderson Chase' when their food arrived, momentarily distracting all three with the unenviable task of identifying what sat on their plates.

"I think this was a duck at some point in its unfortunate life," said Ward. He stabbed at the meat with his fork as though he was expecting it to leap from the plate and dive into the Torri River that burbled close by. When it didn't move, he dug into the potatoes and began to separate the small, orange chunks off to the side.

"I told you ordering the 'Special' was a risk," said Jeremiah as he ran his fork through his curried chicken and was satisfied that the nature of all of the ingredients, at least those not ground into paste, were easy to determine. He had once excavated a whole fish from underneath a rice plate and, though he had been assured its presence was intentional, he had still found the experience unsettling.

Millie ate her stew without even considering it. She had long ago learned that while Mr. Panglossian's concept of which foods belong together was entirely absent, his talent for making the combinations palatable was without question. As there had not been a single meal at the restaurant that left her unsatisfied, she saw no reason to question any aspect of it.

Shrugging, Ward picked up his knife and began to carve pieces off of the meat. "So, now that we've been over my and Jeremiah's escapades, how about you two fill me in on how the two of you met?"

Millie glanced at Jeremiah and raised an eyebrow. Jeremiah gave her a reassuring smile, to which she shrugged.

"There is a story there, but it's not one that a wise person would relate to an inspector of the Constabulary," said Jeremiah.

Ward laughed and managed to try and look incredulous. "Jeremiah, my old friend, I'm sitting here as your friend Radclyffe, not a copper from The Centre. You know you can trust me."

Jeremiah put down his fork and wiped his mouth. "I do understand your stance there, Clyffe, but at the same time I suspect that if I were to tell you of a crime I committed you may feel some obligation to follow through on your duty."

Ward stared at him over a forkful of meat. "Okay, I'll play your game. What kind of crime? Murder? Kidnapping?"

"Nothing so harsh," Jeremiah assured him. "But a crime nonetheless."

Ward shrugged. "The two of you met over a year ago. The trail would be too cold for me to follow on anything lightweight you told me about. So you have my word, I will listen to your story as a citizen, not a constable."

"Well in that case," said Millie, "tell away."

Jeremiah nodded, took a sip of his beer, and sat back in his chair. "It all started on a train…"

Jeremiah checked his pocket watch and tutted, more to himself than to the man sitting across from him on the train. This particular car had circular seating areas set at intervals—four along each side with no walls between them—and crowding at the beginning of the journey had necessitated sharing an area. Despite the fact that the car had mostly emptied along the journey, neither of the men had opted to move for fear of causing insult.

"The train is running slowly again, I dare say," he mused. "We've only just passed Mellick and we should have done so twenty minutes ago."

His companion—or rather, the man with whom he had the misfortune of sharing seating on the train—merely grunted. The portly man had introduced himself as Kingston Frasier, Esquire, upon taking his seat as they left Fleis, acting as he did so that his identity should already be known. After Jeremiah had failed to be visibly impressed with who he was, the man had responded with nothing but guttural noises as they crept across the landscape.

"Are you traveling all the way to Tamarind?" Jeremiah asked. He had made several attempts at conversation to pass the time, and now only made the effort as a formality more than a true attempt at anything informative.

Frasier pulled his gaze away from the passing scenery long enough to say, "Tippoli," before pulling his bowler down over his eyes and falling asleep with startling speed as the train plunged into the tunnel through the Chetan Mountains.

'Thank the gods,' thought Jeremiah to himself as he shook his head and stared out the window at the tunnel walls racing by, 'that's only the next stop'.

He turned up the gas on the wall sconce and returned his attention to his letters, making notes in his small journal.

– Mayor of Zygmunt requests assistance with missing monies
– Lady Mondegreen insists on update on search
– Norris Levon remains uninformative regarding statuette
– Need eggs and milk

He would need to look into each of these on his return to his apartment. Especially the eggs and milk.

The whistle sounded, bringing a startled cough and sputter from Frasier as the man snapped awake and suddenly found energy that had previously been hidden away. The train left the tunnel, flooding the passenger car with light and propelling the large man to his feet, not without some difficulty.

"Well now, it's been jolly good making your acquaintance," Frasier said as he nodded vehemently and collected his bag and umbrella. "If you're ever in Tippoli be sure to look me up."

Jeremiah smiled, amused to see all of the social niceties packed into a single minute. "Indeed," he said, and went back to writing in his journal.

Frasier nodded again, seemingly taken aback by the shift in their positions, and with his signature grunt made his way up the aisle toward the front of the train. He bowled right into a young woman as she came through the door between cars and apologized profusely while she fitted her hat back onto her head and patted his arm to reassure him everything was fine, that there was no injury.

Jeremiah started to look back at his correspondence but couldn't take his eyes off the woman. She had jet black hair, pulled into an arrangement on the back of her head that allowed for a hat to be worn but still showed off its great length. Her dress was royal blue, with a fitted bodice and lace trim, and Jeremiah noticed immediately that one of her sleeves was torn, as if it had been pulled roughly. That, combined with the wild, frightened look in her eyes let him know that in her wake trouble would likely follow.

She looked back over her shoulder and then scanned the car, finally catching his eye before he could look away. That moment was all it took for her face to light up.

"There you are, Horace! You naughty man," she yelled as she marched toward him shaking her finger back and forth.

As she got halfway down the car to him, the door she had come through opened, and a large man squeezed through, ducking to avoid hitting his head. The man looked at the back of the woman and took a step forward before pausing at her words.

"You had me worried sick, my dear," she added.

Jeremiah returned her smile, waiting to see how this whole scene played out. It was obvious that the woman was in trouble, and it was equally obvious that the large man was likely the cause of it. He shifted his weight and felt the reassuring shape of the brass knuckles in his coat pocket. If it came to fisticuffs, he had no qualms about getting a leg up against such a foreboding opponent.

Much to his surprise the woman came straight at him and sat, without pause or explanation, next to him.

"Please help me," she whispered quickly. "That man won't stop entreating me to bed him despite my repeated assurances that I am not only not a prostitute but also a taken woman."

Jeremiah glanced dramatically at his watch. "I'm terribly sorry, my dear," he said loudly. "I'm afraid time got away from me and I neglected to meet you up front as I promised. Can you forgive me?"

He couldn't see what was happening behind her, but he heard the door to the car slam and hoped it signaled the retreat of her assailant.

"Did he hurt you?" he whispered.

"He tried," she answered, nodding toward her sleeve and a red mark on her arm.

Jeremiah chanced a glance over her shoulder and saw that the man was in fact gone.

"I'm happy to report that your aggressor has seemingly given up the chase."

She sighed and sat deeper into the seat. "I'm grateful to you, sir. I do not know what would have become of me if he had managed to catch me away from people. How can I ever repay you?"

Jeremiah shook his head. "There is no need for gratitude, Miss. I'm happy to help. My name is Jeremiah Mountweazel," he said, offering his hand.

"Shelby. Shelby Lillian," she said with a genteel smile. "I'm sorry if I made you uncomfortable by approaching you with such familiarity, Mr. Mountweazel. It was the only way I could conjure to give that awful man the slip."

"In times like these, for a young lady traveling alone, it pays to be resourceful, and if that need should hurl propriety out the window then so be it."

She smiled at his words. "It is fortunate for me that I found a man of such decency at just the right time. And please, call me Shelby."

"Then I should be Jeremiah to you."

She studied him. "It's a pleasure to meet a polite gentleman, Jeremiah. It's a refreshing change from what I usually encounter."

Jeremiah sat up straight and shook his head. "These trains are lovely, but sometimes they can attract all sorts of vagabonds traveling to and fro whose intentions are, to put it mildly, impolite."

Shelby pursed her lips. "Indeed," she said and looked away.

Jeremiah waited a beat. "You still seem troubled," he said.

She studied him for a moment, then nodded, seeming to come to a decision. "I find myself wondering if you might be traveling as far as Tamarind today. That happens to be my destination, and if that loathsome brute comes after me again in your absence, he may see it as an opportunity."

"As it happens, you are in luck. I keep my offices in Tamarind, on The Strand. Have you heard of it?"

She shook her head. "I'm not familiar with Tamarind itself as I've only been there a few times and haven't had the opportunity to tour the city."

"Indeed," said Jeremiah. "It was foolish of me to expect you to be as intimately familiar with the city as I am. Let's just say that though it's not the most affluent part of the city, it is also not the worst part."

"A man of your obvious quality doesn't live in a big house in the city?" she asked with a slight frown.

"I fear not. Perhaps one day I will, but today is not that day."

Shelby looked for a moment as if she may rise, but in the end she stayed in her seat.

"I would be happy to keep you company until we reach Tamarind. If you'd like, I can even escort you to your destination to ensure you get there undisturbed," he said. Her shoulders relaxed, as though her worries were gone.

Shelby nodded. "I wouldn't dream of asking you to invest so much time and effort in someone you just met, sir. If you would see me to the city, I should be fine from there."

Jeremiah shrugged. "It's still two hours until we reach our destination. Perhaps between now and then, you may change your mind."

Before they reached Tamarind they had agreed that it would be best if Jeremiah accompanied her at least until they were clear of the train depot in order to remove the threat of the man following her through the city. It was Shelby who suggested she should treat him to dinner by way of thanks, and Jeremiah told her he knew the perfect place.

The brute who had accosted her had passed through the car twice in the remainder of the journey, both times eyeing the two but saying nothing. After the first time Jeremiah had shifted his things so that his cane was readily available. Should the need arise to pull the sword free, he wanted to be ready.

At the final stop in Tamarind they disembarked and made their way across the platform and into the depot. Where Shelby had previously intended to part ways with him at the station, she now stayed by his side as if they had traveled there together.

He left her briefly to hand a letter to the station master, then led her outside.

"Sorry for the delay, Miss Lillian. My business never stops even when I have things I would rather be doing," he said as she took his arm.

"What sort of business is that?" she asked.

"Acquisitions, mostly. Some research. It's all over the place," he answered. He held his hand out and a carriage pulled to a stop in front of them, the steps descending with a hiss.

"Would you like to be taken to your destination to freshen up, or would you prefer, as I would, to get something to eat now? I find long journeys always fuel my appetite," he asked as the driver waited for directions.

Shelby shrugged. "My rendezvous isn't for some time yet. I would be happy to take you up on your offer now, if you please. I am desperate to find out more about this vocation of yours."

Jeremiah shouted an address over the hiss of the engine and joined her inside the carriage. As it lurched forward he checked his pocket watch. "As I thought. The trains are off by twenty minutes today. No matter."

Shelby tapped her chin thoughtfully and they rode in silence for a few minutes. Finally, she broke the silence. "Acquisitions? What exactly do you acquire?"

"This and that," he answered. "People need things, and I find the things they need. If I do it well and quickly, the people walk away happy."

"And reward you handsomely, I'm certain," she said.

Jeremiah shook his head. "Such matters are not appropriate to discuss."

"But you do well?" she prompted.

He smiled at her and gave a quick nod before glancing out the window. "Ah, we're here. I'm afraid it will not be as impressive as you may have been expecting, but I assure you I have not taken you somewhere unsafe."

The door hissed open and he descended the steps, reaching back in to offer her his hand. She gathered her skirts and took his hand, joining him on the street.

"Hmm," was her only response.

They stood in front of a three-story building, the bottom floor of which housed a restaurant currently filled with dozens of people, ranging from dock workers to traders. The large, open front allowed for the smells to spill onto the street, hitting the two observers with the aroma of curried meats, roasted vegetables, sauerkraut, baked bread, and fish. If the establishment had a clear identity it kept it well out of visible reach.

"If you'll follow me, I can see if Mr. Panglossian can get us a table. I'm sure it will not be an issue."

She looked up at the higher floors. "Your office is above this place?"

He nodded.

"I wonder if I may be given the chance to freshen up after all, before we sit down to eat?" she ventured.

Jeremiah smiled. "Certainly. I should have offered."

He led them to a side door and unlocked it with a key from his pocket.

"It's just up the stairs," he said, gesturing for her to follow.

"I'll have to admit, Jeremiah, that your countenance and your dress did lead me to expect something with a bit more..."

"Finesse?" he offered.

She smiled. "I was going to say 'finery' but that will work just as well."

"Well I trust you will be suitably impressed once you see inside," he said, and he slipped another key from his pocket and opened the door at the top of the stairs.

Inside was a well-furnished sitting room, with shelves lining each wall and several plush leather chairs arranged in front of a large wooden desk. The shelves were mostly filled with books, but occasionally the repetition was interrupted by odd trinkets—a wooden globe, a large jar containing something floating in green liquid, a brass sextant. Shelby stared around the room and her smile returned.

"This certainly is very impressive," she purred.

Jeremiah laughed. "I do try."

She walked over to the single window that looked down on the street below and pulled back the curtain. "Fairly nice view as well. The river?"

"The Torri. Beautiful to look at but I would never suggest jumping in. Mountain water is unforgivably cold."

She laughed and pulled a handkerchief out of her handbag and wiped a smudge off of the window. "I shall have to watch my step should I choose to walk along it later." Staring through with satisfaction, she returned the cloth to her bag and turned back around. "Now, if you can show me where I can freshen up then I would be delighted to join you for dinner," she said.

There was a sudden, loud knock at the door. Shelby jumped and stared at the wooden barrier with a face filled with confusion.

"What?" she muttered under her breath.

"Ah, do pardon me for a moment," said Jeremiah suddenly, stepping past her and opening the door. He exchanged a few quiet words with the person outside and then closed it.

Shelby watched him with suspicion. "What is going on?"

Jeremiah smiled and gestured to one of the two chairs in front of the desk.

"Please sit down," he said. He walked around and sat down behind the desk, pulling some papers from the drawer.

Shelby stood for a moment looking back and forth from the door to him. She walked over, opened the door slightly, and saw the back of a constable blocking the passage.

"What is this?" she asked.

"I have some questions for you, that's all. And it would be best for both of us if you remained here until I get the answers I need," he said, not looking up from the papers. The change in his countenance was sudden and unexpected, with professional forthrightness replacing friendly curiosity.

Shelby shrugged and walked over to the chair, collecting her skirts and settling in. She regarded him with a cold glare that stood in stark contrast to the look she had favored him with until that moment.

"Ask your questions then," she said quietly.

"Are you familiar with a man called Chet Albert?" asked Jeremiah as he finally met her gaze with an unflinching one of his own.

"No, I can't say that I am. What is this? Are you an Authority man?"

Jeremiah laughed. "No, and you can thank the gods that I am not, I assure you. Are you sure you are not familiar with Mr. Albert? If it helps, his cohorts sometimes call him 'Mr. Punch' on account of his tendency toward that sort of action."

Shelby glared and shifted in her chair. "I may be, I suppose."

"Great. Now my next question is, how long have you and Chet Albert been defrauding people with this whole 'damsel in distress' routine?"

She stared at him for a few moments, her eyes narrowing. He waited patiently.

Finally, she laughed and shrugged. "Not long. How did you clock us?"

"Mr. Albert's reputation is well known, as is his distinctive scar on the left side of his head, a remnant of a disagreement he had with a bullet, I am led to understand. And you are hardly the first young lady he has trapped into this scam."

Shelby looked sullen. "I know," she said, staring at the floor.

"You should also know that things will not be going according to your usual plan. He is not waiting on the street to see your signal at the window. He will not be busting through the door so that he can rough me up while the two of you steal all of my valuables. And thanks to the tip I left with the station master, he was picked up by the Constabulary shortly after we left the station."

Shelby perked up at that news. "He's been taken away? Oh, thank the gods!"

Jeremiah studied her.

"That may be the first genuine reaction I've seen from you today," he said.

She laughed a different laugh this time, one of relief mixed with celebration. "You have no idea what it's like to be indebted to a maniac like Mr. Punch," she said.

"Indeed," Jeremiah said. "I have one more question, which hopefully will lead to further revelations."

Shelby shrugged. "And that is?"

"How much do you hate your mother?"

"Lady Lillian Mondegreen contacted me through associates of mine and employed my services to find her errant daughter Millicent about three months ago," said Jeremiah.

She shuddered. "I hate that name."

Jeremiah continued. "She said her daughter had been kidnapped, or taken hostage, or lured away, and I was to use every tool at my disposal to find the poor, helpless girl and bring her home."

"Helpless? Ha!" came her response.

Jeremiah nodded. "Not my assessment of you, either, truth be told."

Her glare melted into a wry smile before returning with force. "Did she tell you why?" she demanded.

"Before we get to that, if it's all the same to you I would prefer to call you by your given name and not the alias you used in your deception."

"Fine, but if you call me Millicent I'll shove that telescope over there somewhere unpleasant. Only that controlling troglodyte of a mother of mine calls me Millicent. It's Millie."

"Well, I was going to go with Miss Mondegreen, but I like Millie much better. Hopefully it brings you some sense of relief to hear that my name is indeed Jeremiah Mountweazel and I have been completely honest with you at every turn of our encounter."

Millie laughed and threw up her hands. "Well, aren't you just a shining knight?"

"My dear Millie, I am no more a shining knight than you are a damsel in distress. I know that and you know that, so drop the pretense of being a victim and this will go smoothly for both of us."

"You never answered my question. Did she tell you why she wanted me back?"

"I was led to believe you were betrothed to be married," said Jeremiah.

"That is correct. I was betrothed, against my will, to be married to a complete bore and simpleton who was, I should add, nearly three times my age. All so my dear mother could have better social connections. I had no choice. I had to leave as soon as the opportunity arose."

Jeremiah steepled his hands under his chin and listened, nodding.

"So one night after she had one too many toddies I dyed my hair, slipped out of the house, and caught the train out of town."

"Unwisely deciding to cast a damning glare back at your mother by using her given name as your new surname and frequenting places that would make the establishment downstairs appear to be fine dining by comparison," Jeremiah said.

"You do what you must," she snapped. "But it didn't take too long to get into debt, which is why I got stuck working with that thug Punch."

"Who lured you into larceny and...other things?" he added.

Millie sat up straight in her chair and pointed a finger at him. "Larceny, maybe, but I'm no whore."

Jeremiah had the decency to look shocked at her use of the word. "Well, it certainly is reassuring that the man had some decency."

Millie cackled. "Him? Oh, he would have had me working on my back to pay off my debt. No, I told him it was either picking pockets and luring in suckers or I would find the highest building I could access and end it all with one step into oblivion."

"Ah, that reminds me," said Jeremiah, rising to his feet and pulling a box out from under a shelf. He set it down on the small table between the chairs and pointed at it. "Please put all of your ill-gotten gains from the train in the box."

Millie groaned and began searching through her skirts, pulling wallets, watches, and handkerchiefs from invisible places. She dropped each into the box, maintaining eye contact with her captor as she did so.

The last thing she pulled out was a small pistol which she pointed at him.

"What now?" she asked. "I will not go to jail, and I will not go home."

Jeremiah stared at the pistol. "Well, I suppose you could shoot me. You might make it as far as Porter Street before they catch up with you. Or, you and I could reach an agreement." He leaned back against the desk, raising his hands in the air.

"What sort of agreement?" she asked.

Jeremiah smiled. "You're good at pretending to be helpless. How good are you at playing pious?"

———o❦o———

Jeremiah poured the tea in two of the three cups, then added milk to his and looked expectantly at his guest.

"No milk for me. It sullies the flavor and cheapens the tea," said Lady Mondegreen with a sneer from beneath her gaudy, yellow hat. The hat matched her dress and the color of both, Jeremiah imagined, was meant to cast a youthful sheen across her unmistakably dour pallor. The end result, however, was to make her seem more jaundiced than young. "I see there is a third place set, Mr. Mountweazel. Does that mean you have located my missing daughter and my journey here was not for naught?" She looked around the room as if any moment something disgusting would brush up against her.

Jeremiah was glad that he had chosen to have the meeting in Tippoli at the beautiful home of his most recent friend, Kingston Frasier, Esquire. Frasier had been more than happy to offer up his office for this use after Jeremiah made such a lengthy trip to return his wallet and watch, which the man had clumsily dropped on the train.

He sat back in his chair and sipped his milky tea, enjoying not only the flavor but also the look of incredulity that crossed the lady's face when he had not waited for her to start.

"I applied my talents—at considerable expense, mind you—to the task and I am happy to say that I have met with some success," he said in response.

"Well where is she, sir? I am eager to have my daughter back, as is her fiancé."

"Ah, well, Lady Mondegreen, on that front there is a bit of a complication."

The woman shook her head. "I do not understand. What sort of a conflagration? Was she burned?"

"Not conflagration, complication, Lady Mondegreen."

"Speak clearly, sir, is my daughter present in this home or not. If you've made me travel this absurd distance to tell me you have failed then I shall have to take this matter up with the Authority."

"I assure you, Lady Mondegreen, that the woman formerly known as Millicent Mondegreen is in fact here."

The woman's eyes narrowed, causing them to almost disappear. "What do you mean 'formerly'?" she demanded.

"Are you familiar with the Order of the White Nettle?"

Lady Mondegreen gasped and covered her mouth with her hands as if horrified that she had allowed such a display of emotion to escape. She sat, mouth covered, eyes wide, and stared at Jeremiah in disbelief.

"She did not! She would not!"

"I'm afraid the woman formerly known as Millicent Mondegreen is now known by her new name, Sister Lelina Xayr, Novice of the White Nettle." He gestured to the door. "Sister, you may enter now, if you choose."

The door to the room opened and in walked Millie, bedecked head to toe in brown with an embroidered white nettle in the center of her blouse. A brown hood covered her head and the lower half of her face, leaving only her blue eyes showing. It was these eyes that regarded Lady Mondegreen with coolness that betrayed nothing of the animosity she felt.

"Oh, Millicent, how could you?" demanded Lady Mondegreen. She crossed the room to embrace her daughter then stopped, suddenly aware of the situation.

"Yes, I see you are fully versed in the dictates of the order, Lady Mondegreen. She is allowed no physical contact for the first three years of her life as a novice," said Jeremiah.

"Good day to you, Lady Mondegreen. I trust you are well," said Millie in the most level tone she could muster.

"Mill—" started her mother, then, "Lulu Naysur?" Lady Mondegreen looked to Jeremiah for confirmation.

"Sister Lelina Xayr, Lady Mondegreen," he offered.

"Laylon Nezur?" she attempted.

Humor shone in Millie's eyes as she watched her mother try and comprehend the sounds.

"Just 'Sister' will do," she finally offered.

Lady Mondegreen straightened up and began smoothing the yellow expanse of her dress—already immaculately ironed—as she struggled for words. She seemed close to tears.

"So your name?" she begged.

"No longer mine," offered Millie.

"But what of your fiancé?" asked her mother.

Jeremiah could see the ire bubble up in Millie's eyes. "As you know," he interjected before things could go sour, "upon joining the order the woman formerly known as your daughter forfeits her name and possessions. Any arrangements she entered into before joining are now null and void, and any property belonging to her becomes property of the Order."

"B—but that's a quarter of the family fortune!" blurted Lady Mondegreen before collecting herself and returning to the task of smoothing her dress.

"If I may offer a suggestion, Lady Mondegreen—and I must admit, it is not my idea but one already in effect, which the very search you commissioned me for threatens to undo—it may be best if you were to declare your daughter officially deceased. That way her portion of the family's wealth will be distributed to the rest of the family and will not be seized."

Lady Mondegreen looked at him intrigued. "Will that work?"

Jeremiah saw Millie's eyes narrow, then relax. They had already discussed the ramifications of this path, and Millie had declared it the best option because keeping a claim on the money 'would cost too much.' He saw in that moment the hardening of her resolve.

"I have little doubt that it would be successful, if handled properly," he said.

"But people know she's alive."

"None but us, and my silence is bought with the payment of my expenses and the location fee we discussed. As for Sister Lelina Xayr..."

Millie nodded. "Millicent Mondegreen is dead," she said.

Lady Mondegreen stared at her for a moment, then shrugged. "One of your sisters will have to marry the man, I guess. If this is the foolish path you've chosen, I have no recourse but to allow it."

"This is the case, for certain," said Jeremiah.

Lady Mondegreen nodded. "Goodbye Millicent, or whatever your name is now. We will throw you a nice funeral."

"Goodbye, Lady Mondegreen. Be well," Millie said in response, and she turned and left the room without another word.

"Children never fail to disappoint you, Mr. Mountweazel. Never have any of your own," said Lady Mondegreen. She placed a cheque on his desk and left without looking back.

"*A*re you alright?"

Millie sat in one of the lounging chairs on the roof garden of Kingston Frasier's house staring out across the fields that surrounded the town of Tipolli, a drink half-finished in her hand.

"Yes, Mr. Mountweazel, I am fine," she said. "I suppose I should be shocked that my mother gave up so easily, but I am not. I am pleased, of course, and for that feeling I thank you."

Jeremiah sat down in the chair next to her. "We left her very little option, you and I. What will you do now?"

She laughed. "You know, for the first time in forever I have no idea."

"I have a suggestion, then, if it appeals to you," he said. He took a sip of his own drink, blanched at the strength, then took another sip. "Come work for me."

"Work for you? Why in the hell would you want me to do that? I tried to rob you."

It was Jeremiah's turn to laugh. "That you did. How many people did that ruse work on before you had the misfortune to encounter a man who was actively searching for you?"

"You would have been number seven. The first six were complete imbeciles, though, and thought only with their libidos."

Jeremiah nodded. "You have a talent for acting and for subterfuge. I could use someone with those talents in my line of work."

"You mean 'Acquisitions'?" she laughed.

"I think you will find that I did not tell you a lie by saying that. Clients hire me to find things or sometimes even people. I have a talent for noticing things, and that has kept me fed over the years. Your mother's payment—which, I should add, was hefty—will set me up for a while, so I can afford to take on help."

"Help?" she said. "I'm not some hireling, Mr. Mountweazel."

"Nor are you a helpless maiden in need of rescue, Ms.—?"

"Oh, don't for a moment think that horrible woman is going to rob me of my name. I will forever be Millie Mondegreen. And one day when I decide the time is right I will surface and announce that my death was misreported and I look forward to watching my mother try and explain her way out of that. So let her spin her tales and pretend to mourn my death and I'll continue on being myself, unless I am in Fleis, that is."

"Your life is your own."

"Exactly," she said. Then she grinned and gave him a sideways look. "But in the meantime, I could use something to do."

Jeremiah smiled. "So?"

"I can leave at any time. I am not indebted to you or anyone. I am my own woman."

"Without a doubt, Miss Mondegreen, and without question," Jeremiah said.

"Well then, what should we work on first?"

Jeremiah pulled the small journal from his pocket.

"I have a few irons in the fire."

Ward looked back and forth between Millie and Jeremiah, unsure which to react to first. For over a year Jeremiah had been working with someone who had tried to con him and seemed fine with the idea. Ward couldn't find a reason to argue either, as in the short time he had known Millie, she had proven to be not only talented but absurdly loyal to the man.

They had retreated from the cold mountain air to Jeremiah's office, brandies in hand and fire roaring in the fireplace. As the story had unfolded, Millie had remained silent. Now she watched Ward with a wary look as though expecting to be thrown into chains momentarily.

"That's some story," he finally said.

"And?" asked Millie.

Ward laughed. "My dear lady, as far as I can see, you found yourself in an unfortunate situation and survived as best you could. Our man Mountweazel came along and helped you out of the trouble, and you've been fast friends since. What business is it of mine?"

Millie visibly relaxed. Jeremiah merely smiled, as though he knew this would be the outcome.

"As a matter of fact, you helped us a great deal. That man Punch had been slipping through our fingers at every turn, and whether you knew it or not, you helped deliver him right into our hands. I remember that night. I only wish I had been the one to knock on the door, so I could have met you sooner."

"Things happen when they are meant to, I suppose," said Jeremiah.

"Punch wasn't in for long, though. I mean, we locked him up, but he was free in a few months. How did you get him to leave Millie alone? He had to be sore about the whole affair."

Millie turned her gaze to Jeremiah. "I didn't know that."

Jeremiah shrugged. "Once Mr. Punch was relieved of the burden of her debt, he was no longer concerned with how she spent her time."

"That's the attention span of a criminal for you. The money is all that matters. The people are merely a means of getting it. It's good you were able to pay him off, Millie. As you know, he's not a good sort at all," said Ward.

Millie started as if she just realized he was speaking to her and smiled at him. "Yes, good fortune certainly came my way on that train."

He stood and walked over to the window. "Looks as though the cold is coming sooner this year," he said as he pointed outside. Light snow had begun to fall. "I should be heading home before Mrs. Ward has my head. Can I offer you a lift, Millie?"

She tossed back her drink and set the glass down on the desk. "That would be most appreciated, Clyffe. Please wait for me downstairs and I'll join you shortly. Jeremiah and I have a brief matter to discuss."

Ward picked up his hat and coat and, nodding to the two of them, let himself out. Once the sound of his boots clomping down the stairs disappeared, Millie turned to Jeremiah.

"I didn't pay off Punch," she said.

"No, you did not," said Jeremiah. He took a sip of his brandy and stood, walking around the desk over to the window. Ward was climbing somewhat clumsily into the waiting steam carriage.

"Did you?"

Jeremiah turned and regarded her. "Technically, your mother did."

"The fee you made from finding me? Oh, Jeremiah, you should have said. I can't let you spend your hard-earned money on—"

Jeremiah held up his hand. "Let me stop you right there."

An incredulous Millie stared and waited.

"Before you came along my life was simple. People paid me to find things, and I found them. Sometimes I had good months and ate like a king and sometimes I had to scrape together enough coins for a mug of Mr. Panglossian's questionable soup.

Despite those monetary fluctuations, everything else about my life was predictable and boring."

He glanced down and saw that Ward had lit up a cigar, the smoke curling up through the light snowfall like dancers through a forest of white.

"And then you came along and all chance of predictability went out the window," he said.

"I will pay you back," said Millie. "You should have said."

He dismissed the thought with a wave of his hand. "You will do no such thing. The debt is erased, so there is nothing to repay," he said.

He felt her hand on his shoulder followed closely by a peck on his cheek. "You're a surprising man, Mr. Mountweazel. See you tomorrow?"

"I look forward to it, Sister Lelina," he said.

With a laugh that bounced around the room bringing light in its wake, Millie swept on her coat, grabbed her things, and disappeared down the stairs.

The Promising Pugilist

⚜

Chapter One

It was cold, bitter cold, and the wind that descended off the steep crags of the Stelin Mountains cut down the Torri like a raptor after prey: merciless and unrelenting. Millie had only lived in Tamarind for a little over a year now, and if her first winter had taught her anything, it was that the figure walking swiftly but awkwardly down The Strand would not make it much farther without having to take cover to warm their bones.

"What do you imagine it is that makes people venture out in this madness?" she asked, leaning to watch the person's progress and feeling the bitter cold through the glass of the window. The fire, luckily, had been stoked, so the apartment was toasty warm, though the air by the window still hinted at the icy torment outside.

"Trying to decide whether to head home now or take me up on my offer of the guest room?" asked Jeremiah, not looking up from his book.

The figure Millie had been watching stopped in front of their building. Whoever it was, they had bundled up to the extent of becoming an unrecognizable lump, so Millie couldn't make out if they were looking up at her or trying to decide whether to brave Cobbler's Rest for dinner.

"Ha! No, there's a person outside who is either too insane to care about the weather or too stupid to know that they may freeze solid if they stay out in this."

Jeremiah slid a bookmark into the book, carefully closed it and set it on the table, and rose to walk over to where she stood.

"Hmmm. I see what you mean. They do seem to be frozen to the spot."

The figure took a step back, then another, and craned their neck up to the point where the viewers could actually make out a pair of eyes. They also saw the carriage that was coming down the road toward the person. Jeremiah and Millie began waving their arms frantically to warn the person, but they were not quick enough. The sound of the carriage finally reached the person and they stepped forward, tripping on the curb and falling on their face.

Jeremiah and Millie watched in horror as the carriage rode over the person's shin and continued down the road as though it was just another bump in the road. Jeremiah grabbed his coat and raced down the stairs.

As he burst out into the night he regretted not grabbing a scarf as well, but his comfort was secondary to the person who sat clutching their ankle.

"Are you alright?" he shouted.

"I think so," said a woman's voice. "That carriage came out of nowhere."

The fact that the woman wasn't screaming in pain flummoxed Jeremiah, but he shoved that confusion aside and knelt down beside her. "Can you walk? My office is right behind us. I'll take you up and call for a doctor."

"There's really no need," she said, turning to him. He could see a pair of bright green eyes staring at him, no sign of pain or anguish in them. "I'll be alright."

"Miss, the carriage ran over your leg. We saw it. I think you may be in shock. Please come with me," he said. He leaned down and helped her up, holding her so that she didn't have to put her weight on the injured leg.

She allowed herself to be maneuvered. "I'm looking for a man that can help me find my brother," she said. "Do you know a Jeremiah Mountweazel?"

Jeremiah barked a laugh as he practically dragged her to the door. "You're in luck, Miss. I just so happen to be that very man. Come up and we'll see to everything you need."

The woman stopped them at the landing, looking up with annoyed resignation.

"Of course there are stairs," she mumbled.

*A*fter an awkward climb up the stairs during which Jeremiah again marveled at the lack of complaint from his companion, he settled her into one of the cushy chairs in his office with the help of Millie.

"Should I send for a doctor?" asked Millie. "How bad is it?"

"Oh, I'm afraid it's broken, but a doctor won't be of any use," answered the woman as she pulled her hood back and unwrapped the scarf that was wound in layers around her head. Shoulder-length blonde hair broke free and she sighed at the freedom.

"Miss, I know that the modern opinion of medicine is skeptical to say the least, but surely you need to be seen by someone," said Jeremiah. He handed her a brandy and drank one down himself to bite back at the cold.

She laughed, bringing confused looks to both of their faces. "Do you have any carpenters handy?"

She pulled up her coat and skirts and revealed to them the source of all the confusion. Her legs, or at least the portion propriety allowed them to see, were made of wood. The left one was cracked straight up the middle and roughly splintered at the bottom.

"I've had this pair for five years without even a scratch, and now this," she grumbled.

Jeremiah stood and scratched his head. Millie fought the urge to laugh.

"You walk on prosthetics," he said at last.

"Well, they weren't lying when they said you were a good detective," said the woman with a wry smile.

Millie did laugh then, loud and uncontrolled, until an accidental snort brought her back around. Jeremiah scowled at her, but it quickly turned into a grin as the seated woman joined in. He walked around, sat down behind his desk, and poured himself another drink.

"So, Miss…?"

"Quinlan. Nora Quinlan," she said. She smiled at him, and then at Millie who flopped down into the chair next to her. "I was told by one of the nurses at St. Dismus that you proved useful in locating a man who was in their care. I am hopeful that you will be able to help me in a similar fashion."

She reached up her skirt and pulled something, then something else, then she slipped the damaged leg out. It did not have a hinge, so it was just for the lower portion of the leg.

"I'll have to take this to Papa for a repair, but not before I find out what happened to Declan."

"And Declan is your brother's name, I presume?" asked Jeremiah.

"Yes, my foolish, foolish brother."

Millie reached out to her. "Do you mind if I have a look?"

Nora shrugged and handed her the prosthetic. Millie began to examine it.

"Why don't you tell us what happened to your brother?" said Jeremiah.

Nora sat back and sipped her brandy. "Where to begin? I come from a small farming community just off the rail south of Peyze. Where I'm from, you grow up on the farm, you work the farm, you die on the farm. If you're lucky you meet someone to marry so that you can have babies of your own and raise them on the farm."

"I'm guessing that life wasn't for you," said Jeremiah. He glanced over at Millie who was examining the leg with great interest.

"Oh, it was. Very much so. I had dreams of finding myself a big, strapping farmer lad and starting a family. I would have at least seven children and raise them to look after the pigs and bring in the wheat. It seemed like an idyllic life. Until one day an accident took the bottoms of both of my legs."

She spoke of it so matter-of-factly that Jeremiah was at a loss for how he was supposed to react. He finally opted to continue to nod thoughtfully.

"After the accident it took me a while to recover, and then it took me even longer to get back on my feet, so to speak." She grinned at her own joke. Jeremiah smiled.

Millie barked a laugh, then looked up from the leg. "Sorry, please continue. I'll be right back." She slipped out of the room with the leg.

Nora watched her go, holding her hand up as if to stop her, then shrugged and returned her attention to Jeremiah. "Where was I?"

"The accident," offered Jeremiah.

She pursed her lips in thought, then continued. "My father made my first legs, and every subsequent pair, improving each time. We had a pony that I used to get around, and after a while I got into a rhythm with things, but it felt off. I couldn't settle back into my routine or my previous way of thinking."

"So you left?" asked Jeremiah.

"I did. It was a hard decision, but I knew I couldn't stay there. The people in my community were all very kind, but I could see the pity in their eyes every time they looked at me. They didn't see the fact that I learned to walk again, that I helped my father fashion better and better legs until I was so skilled with them a casual observer wouldn't even know they weren't real by the way I moved. I knew I had to leave, so I did."

"Where did you go?" asked Jeremiah. He knew she was taking the long route to the point of the story, but he didn't mind. She had a very pleasant, calming demeanor despite her brush with death and he found he enjoyed it.

"An uncle in Mellick offered to put me up at his place and find me work at a hospital in the city. I took him up on it, and I trained as a nurse. I got to be so good at my job that they put me in charge of the ward. My parents came to visit me a couple of times. Once, they even brought Declan and my sister Aoife too. That was their mistake, at least as far as Declan went."

Millie came back in with the leg. The repair work she had done wasn't perfect, but the splinters were all gone and the crack was sealed with something black. She handed it to Nora.

"Not my best work, but not my worst. You'll need to have it properly fixed, but this should hold you over until then," she said, returning to the chair.

"How did you—?" started Nora.

"I live over a theater. My friends there are experts at patching things up for the show. I may have picked up a thing or two," she said with a shrug.

"Millie is a woman of many talents," said Jeremiah. "Now if you could please continue, Miss Quinlan."

"You've seen my legs, Mr. Mountweazel. It seems appropriate that you call me Nora now."

Millie laughed at the blush that rose to Jeremiah's face.

"Well then, I must be Jeremiah to you, Nora. Please continue."

"Aoife didn't like Mellick. She complained endlessly about the noise, and the smell, and all the people. She couldn't wait to get back home. Declan, however, he was enthralled." She shook her head with a sad smile. "I get it. I really do. The city is a living, vibrant place with endless opportunity for adventure. The farm, by comparison, is a boring, mundane waste."

As she spoke she examined the leg and, satisfied, began the process of reattaching it. Jeremiah found everywhere else to look while she did so.

"So Declan ran away?" asked Millie.

"Well, he's seventeen, so you can't really call it that. When I left, it was to find a life outside of the one that realistically I had lost. My parents supported my decision and gave me their blessing. When Declan left it was under a dark cloud. My parents thought he was being foolish, and told him he should stay. I found this out later, though. All of it. He knew I had gone west to Mellick, so he went east. He wanted to make his own way, he said."

"And that brought him to Tamarind, you think?" asked Jeremiah.

"It seems the natural conclusion," Nora said. "I hardly think he would have found anything interesting in Thorpeworth. No, I know he's here. Trouble is, I don't know where. Or if he's okay."

Millie was no stranger to leaving home, nor was she a stranger to being sought. Her mother's search for her had led her and Jeremiah to their partnership, after all. "You know, sometimes people go out on their own and do just fine," she offered.

Nora smiled. "My brother is hotheaded and brash. He got in so many fights in our little community that we used to joke that he would have to move to the next town just to have someone new to hit. I know it makes me sound like an overprotective older sister, but I'm truly worried that some harm has come to him."

"How long has it been since he left home?" asked Jeremiah.

Nora sighed. "Six months."

Millie whistled. "That's a cold, cold trail."

"I know," said Nora. "My parents didn't tell me he had left home. I think they thought he would get it out of his system and come back, but when he didn't return after a few months my mother got worried and wrote to me. And now my father is sick."

"Oh, no," said Millie.

"They need him back on the farm to help, and they can't go look for him because my father cannot travel. That leaves it up to me. I applied for a transfer to St. Dismus so that I could be in Tamarind, and when I got here tales were still being told about the Sudworth boy and how you had helped reconnect him with his family, so here I am."

She sat back and finished her brandy with a satisfied sigh.

Jeremiah sat with his chin on his steepled fingers for a few moments contemplating her story. Millie knew now was not the time to interrupt his thoughts, so she wandered back over to the window and watched the snow that had begun to fall.

"Can you help me, Jeremiah?" asked Nora. "I just need to find him and make sure he's alive. I need to tell him about Papa so that he can know. I'm not interested in dragging him kicking and screaming back home. I just need to know he's okay."

Jeremiah lowered his hands and smiled. "I would be delighted to look into this for you, Nora. It looks as though the snow has started, so I suggest you return to wherever your quarters are and I will contact you when I know more, if you find that acceptable? Can you walk?"

Nora stood and tested the leg. "Your wife has done wonders, truth be told. I can hardly tell it's been damaged."

Millie broke into laughter.

Jeremiah smiled. "Despite her obvious comfort in my home, Millie is my colleague, not my wife. Though I would like to think the concept is not quite so hilarious."

Millie tried to fake a straight face and only held it for a few seconds before laughing again. "Just call me Mrs. Mountweazel," she said.

Nora looked between the two of them and shook her head. She held her hand out to Jeremiah. "I thank you for your time, Jeremiah."

As he took her hand she held his eyes for a long moment.

"It's my pleasure, Nora. I will be in touch soon."

Millie looked back and forth between them with a grin. "I can flag you down a carriage if we hurry. They may stop running soon."

"Thank you, that would be lovely," said Nora, releasing Jeremiah's hand and walking to the door. She bundled herself up again until she was unrecognizable as human. "Good evening to you, sir," she said through muffled layers.

Millie let her go through the door and begin the descent down the stairs before turning to Jeremiah and giving him a playful look. "Making eyes like that at another woman. It's enough to make a wife jealous," she said.

"I have no idea what you're talking about, Millie, my dear."

She laughed. "Right, I'm off. Have to get home to Tipsy in case the roads get clogged. See you tomorrow, if the weather allows it, husband."

The look on his face brought an even louder laugh from her that echoed down the stairs and into the cold night.

$$\diamond$$

Chapter Two

As luck would have it, the winter storm that Millie feared was looming did not descend that night. Through his bedroom window Jeremiah could see the city was blanketed in snow, with only the icy depths of the Torri River uncovered. Soon it would be cold enough to possibly freeze the river, but that day was not upon them yet. Still, the roads looked passable, so they would be free to travel as needed.

When he descended to his study he found Millie had already arrived. She stood at the window, as usual, and watched the world below.

"It's so beautiful when it snows," she said. "When I was a child we hardly saw snow in Fleis. I can remember only two or three times where we woke to find the world gone white, and even then it was barely a dusting."

"As you know, it snows plenty here," said Jeremiah. He joined her by the window and looked down at the street again.
"It almost makes the town look clean, at least until the carriages chew up the road."

Millie smiled. "Clean, crisp air and nary a soul on the street. Beautiful."

A low grumble broke the silence that followed.

"That your stomach or mine?" she asked.

"Likely both," said Jeremiah. "Let's head downstairs and see what questionable creations Mr. Panglossian has concocted today." He walked to the door and grabbed his hat and coat.
"Care to brave the brief cold or do you need to cocoon yourself?"

He gestured to the chair, upon which sat a pile of at least seven multi-colored scarves.

Millie picked a blue one from the pile and wrapped it around her neck. Its color matched her eyes exactly, making them stand out amidst her tangle of red hair. "One will do. It's just a quick hop."

Moments later they were down the stairs and inside the lower level, taking up seats at the table in the corner. During the cold months, when the restaurant was reduced to indoor seating, they always chose this particular table by the window so they could still watch the sparse number of people coming and going.

The waitress came over to their table and set down two glasses of water. "Good morning Mr. Mountweazel, Miss Mondegreen. What can I get you?"

"Good morning to you, Elodie," answered Jeremiah as he studied the menu. "What do you recommend?"

"I recommend not having the eggs. Trust me on that," she said.

"Is everything alright, Elodie?" asked Millie.

Jeremiah looked up and realized why his companion had asked that question. One of the defining traits of the waitress Elodie was that her smile was as constant as the sun, and equally radiant. A person who entered Cobbler's Rest in the worst of moods would be hard pressed to leave without feeling their gloom turned to cheer after just moments of talking to the young woman. This morning, however, her usual disposition was replaced by something more grim.

She sighed. "I'm fine. Everything is fine," she said, though her eyes betrayed her lie.

"Are you sure?" asked Jeremiah.

She smiled, though it was merely a pretense. "Of course. Now what looks appealing to you this morning?" It was clear they had gotten the full limit of what she was willing to offer regarding her mood.

"I'll have the breakfast burrito, but please have him hold the codfish," said Jeremiah.

"Okay, but he won't be happy," said Elodie.

"I'll have the eggs," said Millie, setting down her menu.

Elodie looked at her. "Are you sure? There's something blue in them I can't identify."

Millie laughed. "Every day is an adventure with Mr. Panglossian, eh?"

Elodie sighed again, although only a brief one. She looked back toward the kitchen. "He is a wonderful man."

After she wandered back to submit their orders Millie knocked on the table. "I wonder what rained on her parade. Do you think it's the weather?"

"I don't know. Maybe it's that or something more personal. It's hardly our concern, though."

Jeremiah glanced out the window and chuckled. "There's our man."

Part of the secret to Jeremiah's success in his profession was knowing that he didn't need to know everything, he just needed to know the people who did. If he had questions about flowers, he would talk to Millie's friend Mr. Yonic. If he had questions about exotic cuisine, Mr. Panglossian was the man to ask. Knowing who knew what was key.

Finding himself in the position of needing to track down a person with no starting lead other than a name and description, Jeremiah knew the best person to start with was the lad who was currently loping by the restaurant. He walked along the stone wall which separated walkers on the footpath from the icy waters of the Torri, several parcels and bags clutched in his arms.

He was a useful lad, clever and strangely capable of finding any sort of items that were requested. He was hard to miss whenever he was spotted in a crowd walking down the street in his bouncing gait, all gangly arms and legs like a newborn gazelle. At birth he was given the unfortunate name of Tarquin Rantipole, and the world has never let him forget it.

Jeremiah excused himself and headed out into the cold to greet the boy before he could pass, which wasn't difficult as the lad was currently looking into the restaurant with the peculiar air of a person trying to look like he was not looking into the restaurant.

"Tarquin, my boy, how fortuitous for us to meet so unexpectedly," said Jeremiah.

The young man started, pulled from his conspicuous study of the window by the familiar voice. "Mr. Mountweazel, sir," he said, louder than he meant and then, looking around, he lowered his voice. "Is there something I can do for you?" He tapped the side of his nose conspiratorially. The packages in his arms, resistant to being restrained by the young man, began to slip this way and that, and Jeremiah helped him regain control of them.

Jeremiah smiled and carried a few of the parcels as he put his arm around the boy and strolled with him down the path. He realized as he did so that Tarquin was now somehow taller than him, if only by an inch or two. He was practically a man now, which gave Jeremiah pause since he always thought of him as the young boy he had met years ago in an alley in The Bottoms.

"I've been hired to find a young man that wouldn't be much older than you," said Jeremiah. "I was hoping you would put the word out and see what information you could find for me."

Tarquin nodded, a bit more than was necessary. "Of course. I mean, I have some things to take care of, but I can help you out if you need."

"Good lad," said Jeremiah. "His name is Declan Quinlan, although he may be using an alias. He originally hails from north of Peyze." He reached into his pocket and took out the photograph Nora had loaned him. "This is him in the center."

It was a family photo, and he had promised to keep it safe. The parents stood in the back: large, robust father and sturdy, kind-faced mother. In front stood the three children, Nora and Aoife on either side of Declan, who stood with his arms crossed in front of him, clearly resistant to the photo being taken.

"Can I take this?" asked Tarquin.

"Sorry, no. I need it," said Jeremiah.

"No matter," said the boy. "I'll remember. I'll ask around and see what I can find."

Jeremiah stopped and patted him on the back. "I have to get back. Thank you, Tarquin. You're growing up to be quite a remarkable young man." He positioned the parcels he carried on top of the pile.

Tarquin flashed a grin that looked more like a grimace and nodded his head before heading down the path. Jeremiah returned to the restaurant confident that he may have at least a lead or two soon.

Millie chased something blue and gristly around her plate. "I should have listened to Elodie, I think," she said.

Jeremiah looked at his own plate, shaking his head but chuckling at the fish head that stuck out the end. "Always an adventure."

Chapter Three

Though Tarquin was usually a help on cases he could hardly be the only source of information they relied upon. As they powered through their mystery meals they discussed the possibilities.

"You should go talk to Ward and see if the boy has ended up under the river," said Millie. "It wouldn't be the first time an innocent youth has ended up on the wrong side of the law due to bad choices, as I well know."

Jeremiah chuckled. He had had his own scrapes with authority, though none in recent years, at least officially.

"A sensible approach. And what will you do while I'm on this assignment?"

Their partnership worked because he never once held it over her that since the business was his she technically answered to him, not the other way around.

"I'll ask around in The Bottoms. I mean, if he's as much of a hothead as Nora made out he might have made a name for himself already, or…" she trailed off.

Jeremiah followed the thought thread. "Let's hope it hasn't gone that route." He stood and left a few bills on the table, more than enough to cover the cost of their meal and a sizable tip. "Shall we meet for dinner and compare notes?"

"See you then," said Millie.

They walked together as far as the next street before Millie bid him farewell and cut down an alley. Though the alleys in this part of town were hardly filled with dangers, Jeremiah always worried about her tendency to choose the less populated paths out of fear of some cutthroat or thug attempting to assault her. It wasn't that he feared for her safety, it was just that the mess of dealing with the Constabulary after Millie was through with the villain took longer than he ever appreciated.

It wasn't an especially long walk to The Centre, but the cold made it seem longer and by the time he reached the bridge to cross over onto the island he could no longer feel his hands. He picked up the pace, rushing up the steps and through the doors without delay.

The lobby was filled with an assortment of people all creating a cacophony that filled the large room. The shouts of a defiant criminal mixed with the angry rant of a wronged neighbor. These pulled a crying baby and coughing vagabond in to make a symphony of agony that was clearly working its magic on the poor clerk behind the counter.

Jeremiah spared him additional noise by silently nodding to him and heading towards the stairs. He was well known at this point to be a friend of Inspector Ward and according to Ward could "damn well come up and knock without all this blasted ceremony."

As he left the stairs and walked down the hall it occurred to Jeremiah that it was far too quiet. Normally by this point he would be treated to shouts from his friend, generally in the direction of his secretary but concerning someone else. The eerie silence that greeted Jeremiah made him think Ward was either asleep or simply not in.

As he neared the door to his office, though, he heard a familiar low rumble that could only come from the grumbling frustration of his friend. He knocked and opened the door to find Ward sitting at Miss Slater's desk, hunched over her typewriter.

"Stupid machinery isn't built for shit. I don't know how she uses this damned contraption," he mumbled, not looking up.

"Well this is new. Miss Slater out sick today?" said Jeremiah as he hung his hat on the deer antler coat rack that occupied one corner of the front office.

Ward looked up. "What? Oh, it's you, Jeremiah. You wouldn't know how to use this infernal device, would you?"

Jeremiah smiled. "Of course I do. My question is, why do you need to when you have a perfectly capable secretary?"

A loud "Hah!" came from behind the closed door to Ward's office. Ward glared at the door and visibly bit back a response.

"My secretary is, as you say, perfectly capable, but she is also unwilling to receive any sort of instruction and is prone to fits of temper."

Jeremiah chuckled as Ward's own temper was legendary in its shortness. "Let me guess, you told her to hurry up and she told you in so many words that you could type the letter yourself."

Still glaring at the door, Ward nodded.

"Think I might be able to interrupt your professional dispute to ask for your help?" offered Jeremiah.

Ward stood suddenly. "Of course I'll help you, my boy. And since duty calls, perhaps it would behoove someone else to take care of typing up this letter." He stared at the closed door and waited.

Miss Slater's thick brogue finally broke the silence. "It'll be there waiting for you when you get back."

Ward huffed and started to say something in return, but Jeremiah put his hand on his shoulder. "Let me save you from yourself," he said. He held out the photograph of Nora's family. "The boy in front. He's missing. His sister, the one on the left, is looking for him. Can we check below the river?"

"Miss Slater, I'm going out on official business," shouted Ward in his bellowing baritone.

He received silence in reply.

"I would consider yourself lucky," said Jeremiah.

"Indeed," said Ward.

As they headed down the hall and down the stairs, Jeremiah filled him in on the particulars. He surmised that a boy so prone to fisticuffs would quite possibly be resting in the cells on the bottom floor of The Centre. Ward agreed and led them through the numerous security gates to the circular pathway that ran between the outer cells, called the Drippers, and the inner ones, called the Crushers. If the structural integrity of the seven story building ever failed, drowning or burial awaited those unfortunate enough to be housed there.

At least that was the threat. The building, as it was, was remarkably sound.

Their circuit proved fruitless, however. Jeremiah tried to be discreet as he glanced down at the photo and studied the faces, most glaring, of the occupants of the cells, but the face of Declan Quinlan was not among them.

"Cheery bunch you have down here," Jeremiah said to Ward as they passed through the first security checkpoint to head back upstairs.

"It's the constant sound of water. It's soothing to some, to others it's a reminder that one sprung leak and they're sitting in a locked cage that could quickly become submerged," said Ward, making no apology for the situation. "It's the main reason why people try hard not to gain a second visit."

Jeremiah recalled Tarquin telling him of a night the boy spent under the river. He said it was all he needed to make him want to do better in life.

"So our bruiser isn't locked up with you," said Jeremiah. He stared at the picture, trying not to be distracted by the smiling face of Nora, and studied the boy's face. Declan looked like the kind of kid who would sooner throw a punch than have a conversation. Nora hadn't said anything to make him think otherwise.

"That means you only have a whole city to search. Easy as pie," laughed Ward. "Come on, I'll have Rassom make a sketch from your picture and I can make sure it's in the pocket of every Constable until we find this lad."

"That would be champion, Clyffe."

Constable Rassom was a tall, slender man with a pencil-thin mustache and sharp eyes. He took one look at the photo, pulled out a pad and pencil, and quickly sketched an almost picture-perfect replica.

Ward walked out with Jeremiah when he left. "Wouldn't do to get back before Miss Slater cools down," he joked.

"You know, you really should be more appreciative of her, my friend. She does more for you than you think," said Jeremiah as they stood on the front steps and watched the people and the rivers flow by.

"Damned if I know what sets her off," grumbled Ward.

"I suspect it may have something to do with whatever had recently set you off. You do tend to be a bit…reactionary."

Ward laughed. "Truer words have never been spoken. You're right of course. I'll go up with my tail between my legs and restore order to my office."

"Good man." Jeremiah donned his hat and shook his friend's hand. "Do let me know if you hear anything about young Declan."

"Of course, say hello to your young protégé for me."

As Ward disappeared into the building, Jeremiah continued to look around. From this point in the city one could see the divisions made more real by the rivers that criss-crossed through the city.

He looked out to the east, into the section called the Gardens, and tried to picture a farm boy finding a place there. Sure, he may have found employment in one of the big houses, but Jeremiah doubted the boy's temperament would allow him to keep such a job for long.

To the north, work could be found in trade or possibly in the mines that barely ran anymore. The Authority was another possibility, but as Jeremiah glanced down at the photograph he found it difficult to imagine Declan in one of their crisp, white uniforms doing what he was told.

The Bottoms, he had to admit to himself, seemed the likeliest place young Declan would be found. He hoped for the boy's sake, and for the sake of his beautiful sister, that he would be found alive.

Jeremiah looked at the younger version of Nora in the photograph. He had to admit to himself that the woman he met in person stirred something in him that he thought lay dormant, and he didn't find the feeling unpleasant in the least. His tendency was always to occupy himself with work when he had it and books when he didn't, so a distraction would be welcome, although he was loath to consider her by that word.

There was the tricky matter of her missing brother to consider, though. If he pursued her in any way but his search for Declan came up with unfortunate results it would create a situation that could only be described as unprofessional. He didn't want to chance putting himself or Nora in that situation.

Still, he thought it would be prudent to inform her of what had been done so far. Surely that wouldn't cross any lines.

With something of a spring in his step Jeremiah headed to the healing hall of St. Dismus.

Millie loved alleyways. There was something magical about the passages that appealed to her sense of discovery. A person could have a pristine house, all gold and lace and perfume, but out back was where the truth lay. Out in the rear, where the trash held treasure and servants furtively grabbing a smoke had loose tongues, was where it all came into the light.

When she was in Jeremiah's company she strolled down the street with him in a manner that wouldn't draw attention. He was fixated on maintaining a demeanor of luxury, though they both knew some months were more of a struggle than others in regards to things as simple as food, or as necessary as bourbon. She could understand that, coming from that world herself, but it never felt right to her. The shadows called and embraced her. The dark, dingy, discarded places and people lit a fire inside her that she hoped would never be quenched.

When she had first landed in Tamarind, her explorations had led her into trouble more than once. But trouble was a creature with which she was intimately familiar and as easily as she had found her way in, she had found her way back out. Now when the people whose vocation revolves around accosting naive travelers in shadowy corners see her coming, they step out of the way and let her pass lest they end up like the last one. It was always easy to pick out if a mugger was new in the city. They were the ones that tried to stop her and demand her valuables and soon found themselves swallowing teeth.

If Jeremiah was checking with the Constabulary then she would check in with its counterpart, that criminal underbelly that itched the body of every city but avoided all attempts to be scratched. She found Mr. Yonic rolling his flower cart down the street in the middle of a crowd that was likely half pickpockets and half victims. He was bundled against the cold with a furry hat that looked as though it may possibly still be alive and a long, brown coat that stood in stark contrast to the rainbow of colors that decorated his cart.

"My dear Millie, how are you today?" he said. He pulled a yellow rose from an arrangement and offered it to her. She sank it into her hair on the left side, indicating she needed a private conference.

"It's a beautiful day, Mr. Yonic, a beautiful day indeed," she responded.

He nodded, then quickly tilted his head towards a side street as he turned his cart and wheeled it in that direction. Millie continued on down the street but circled back up an alley to meet him.

"I'm looking for a boy. Almost a man. Bit of a thug," she said.

"My dear girl you've described almost half of The Bottoms," he said, a wry smile cutting across his face and puckering the scar that ran down his right cheek.

Millie laughed. "Right. Let's see. Farm boy from Peyze. Bit of a temper. Left home a while back. Name is Declan Quinlan."

"Have you checked the morgue? Newcomers don't often fare as well as you did, dear girl," he said. As much as she liked Yonic, his condescending manner could be very off putting. Still, he had helped her immensely on more than one occasion, so she was willing to put up with it.

"Of course," she lied, adding it to her list of places to check. "No dice, so I just thought I'd check and see if you knew anything."

"None of it rings a bell at the moment, though as I said, you're not narrowing the field down to any satisfactory degree. If he's hot headed, he may have found his way into the fights, although which one is the question. Fighting rings are as common as knives in these parts."

Yonic began to look around and Millie knew her private time with the man was almost up. "If you hear anything about anyone with that name, please let me know through the usual channels. I'll make it worth your while as usual."

"Our friendship is always to my satisfaction, my dear. You may trust that aiding you is one of my highest priorities just as I trust that aiding my purse is one of yours."

Millie nodded, gave him a quick smile, and sprinted off down the alley as he wheeled his cart back into the road whistling a happy tune.

She thought about the fights. She had been to more than one in The Bottoms. She had even considered stepping into the ring herself, but in the end had thought better of it. The Constabulary left them alone, so long as no one died, and to appease the law it was declared that none of the fights would be to the death. But people still died.

More died than anyone would ever admit. Disposing of a body was never a problematic thing in The Bottoms. Choosing which method to use was the only real challenge.

Millie shuddered and drove the thought from her mind. They would find Declan. She was sure of it. They just needed a lead.

As she made her way back to her apartment she was unsurprised to find the stage door to the theater closed. In the summer it would always be open, watched by a giant of a man called Bert who was built like a wall and acted in that capacity to anyone who was not allowed backstage.

She thought about running upstairs and warming up. Tipsy would no doubt be impatiently waiting for some attention, if not more food. She would have to wait, though, as Millie made up her mind and knocked on the door with three short raps, two pounds, and three more short raps.

Moments later the door opened and the enormous hairy head of Bert stuck out. He looked around, confused, then almost as an afterthought looked down, spotting her. She probably could have slipped in without him knowing as he sometimes seemed to forget not everyone was as tall as he was, but it was him she wanted to talk to.

"Hiya, Bert, my old chum," she said.

"Oh, Millie, hey." He was a man of many words, Bert.

"Wondering if I can't bend your ear for a moment."

He nodded and stepped back so that she could enter.

No matter how many times Millie visited backstage it always amazed her, the costumes and curtains, draped hosiery and wigs, and the overwhelming smell of greasepaint created such an immense level of chaos and beauty that she always gasped when she saw it. Bert, for his part, was unaffected.

"What's up, Millie?" he asked. He settled back down in the chair that served as his regular place in the center of the chaos. It creaked, screaming out to the world that one day, one day soon perhaps, it would finally give in to the abuse it so constantly suffered and splinter into a thousand pieces. That day, however, was not today.

"So, I was wondering if you could help me out. I'm trying to find a friend and I think he may be involved in the fights."

Bert presented a blank look to her on a face decorated with the trophies of years of fighting. His lip was currently split and his eye was a deep yellow from a shiner on its way out the door. His appearance was as fluid as the Tarsain, in that every time you saw him some new aspect of his visage would have changed due to pummeling. In short, no matter how much he pretended to be unaware of the fights, his face declared otherwise.

"Why are you asking me, Mille? I'm a lover, not a fighter." He grinned slightly and gave her a wink.

"Well, hypothetically, if a person wanted to get involved in the fights, is there a particular someone with whom they would get in contact?"

Bert shrugged. "Beats me. I mean, my friend Alban Teel wouldn't know either. He's not the sort to hang around the Oyster at all. Don't bother with Stace Kimball over at the Char Pit either. And I doubt Mr. Punch would know. He's not starting up a new show over in the warehouses." He was grinning, and Millie was grinning with him until the last one.

"Wait, Punch is back in town?" she said.

Bert stopped, momentarily trying to decide if he was still pretending to deny things or if he should just go on with a normal conversation. "Do you know him?"

Millie thought back to the time she spent with the man known as Mr. Punch swindling men on the trains. It was a period of her life that she cursed, right up until the point where it led her to meet Jeremiah. "I've encountered him before," she said.

Bert leaned forward and looked around, even though the two of them were the only ones in the room. "Word is he's gone legit. He's got a city-sanctioned fighting ring and everything. Not a back-alley sort of thing, but with proper seating and an actual raised ring."

Millie nodded but her mind was miles away as Punch held her to the wall by her throat and told her he could snap her neck whenever he wanted to. She wondered if he would recognize her if he saw her. It would not do to go into his circle as Millie Mondegreen.

"Hey, thanks Bert, you're a gem," she said.

"Sorry I couldn't help you any, Millie," he said, taking up the pretense again. "Best of luck finding out anything useful."

She was out into the cold and climbing the stairs before the door closed. This case was her focus, but if she could find out anything on Punch, anything at all to put him away for good, she was damn well going to get it to Ward.

Chapter Four

When Millie arrived later that day at the building which housed both Cobbler's Rest and Jeremiah's offices, she was taken aback to see that the restaurant was closed. She couldn't remember a time in all her days of coming to this building when the doors had ever been closed against anything but the cold.

A sign hung on the door that simply read "Closed Sorry."

She climbed the stairs and heard voices as she approached the top landing. She stood with her hand on the knob and tried to overhear, but the voices were all too low, so she shrugged and let herself in hoping that it was Ward who was visiting so she could fill him in.

Inside, Jeremiah sat behind the desk and the lanky form of the boy, Tarquin, paced back and forth.

"It's three so far, if you count the boy you're looking for. All of them snatched up in the middle of the night and none of them seen since. Some are saying they're being hauled off to the Cistern to mine for gold."

Jeremiah sighed and waved Millie in. "Tarquin was just telling me that some other young people have gone missing," he said. "He was also allowing me to benefit from the erroneous conclusions he has drawn based on this information and the thoughtless waggings of tongues."

"But Mr. Mountweazel, I asked around. People have gone missing."

Millie sat and contributed nothing to the conversation, her thoughts dancing along the threads that Tarquin's assumptions wove around the room. Suppose young people were being kidnapped. Suppose it was Punch. It was his modus operandi to trap young, naive people into his service and keep them there under threat of death or worse.

"Millie?" said Jeremiah. He was watching her with a face full of concern.

"Sorry, I was miles away," she said with a start. "How many did you say, Tarquin?"

"Three. There's your Declan guy, then a boy down on Philosopher's Lane and a girl down Keebler Street by the big tree," he said.

Jeremiah watched her. After a moment's pause he turned to Tarquin and smiled. "I would caution you against drawing conclusions without facts, my boy, but I thank you for the facts you have brought me." He reached into his drawer and retrieved a few coins which he handed to the boy. "Please come back if you hear any other information that may be connected to the things you have discovered."

Tarquin nodded, looked as though he was going to say something else, then turned and walked to the door, opening it swiftly.

Mr. Panglossian, the proprietor of Cobbler's Rest and Jeremiah's neighbor, stood at the top of the landing with his hand raised to knock. He looked confused at the disjointed sequence of events that resulted in the door being answered before he had asked, and then shrugged and pulled his cap off.

"Begging your pardon, Mr. Mountweazel," he said. The usual smiling face of the man was as twisted with worry as his hat was twisted in his hands.

Jeremiah stood and walked around the desk. "Not at all, Mr. Panglossian. Please come in out of the cold." He gestured to one of the chairs in front of the desk.

As he took the offered seat, Millie poured some bourbon for all but Tarquin, who lingered by the door. Mr. Panglossian looked surprised as she presented the cup to him, then sniffed it and took a sip, shuddering as it burned its way down his throat. He relaxed slightly.

"That'll warm you up," she said. She tossed back her glass and took the other chair while Jeremiah leaned back against the desk.

"What can we do for you, sir?" Jeremiah asked. He liked Panglossian. The unbridled optimism of the man gave him hope, and it was an odd thing to see him look troubled.

"It's my daughter, you see," stated Panglossian. "She's missing."

Jeremiah and Millie exchanged a confused look.

"I didn't know you had a daughter," said Millie. She reached out and took the man's hand, squeezing it softly.

Panglossian nodded, holding his hands up in apology. "It's true, I have none. But had I the choice, Elodie would be my flesh and blood," he said.

"Elodie? You mean the waitress with the long, black hair that always smiles?" asked Millie.

Panglossian nodded. "The same. Were I to be so blessed as to have a child, she would be the one I would ask the gods to grant me. She brings sun to my dark skies and laughter to my heart." He began to cry, letting out long, drawn-out sobs.

Millie moved over to sit on the arm of his chair and began to pat him gently on the back as he cried. She looked at Jeremiah and raised an eyebrow.

Tarquin cleared his throat. "I'll just be off then," he said, not looking up from the floor. He slipped out without further ceremony. Jeremiah watched him go before returning his attention to his neighbor.

Jeremiah tapped his chin and moved around to sit behind the desk again. He pulled out a pad and quill and cleared his throat. "Tell me what you know."

Panglossian looked at him hopefully through wet eyes. "I do not have much in the way of money, Mr. Mountweazel."

Millie laughed. "Like we would take your money. We're neighbors. Neighbors help each other."

Panglossian smiled up at her, then pursed his lips as he thought. "The last time I saw her was earlier today. She worked a long shift and was terribly tired, so I told her she could go home early." He pointed at the wall that divided his apartment from Jeremiah's office. "She lives with me, you know, while she's getting some money saved up."

"No, I did not know that," said Jeremiah. "How long has she been living here?"

"Just two months. She came to work one day crying because she had been evicted. I pay her what I can, but it's never enough when there are bills to pay, you know?"

Jeremiah thought back to the harder times when he had often considered pushing the piles of unpaid bills into the waste paper bin instead of confronting the fact that he could not pay them. "I do know," he said.

The old man nodded. "So I told her to stay with me. I have a guest room, so she's my guest. She helps out around the place, keeping things clean, and works for me in the Rest."

Millie frowned. "I don't want to ask this question, Mr. Panglossian, but you said she was saving up money. Do you think it's possible she saved up enough and simply left?"

He patted her hand. "You are not wrong to think such things, but if you knew my Elodie then you would know how very unlikely, even impossible, that is. The girl dotes on me, and I her. She has been happy here. She tells me all the time how I am like the father she never knew. I just can't believe she would leave without saying goodbye."

"So you sent her home," said Jeremiah. "When did you notice she was gone? Surely you have customers pulling your attention."

Millie shot him a look that he recognized. She was often on him about being more sensitive to people when they were upset, and that look was a warning that he was approaching being unintentionally rude.

"She sings, my daughter. She sings like an angel. When I climb the stairs I can always tell she's home when I hear her beautiful voice drifting down to greet me. Today, there was no singing. I went up to check on her, and there was no joy waiting for me when I opened the door."

"Was anything missing along with her?" asked Millie.

"Like did she pack a bag or take all of her things?" asked Jeremiah, earning him another look from Millie. He shrugged and gestured for her to continue.

"Her things are gone. She didn't have much, but what was there is gone." He began to sob again.

Millie rubbed his back and made soft shushing sounds until he got himself back under control. "Is there anyone you suspect may have wished her ill?"

"No no no no no," he said, shaking his head. "Elodie is someone who everyone loves, some of them too much, but no one would want to hurt her. She has never so much as raised her voice in anger that I have seen."

"What do you mean, 'some of them too much'?" asked Millie.

"You know what it's like. She's pleasant to everyone. She smiles at the boys and they melt. They come around and bring her flowers and presents and want to take walks with her, and she tells them no and they go away and come back trying harder. Sometimes she comes to me and says they are being rude, and I tell them they are no longer welcome around my restaurant."

Millie raised an eyebrow at Jeremiah again and he nodded. "Any boys in particular?"

The old man shook his head. "You know me. I'm friendly with everyone, but these boys all look the same. I saw one last week stopping her in the alley while she was taking the trash out. He was in the shadows, hunched over like a thief, and she kept moving away from him like she was afraid. As soon as I saw this I came out to see if she needed help and he ran away."

Jeremiah wrote quickly on his pad. "This boy seems like a likely culprit, but since you didn't see him I can't very well pass a description around town," he said. Millie hit him with a scowl. He ignored her and smiled at Mr. Panglossian. "Tell you what. I will make some inquiries and see what I can find out. I don't have a lot to go on, but anyone who has seen Elodie will surely remember her, and that may help."

Panglossian stood and stuck out his hand. When Jeremiah shook it, Panglossian grabbed his hand in both of his and shook it vigorously. "You come to dinner whenever you want, Mr. Mountweazel. And you, too, of course, Miss Mondegreen," he said, smiling back at her. "I make you the most special dish of all, on the house."

Millie stifled a laugh as Jeremiah fought to keep the smile on his face.

"I look forward to it."

The old man left, his spirits raised only slightly by the promise of help. When he was out of earshot Millie sat back down and stared at Jeremiah.

"That makes four."

He sighed. "I'll grant that there do seem to be an absurd number of people missing, but they're too far apart for me to consider it a pattern. Philosopher's Street and Keebler Lane may be close to each other, but they're in The Bottoms, and Elodie lived here. On top of that, we don't even know where Declan laid his head or if he's actually missing."

"So you think it's a coincidence?"

He tapped his chin and stared at the door. "Maybe. Maybe it's something else."

Millie groaned. "I do so love it when you decide things and don't tell me what they are."

Jeremiah stood and picked up his hat from the desk. "Some food will do the trick. Let's see if Mr. Panglossian is managing without help."

It was Millie's turn to sigh. "About that. We may be in for a walk."

"Keeping in mind that I, as you know, generally like to wait until I know all the facts to voice any conclusions, I have a theory," said Jeremiah as they walked back from a restaurant four blocks away. Every restaurant in town paled in comparison to Cobbler's Rest because none of them could keep up with the eclectic variety. Granted, most of them didn't try to because, in most cases, diners didn't want eel in their corn, but Jeremiah and Millie had grown so accustomed to it that the place they had just been to held no great memories for them.

But they were fed, and with that usually came the brain space Jeremiah needed to work things out. It amazed Millie that a sandwich could sometimes be the difference between a case being a complete mystery and it being absolutely resolved.

"I have one too," said Millie. "Who goes first?"

Jeremiah shrugged. "You go ahead."

"I know that you don't think there's a connection in the disappearances, but I can't ignore it. I think people are being taken for some nefarious purpose, whether it be the fights or the mines, and once we sort out who is doing the taking we can shut it down."

Jeremiah nodded. "And you think this organization chose to take two people from a nicer part of town, a waitress from The Strand, and a boy from out of town?"

"Who knows how many more there are, though? Think about it. People may have been going missing for months and we're only just putting it together."

She looked so certain, so determined, that Jeremiah didn't want to argue with her.

"You're worried about Punch, aren't you?" he said, sussing out her motivation.

"I just know what he's like. This is his way of doing things," she said. She glanced around at their surroundings and gave him a confused look but he kept walking forward without returning her look. "And with him back in town we can't ignore the possibility, even the probability, that this is him."

"I understand. But you know you are out of his concern now. His fee has been paid."

She smiled. "Yes, Mr. Mysterious Benefactor, I know you settled the tab, but that doesn't matter to a man like him. He went to jail because of me. He won't forget that. Where the devil are we going, anyway?"

"We're almost there. If you can bear the cold a little longer while I explain my theory."

They settled on a wall, not in the light of the gas lamp, but in shadows cast by a large tree that hung over them protectively, leaving the ground beneath less covered by snow.

"I await your amazing insight," she said.

"First of all, and I can't believe I've never asked you this before, but do you believe in fate?" he asked staring off into the distance.

"What, like the 'everything happens for a reason' type of fate, or the 'they were destined to be together' type?"

"There's a difference?"

"Of course there is. The first kind is the fate that everyone turns to whenever something bad happens. They equally turn to it whenever something good happens. It's like a catch-all for laying the blame on an invisible force instead of acknowledging the effort of the parties involved. A man reading the paper walks out in front of a carriage and is run down and people try to comfort the family with the idea that it happened 'for a reason'. His widow meets a man at the funeral who comforts her, leading to the two of them falling in love and her finally being in a relationship with a man that doesn't like to slap her when he drinks, and everyone nods and says 'see, I told you so.' It's all fate's doing, never mind the people involved."

Jeremiah laughed. "You've given this more thought that I expected."

"Then there's the people who see a man and a woman meet on a bridge. Maybe she drops a glove and he picks it up for her. Maybe their eyes meet and they begin to talk and before long they are getting married and people want to wonder what would have happened if she hadn't dropped the glove. Would they have never met? Would they end up married to other people?"

"That ignores the players, as you say," offered Jeremiah.

Millie nodded vigorously. "Exactly! They claim it was fate that brought them together, not the fact that she is a clumsy person who drops things all the time and he's a perfect gentleman who would stop to help someone."

Jeremiah pursed his lips. "So you don't believe in fate, then?"

"I believe in people and the fact that the actions they perform have consequences, good or bad," she said. "For instance, the consequence of sitting under this tree in the cold is that I will not be able to feel my feet anymore, whereas if we were to stand and start walking again, preferably to your study where I can make something hot to drink, I may just save my toes from an icy demise."

Jeremiah let out a long exhale, his breath fogging in the air and drifting away.

"Tarquin was lying."

Millie shot him a look. "Why in the hells would he do that? You're so good to him."

"That's a good question, and the answer either lies in the fact that he has a good reason or he has suddenly become a bad person. I'm inclined to believe the former."

Millie rubbed her hands together to warm them. "So he was lying about the missing people?"

"I believe so," said Jeremiah. "I think he was trying to set up an explanation for something else—and he might have pulled it off, too, if he hadn't tried it on me, and if he weren't such a terrible liar. When he's telling the truth he just comes out with it, plain as day. When he's lying he becomes emphatic and insistent, and far too detailed."

"So I'm confused about what this has to do with fate," said Millie. "Perhaps my brain is frozen."

"When I rushed out to flag him down yesterday, he dropped some packages. I noticed when I picked them up and carried them for a while that one had torn open so I could see its contents. It didn't register as important at the time, but now I think—and I hope to be proven right soon so that we can go warm up—that what I saw was very important."

"So did fate lead you to that discovery or something else?"

"An academic discussion really, because the more important question is what motivation he would have for lying to us except to, as I said, set up an alternate explanation to whatever conclusion we may have drawn when we heard the news."

Millie scrunched her brow. "What news?"

Jeremiah shushed her and pointed. Coming up the path was none other than Tarquin himself, and when he reached the door of a dilapidated cottage he knocked a series of sharp knocks, then a couple of hard ones. It reminded Millie of her own special knock at the theater.

The door opened and the light from inside poured out onto the street, illuminating the girl who had answered.

"Elodie?" whispered Millie.

"The same. My supposition is that our young friend and Mr. Panglossian's adopted daughter have gotten themselves into a bit of a situation, and Tarquin, misguided though he is, is doing his best to make it right. The problem is, he lied to me, and that must be answered. But not tonight." He stood and stomped his feet. "Come on, I'll make you some tea."

They walked down the path toward Jeremiah's rooms.

"So that's what the fate thing was all about. You somehow had the answer to the mystery before the question was even asked," said Millie.

"Exactly," he said. "So do you believe in fate now?"

"No, but I believe in comeuppance, and I want to be there when you call him out on this."

Chapter Five

Mr. Panglossian's lights were all out when they got back to the building. They had a debate on whether to wake him, but ultimately it was decided that a note slipped under the door would be the best approach. Neither of them really knew what the old man's life was like in his private quarters, only the persona he showed in the restaurant.

Jeremiah wrote out the note for Millie to take over.

"Mr. Panglossian. Elodie has been found and I assure you she is in good health. I will fill you in on the details in the morning."

"Don't you think you should put more detail, like the fact that she's, you know…" asked Millie.

"That is not my news to tell. Right now I just want to reassure him she's safe."

"Fair enough," said Millie. She grabbed the note, shot down the stairs, and raced across the snowy patio to the door on the other side of the building. She was surprised to find it unlocked.

"Poor old guy probably thinks she might come home tonight," she said quietly. She slipped up the stairs as quietly as the wind and slipped the note under his door. She half expected the door to fling open and him to come racing out begging for details, but there was no response. She wondered how the man had become so attached to the girl and she realized that despite the hundreds of times she had been fed by him she did not actually know that much about him.

In the short walk back to Jeremiah's rooms, darker thoughts crowded her head. They all revolved around the complete bastard who called himself Mr. Punch. Jeremiah may be right that Punch isn't kidnapping people, but his stink still seemed to waft up every time she thought about the missing boy Declan. She wasn't sure why she was so convinced, but every part of her told her that going after Punch would give them the answers they needed.

Now she just needed to convince Jeremiah.

She found him sitting behind his desk flipping through a collection of telegrams. "No one seems to know anything certain," he said, looking up from the tiny, square pieces of paper. "There are a few leads that may be him or may just be someone that looks like him. I can't say he's all that remarkable, our lad."

"He's a fighter," said Millie simply.

Jeremiah set down the telegrams and looked at her over his reading glasses. "True."

"And we know there are fights in town, especially a new one run by—"

"You're convinced it's Mr. Punch without any evidence," he said.

"No evidence except my experience," came her retort.

Jeremiah knew better than to argue with her when her mind was set.

"What do you propose?"

"I'm going in there and finding out what I can," she said.

"Punch will undoubtedly be delighted to see you."

She flashed him a winning grin. "Oh, my dear Jeremiah, don't you fret. Millie Mondegreen will not set foot anywhere near that awful man." She stood and walked over to the mirror that hung on the wall behind the door. She pulled her hair back and pressed it down to her head, a herculean feat as her red mane was generally as tamable as a bucket of snakes. "What do you think? Trevor? Willis? Ooh, maybe it's time I was a Desmond."

Jeremiah sighed. "I'm not going to talk you out of this, am I?"

Millie let go of her hair, crimson curls dancing in every direction, and walked over to lean on the desk. "You are not, but I appreciate your concern. You know I know how to take care of myself."

"I do."

"So I slip in, make some subtle inquiries, and come back with information. If it's useful, we act on it. If I find nothing, I grant you permission to say you told me so as many times as you want over the following week without rebuke."

Jeremiah laughed and shook his head. "In and out, no lingering, no confronting Punch."

She shot him a look.

"Please," he added.

"I'll be careful. In the meantime, maybe you can drop in on your lady love again," she teased.

"I merely went by to bring her up to speed on where the investigation was, nothing more."

"Riiiiight," said Millie. "And Mr. Punch is a legitimate businessman now. Any other tall tales you want to hit me with?"

Jeremiah managed to look appalled and then cleared his throat. "Supposing I did have something of an interest in getting to know Miss Quinlan to a more familiar degree. Any advice?"

Millie stared at the ceiling and rubbed her chin for a moment. "Don't wait. I know you, and I know you're trying to be all sensible, but if you wait until this is all said and done you may miss your chance."

"What if we can't find her brother?"

"Then you're the shoulder she can lean on. Go for it, Jeremiah. I hate seeing you sitting here all alone most nights when you could be impressing some lovely lady with your extensive knowledge of fall foliage and the migratory habits of herons."

Both of them laughed.

"Thank you, Millie."

"You'll thank me more when I solve this case for you. I'll be in touch tomorrow after my reconnaissance." She picked up her pile of scarves from the chair and wound them around her head and neck. "See you soon."

When she left, Jeremiah slipped the picture out of his pocket. Most people assumed he and Millie had some sort of romantic relationship, but neither of them felt in any way inclined toward that. What they had was a friendship beyond definition, and he was grateful for it.

He stared into the smiling eyes of Nora in the picture. Sure it was her five years ago, but the smile was the same. The eyes were the same. He felt that flutter in his chest. Maybe he would tell her. What could he lose?

He had a case to solve, though. No time to get distracted. He slipped the picture back into his pocket and sighed. Millie was probably right, but he needed to focus. After he saved her brother he would ask her to dinner. For now, it was work.

Jeremiah picked up the pile of telegrams and began to read through them again.

Millie didn't want to wait, but these sort of things don't usually happen in the middle of the day. No, the night called to her, and she was ready to listen.

But first, a cat nap.

She splayed out on her bed, which was only recognizable as such because of the three posts that stuck up from the corners, the fourth having been snapped off long ago. Clothes, books, costumes of various shapes, sizes, and genders all decorated the top of the surface as well as the chair next to it, the night stand, and three-quarters of the floor. It wasn't that she had a tendency toward hoarding, it was just that the apartment was ludicrously small, having only the one room that served every use, save one which belonged to the tiny bathroom off one corner.

She loved it, though. She could hear the sounds of the Callipygian Theatre getting into full swing downstairs, loud brash music playing to accompany some amazing act. Some thought living over such a raucous environment would drive any hope of rest from the occupant's life, but to Millie they were the soothing sounds of chaos which sang her lullabies.

She closed her eyes and controlled her breathing, smiling as the familiar weight of her cat, Tipsy, fell onto her chest.

"Hey baby girl," she said, scratching the cat's ears. "Mommy has to think."

Tipsy began to clean her paws and Millie closed her eyes again and began to breathe deeply. It was a trick Jeremiah had taught her, to clear her mind and only let in the things she wanted to be present and focus on them.

She saw Declan's face from the photograph and tried to imagine him talking to her. When that failed she pictured him raising his fists and punching, dodging return blows before throwing a few more. That she could see clearly. She saw Punch's face then. She saw him the night he told her she would have to pay off her debt with her body. She saw the look on her face when she told him she would die first. She felt his hand around her throat, squeezing.

She struck out in her mind and drove her fingers into Punch's eyes, relishing the squish as she blinded him, hearing the deafening roar of his scream as he clutched his face. If only she had done that in real life instead of just crying.

Things were different now. She was free. Punch had no hold over her. Jeremiah had seen to that.

He couldn't remove the guy from her mind, though. She had to do that. She would do that.

When she opened her eyes two hours had passed. She got up, disrupting the comfort of her companion who mewed loudly and burrowed into the blankets, and sat down at her cluttered dressing table.

In thirty minutes she was a balding, middle-aged man with a slight overbite and overgrown nose hair. She stood, bound her chest, donned a false belly which also served to hold some tools, and picked through the pile of clothes until she found the perfect outfit to pass herself off as a regular slum-dweller with a little money to his name.

"Well Tipsy, wish me luck," she said, taking a bowler from the hatstand and heading out the door. The cat hardly lifted her head.

She wasn't planning for this to be an infiltration, only a reconnaissance. She wanted the full measure of the place. As the cab pulled up to the address Bert had 'not' given her, she knew she was in the right spot because all signs pointed to the fact that she wasn't. There was no line of people waiting to get in. There were no drunks carousing outside the building. Everything was buttoned up nice and neat, which meant the show was inside, away from the eyes of any passing Constabulary.

She paid the cabbie and crept down the alley, then remembered that she didn't need to creep. She had the password thanks to Bert, and she had the appearance of a man who was meant to be there. As she made it further down, the noise finally reached her ears: shouts of a crowd and the occasional bell, not to mention low thuds that likely meant a body had fallen.

Millie held herself differently, embracing the gut she now possessed and walking as though she was proud of it. By the time she got to the door and hammered on it with her walking stick, Desmond Cully was the man asking for entry.

The hatch slid open. No one spoke, but the sound of the crowd came washing out in the darkness.

"I'd like to buy some roses," she said loudly enough to be heard.

The hatch slid shut and the door opened. The man in the shadows didn't say a word to her, he just gestured down a hallway and went back to sit in a chair in the corner where a lit cigar waited.

As she moved down the hall into a large, open room the sound became deafening. She was walking along an upper floor balcony looking down into a space below where a ring was set up, its walls made of fencing instead of ropes. A large crowd, possibly hundreds of sweaty, shouting people, encircled the ring in which two men were currently pounding on each other.

Millie was about to take the stairs to the floor when a door opened farther along the balcony and three men walked out, two of average height and one much larger, and positioned themselves along the railing to watch the fight below. Her breath caught in her throat as she recognized the large man as Mr. Punch.

Seeing him brought it all back, all the threats, all the abuse. She felt dizzy and grabbed the rail to hold herself up, and when he looked over at her she thought she may pass out. He didn't linger on her, though, and she remembered that she was not herself, at least not outwardly, and that the brute had no idea who she was. To keep from drawing attention to herself she watched the fight again.

This was not your standard boxing match by far. One of the men was wearing gloves, but the other was bare-fisted and kept throwing kicks which were only barely blocked. It was clear there were no actual rules, as all propriety was left at the door and the two men traded jabs, kicks, elbows, and even bites in an effort to take each other down.

Money was held in the air by eager gamblers, snatched by bet-takers who scribbled on tiny notebooks. Mr. Punch watched it all with a grin that Millie knew was nothing but cruel.

The boxer fell and the other man went down with him, punching him repeatedly in the face until the man stopped moving. A man who had been there ostensibly as a referee but only took interest when the fall came about, ran over and pulled the gloveless man off the unconscious boxer, holding his hand up in the air in declaration of victory.

The crowd erupted with unbridled joyful bloodlust.

The ring was cleared of the victor and the comatose loser, and two more men entered the ring. Millie saw Punch tap one of his companions on the arm and point at them, saying something which made them both laugh.

As the referee shouted introductions at the crowd, Millie scanned the area she had seen the fighters exit. She had hoped to catch sight of Declan, of course, but she didn't think it would be that easy. She would have to head down there and see about getting behind the scenes.

The bell rang and the two men began to fight. Millie made her way down the stairs and through the crowd, careful not to bump into too many people for fear of losing her bald cap or some other mishap. Disguises were difficult to keep in order in close quarters.

The sounds of fists on flesh turned her stomach, but she feigned interest as she moved slowly through the crowd, even handing a few bills to a bet-taker and calling for the taller of the two to win. She was handed a slip of paper and she continued on, entering the hallway that had served as the fighter's entryway.

"What are you doing back here?" said a voice.

She turned to see a shaggy-haired man with a lit cigar dangling from his mouth staring at her.

"Pardon, but the crowd was a bit too oppressive," she said in a deep voice. "I needed to get some air. Is there an exit this way?" She pointed down the hallway.

"Yeah, sure, whatever," he said. "Just don't harass the fighters or I'll throw you out on your ass." He turned his attention back to the fight which was still going on, much to the delight of the crowd.

The rooms on either side of the hallway were open, lacking doors of any sort, and she could make out men waiting to fight as well as men who had already fought, some looking more worse for wear than others. She spotted the boxer who had been unconscious being yelled at by another man as he tried to drink water and kept vomiting it back up.

There was no sign of Declan, much to her disappointment. Most of the people here were older, seasoned fighters, probably survivors from the street fights that existed all over town before the Constabulary cracked down on them.

Millie cursed under her breath and made her way back to the floor, just in time to see something she later wished she had missed. The taller of the two fighters kicked high, landing a solid hit on the chin of the other. His head flew up, blood shooting into the air, and he fell backwards onto the fence hitting his neck with a loud crack. He hit the ground and did not move.

Millie stared at the fallen man as the referee came over and examined him. He looked at another man, drew a line across his throat, and went over to declare the taller man the victor.

Two men lifted up the body and dragged it down the hall past Millie. She could tell just by looking that this was his last fight. She looked down at the ticket in her hand, a winning ticket, and felt sick. Then a sound reached her over the crowd that ran up her spine: Mr. Punch's bellowing laugh.

He stood on the balcony, gesturing to his companions and mimicking the killing blow, and all three men laughed to bring the rafters down. They turned and went back into the office, their entertainment over.

Millie thought she may vomit and decided to leave. She pushed her way through the crowd clutching her winning ticket as though it were a weight around her neck that she had to hold aloft. People bumped her this way and that but she didn't bother with it all, eyes focused on the stairs, which she climbed as rapidly as she could around drunken men screaming for blood as the next fight began.

Her heart nearly stopped as she reached the top of the landing and saw Punch descending the steps toward her. She dodged to the right, giving him a wide berth, and kept her eyes down, passing him without incident. She chanced a glance back and saw that he had stopped and was staring at her for a moment before a man bumped into him, drawing his attention and his ire.

Millie fled as quickly as she could without seeming conspicuous. Once out in the alley she found the shadows and clung to them as she took deep breaths and tried to calm her heart.

Punch came out into the alley and looked down each direction. He had that look on his face he always got when he was curious, which was only slightly less grim than his angry face. With a grunt and a shrug he went back into the building and Millie disappeared into the night.

Chapter Six

"I had my revolver with me. I could have just ended him right there. I would have been doing the world a favor."

Millie sat in one of the cushy chairs in Jeremiah's office and he sat in the other. He had made them tea as soon as she came in that morning and encouraged her to tell what she had learned. As her story went on he moved around to sit next to her.

"You're not a murderer, Millie," he said.

"Is it murder, though, to remove someone as awful as that beast from the world?" she asked, almost pleadingly.

Jeremiah took the teacup from her shaking hand and set it down, keeping her hand in his. "Yes. Shooting a man in a dark alley in the middle of the night is most definitely murder, even if he's the worst type of human being. Believe me, you would be haunted by it for the rest of your life, no matter how justified."

Millie looked up at him and wiped the tears that had been welling up in her eyes away with her free hand. She sat up straight and picked up her tea again. "Well, if Punch is claiming to be running a legit club the dead guy from last night would discredit that in a heartbeat," she said as she sipped it loudly.

Jeremiah sat back. "You know as well as I do that they'll never find that body. That poor man likely went to a watery grave, if he didn't become pig food."

Millie shuddered. "So what now? Declan wasn't there. It's possible he just wasn't there last night, but how can we know for sure?"

"Ah, about that," said Jeremiah. He reached over and picked up a telegram from his desk and handed it to her.

It read: 'According to an informant, your boy is a regular at the Char Pit. Ward.'

"We've found him then, and I had to see that bastard for nothing," Millie said quietly.

"Not for nothing. We know where Punch is now, and what he's up to. We'll get him, Millie, or help get him. Trust me, we won't let that piece of filth haunt your new life."

Millie smiled at him. "Shall we go and pick up your lady love and take her to see her brother?"

Jeremiah laughed. "She is not that. Not yet anyway. But yes, we should."

As they exited the building Mr. Panglossian came hobbling out of the restaurant bundled in a patched coat and wool cap. "You found her!" he shouted as he waved them down with the note Millie had left.

"Ah, yes," said Jeremiah. "She is safe, I assure you. And I promise you that after we resolve our current business I will see you reunited with her."

Mr. Panglossian took his hand and shook it vigorously. "I thank you many times, Jeremiah. Come, let me get you something to eat."

"Back open, then?" asked Millie.

He blushed. "Nothing good comes from moping. Cooking makes me happy, so I cook."

"Well we will hopefully come see you at lunch, Mr. Panglossian," said Jeremiah, "but at the moment we are needed elsewhere."

The man nodded. "Ivan. You call me Ivan now," he said. "Ivan."

"Ivan it is," said Jeremiah. "See you soon."

"You're getting extra fish heads in your next soup, my friend," laughed Millie.

"Can't wait," he said, and he flagged down a passing cab.

Millie and Jeremiah stood in the exact same spot she had with her sister months ago. They looked down at the same care ward, although the patients were all different, as were many of the nurses.

"Nora describes this place as transitional. They care for anyone and everyone, no matter where their injuries were acquired, and most patients are out in less than a week, although some take longer." Jeremiah leaned on the rail and watched the nurses move between the beds in a ballet of care.

"Is it transitional for the nurses, too? I hardly recognize anyone from last time," said Millie.

They had been told to wait until Nora could be pulled free from her duties. Jeremiah was familiar with the requirement from his previous visits.

He sighed. "Indeed. The pay is poor and the hours are long. Most move on to private care or burn out altogether."

Millie looked at him, reading the concern on his face. "Tell her."

He nodded. "Soon. For now, let's give her the good news."

"Jeremiah, and Miss Mondegreen as well. This is a pleasant surprise," said a voice behind them. They turned to find Nora coming into the room wiping her hands on her apron.

Jeremiah's smile was radiant when he saw her, and the nurse smiled back at him hardly taking notice of Millie.

"There is news," said Jeremiah.

"You've found him?" she asked. Her eyes shone with excitement and she reached out and took each of their hands. "Please tell me he is well."

"We believe we know where he is, and we're going to go and prove our theory correct, but I didn't want to pass without giving you some news of hope," said Jeremiah. She had released Millie's hand but still held onto his.

"Jeremiah has been kind enough to keep me regularly apprised of how the search is going," Nora said to Millie. "It has been most appreciated."

Millie grinned.

Jeremiah shot her a look and moved over to sit on the bench by the wall with Nora. "My friend in the Constabulary assures me that Declan has been spotted fighting in bouts at a place called the Char Pit. Further inquiries reveal he is doing quite well."

"Further inquiries?" asked Millie.

Jeremiah smiled. "Yes, I asked young Tarquin to confirm the telegram for me. He was most surprised to see me at the door of his current home, and most eager to keep me from coming inside, so he agreed quite readily."

"I bet he did," laughed Millie.

Nora watched their exchange with great interest. "So, this Tarquin lad works for you?"

"He's been a help on a number of occasions throughout the years," said Jeremiah.

Millie nodded her agreement. "And he's currently in hot water, though he does not realize it yet."

"Be that as it may, he was very helpful and took a cab down to the Char Pit to confirm the information. He says Declan is what Stace Kimball, the proprietor of the club, describes as 'a force to be reckoned with in the ring.'"

It was Nora's turn to laugh. "That's my brother, alright. A force indeed."

"We were heading over there now to contact him and let him know you were in town. I thought you may want to accompany us," said Jeremiah. The hopefulness in his eyes gave Millie the arduous task of choosing between giggling and saying 'Aw!'

Nora smiled and patted his hand. "I cannot leave at the moment, or even for a while. There was an airship accident and many people were injured. It took quite a bit of persuading to give us these few moments."

Disappointment crossed Jeremiah's face and just as quickly was forced away. "Well then we shall go and confront your brother with how much he has worried his sister and attempt to bring him your way."

"I'll drag him here by his cauliflowered ear if I have to," added Millie.

Nora smiled, patted Jeremiah's hand, and stood. "I am grateful to you both for all you have done for me. You will find him a stubborn boy, but if you would please tell him when you see him that our father's condition has worsened it may sway his decision."

"I'm sorry to hear that," said Millie.

"As am I," added Jeremiah.

Nora and Jeremiah held eye contact for what felt like an eternity. "I thank you," said Nora finally, and she turned and left the room quickly.

"Tell her," said Millie.

"I will," said Jeremiah.

"Good. Now come on and let's collect her brother."

Jeremiah and Millie stood in front of the charcoal black building that served as the home of the fighting club known as the Char Pit. It gained its name from the block on which it stood, a block historically plagued by a series of fires that led most in the area to declare the plot cursed, an attitude which led Stace Kimball to be able to purchase the entirety for a ludicrously small amount of money.

"How do you want to do this?" asked Millie.

"Do what?" asked Jeremiah.

"Get in there and find Declan. Should I slip around back and jimmy the lock, or—"

Jeremiah laughed. "I do appreciate your talents, Millie, but sometimes you get so caught up in them you forget that this is a legitimate training facility with open access to the public during the day, and since the sun is currently beating down on us, providing no heat, mind, we can simply walk in."

He turned the knob and entered the facility, leaving Millie to glare at the back of his head, shrug, and join him.

The smell of sweat and smoke was overwhelming at first and both of them struggled to see into the dark building. As their eyes adjusted to the dim light and the fug, they could see three separate rings positioned across the massive floor, and down the walls on either side were punching bags, weight racks, large, metal drums, and dozens of men screaming at each other as they trained and sparred.

"Lovely place," muttered Jeremiah.

"Aren't you glad your lady friend didn't come with us?"

"Indeed," he said.

There was an office with a counter, and behind that counter sat a woman drawing deep on a cigar and staring at them.

"And what brings two high-falutins down to our corner of the world?" she asked as she exhaled a cloud.

Jeremiah stepped forward and tried to ignore the burning in his lungs. "I'm looking to talk to Stace Kimball about a fighter named Declan Quinlan. I'm told he fights here."

"And who the hells might you be?" she asked. She spat onto the floor behind the desk, and Jeremiah shuddered to think what horrors that surface might contain.

"I am Jeremiah Mountweazel, and this is my colleague Millie Mondegreen," he said.

"Funny names," she said without blinking.

"Do you think so? What's your name?" he responded.

"Folks call me Luz. That's all you need to know."

"Nice to meet you, Luz," said Jeremiah. He held his hand out as if to shake hers but did little to disguise the bill he held in his palm. "Do you think we might be able to speak to Mr. Kimball?"

She picked it out with her long, bony fingers without accepting the handshake and took another deep draw on her cigar, which she exhaled in his face. "Wait here."

"Charming lady," said Jeremiah as he stepped back to confer with Millie. "I think if I play my cards right I may just have a chance of dinner with her."

Millie laughed. "She does seem to be smitten. What will Nora think?"

A man came around the corner walking directly toward them but stopped to bark instructions at a man hitting a bag before coming over to them.

"I'm Kimball. What's this about?" he demanded. He pulled a cloth from his pocket and wiped his brow. "Make it quick. As you can see, it's training time."

"Mr. Kimball I understand you have a fighter working with you named Declan Quinlan. I've been asked to deliver a message to him from his sister," said Jeremiah.

Kimball looked him over. "And she couldn't bring it herself?"

Jeremiah forced a laugh. "Nothing of the sort. You see she is indisposed at the moment with other obligations."

Millie saw Kimball's face harden. "Look, Kimball, are you going to walk us over to Declan or stand around wasting our time all day," she said. "I thought you had things to do."

Jeremiah looked at her in shock. Kimball laughed.

"He ain't here, damn him," he said.

Jeremiah's look of shock turned to dismay. "What do you mean?"

Kimball wasn't looking at him anymore, only at Millie. It was as if Jeremiah had ceased to exist. "He came in all full of himself. Said he had a better offer for more money and was going to take it. I told the kid, look, you're good, but you don't want to go messing around in the wrong circles. Stick with me and I'll get you set up golden."

"He didn't listen a bit, did he?" said Millie, matching his tone.

"These kids today. You wave a little money in their face and they forget how to be smart. I told him that money wasn't the path to success, making a name for yourself is. Stick with me and people will be shouting your name for years to come. Go down that other path and they'll forget you the first chance they get." He shook his head with disgust.

Millie's heart sank. She knew the answer to the question before she asked it, but she forced herself to ask it anyway. "Where did he go, Kimball?"

"Your boy Declan now works for that upstart Mr. Punch."

Chapter Seven

"What was that about fate again?" asked Millie as they waited for a cab.

"Don't tell me you're suddenly a believer," answered Jeremiah.

Millie laughed. "No, but remember when I told you that I knew in my gut Punch was involved in this? I hate it when I'm right." She studied Jeremiah's face as he stared off in the distance. "What are you going to do?"

"I have to tell her, and we have to get him out of there before he gets in too deep or she'll never forgive me."

Millie shoved him. "Her brother is an adult, Jeremiah. She's not going to blame you for his bad life choices."

He shrugged. "I doubt she'd be willing to have dinner with me if she has to bury her brother. She'll see me as nothing short of a failure."

Millie's jaw set. "Utter nonsense. Besides, we haven't failed yet. We know where he is. We just have to go get him."

"But that's the thing. He's not being held prisoner. He went of his own accord," said Jeremiah, desperation in his voice. "Even if we go there now, find him, and tell him Nora is looking for him he could very well do nothing with the information."

"And then our duty is well and truly discharged," Millie cut in. "She asked us to find him and we have found him. His safety is not our responsibility."

Jeremiah gave her a side eye. "You don't really believe that, do you?"

Millie groaned, then balled her fists and screamed at the top of her lungs. It gave some indication of the area in which they found themselves that no one even stopped to notice.

"Of course I don't, you lummox. I was just trying to make you realize it wasn't all on you," she yelled. "Right, so you go tell Nora the latest and I'll swing by my place, get my Desmond on, and head to Punch's dive. With any luck I can slip in, talk some sense into Declan, and have him back at the office by the morning."

Jeremiah shook his head. "It's not all on you, Millie. I'll come with you."

"Jer, you know I have complete faith in you and your abilities. Your brain is ridiculous when it comes to putting pieces of a puzzle together and seeing what other people can't see, but when it comes to The Bottoms, you don't have a clue."

"What are you talking about?" he demanded.

"You're in there trying to sweet talk a lady who looks like she eats babies for breakfast and when you finally do get Kimball to come over, you treat him like a gentleman. Well I have news for you, my friend, he is not a gentleman and he never will be. Most of these people never will be," she gestured around at the surrounding buildings and people wandering by. "You have to know how to deal with them and that is a skill I have."

Jeremiah sighed and nodded.

"So go tell Nora the latest, and let me do what I do best."

He looked at her, hands on her hips and jaw set in determination and knew that he was beaten. "You're really too good for me, Millie," he said, resignation in his voice.

She smiled. "Don't you forget it, bub."

She had the cab drop her off blocks away from the warehouse and took to the alleys. Her movements were furtive, but changed to casual when the occasion arose, so as to not draw the attention of anyone who could be connected to Punch's establishment.

The hallway that she had searched had led to water, and since it was this close to the shadow of the Morlins, she knew it was the Torri that ran behind the long chain of buildings. That being the case, she should be able to find the back door and let herself in, assuming no one was in the way. She patted the false belly she wore and felt the reassuring shape of her revolver as well as the telltale weight of the knives sheathed in both of her boots.

The portion of the populace that gathered along the river were some of the poorest in the city. Most of them made their livings fishing things of value from the river, washed down from the more affluent homes across the water. This time of year, however, pickings were slim, since none of them had the means or equipment to dive into the depths when the river was nearly frozen.

She felt an uncomfortable awareness of the good things she had in life as she passed by clusters of people gathered around burning barrels. She wasn't well-off now, but her entire life had been spent in luxury until she had fled home. The amount of waste her family committed and ignored made her sick. If she had the means, she would take the food that was needlessly discarded, sometimes on the whim of her fickle mother, and bring it all here so that these people could simply survive.

Millie gritted her teeth and walked on, focused on the task at hand. The rest of the world would have to wait. Tonight she was only interested in saving one young man.

Did he need saving? As she told Jeremiah, Declan was an adult. He could make his own decisions, and if those decisions put him under Punch's control that was his own fault, wasn't it?

Her own bad choices came back to haunt her. Had she deserved to end up under his control, or had things been stacked against her to the point where she would have ended up there inevitably, no matter what she did?

"There's Jeremiah's fate question again," she grumbled quietly to herself as she located what was likely the back door.

She glanced around, checking to see if there were any guards to worry about, but saw none. In her pocket sat one of her sets of lockpicks, so she knew she could get in. The only question was, would she be able to get in unnoticed.

Before she could arrive at a decision the door opened and a man walked out lighting a cigar. He walked past her without paying her any attention, grumbling to himself. Millie slipped through the door.

The hallway was poorly lit and busy, with most of the doorless rooms on either side spilling forth men who traded barbs with the occupants of the rooms and gave each other silent signals. Millie watched the dance with intense curiosity, trying to determine what plans and decisions were being made and who actually knew what they were.

"That one's a knocker," said one man, tapping the side of his head.

"We've got a real winner over here," said another, giving a thumbs down that contradicted his words.

She could hear sparring going on in the arena and shouts from various people as they reset for the evening. She casually strolled down the hallway, glancing into the rooms but trying to appear as if she was both uninterested in what was going on, and also meant to be there.

Then she saw him. He was older than he had been in the photograph, and his face was a bit more puffy with a cut still healing over his eye, but there was no doubt it was him. She stepped into the room and the boy looked up at her.

"Is it time for my warmup?" he asked. He was trying to give off an air of toughness but she could sense the fear lying under the surface. She wondered if it had hit him yet that he was in over his head.

"Declan Quinlan?" she asked.

He gave a start of surprise. "Y—Yes, that's me. How did you know my name?"

"My name is—" she almost said Millie Mondegreen. "My name is Desmond Cully, and I've been sent by your sister," she said. She didn't know whether showing her hand was a good idea, but in all her conversations with Nora the impression she always got was that the two of them were fond of each other.

"Which one?" he asked. He began taping his hands in preparation for his sparring session.

"Nora. She's in Tamarind. She says your father is very ill."

Declan stared at her so long she thought he had been struck dumb. "Hang on, who did you say you were again?"

"Who I am is unimportant," she said. "What's important is that if you fight here you may die."

Declan laughed. "That's a danger no matter where you fight."

"But here it's almost a certainty. All it takes is falling out of favor with the man in charge and you will leave the ring as a corpse."

He shook his head and hopped up off the table he had been sitting on. "Mr. Punch says he'll take care of me. He says I'll be a big name. And with fame comes money and with money I can make it so my parents don't have to slave away trying to grow food from dry land. I can make it so that my sister Aoife doesn't have to marry some braindead farmboy and sling out children."

She shook her head and grabbed his arm. "Look, I get it. You've been promised things. But it's all lies. You are fodder and you will be treated as such. Trust me on this."

"Who the hells are you?" he demanded, snatching his arm away.

"A friend. Now come on, we can slip out the way I came in and get you to Nora. We can have you on the train by tomorrow." She tried to take his arm again to pull him toward the door.

"No! I'm going to fight and make my way. What, did Kimball put you up to this? I told him I was sorry, but Mr. Punch can do more for me. It's no good him trying to get in my head and mess things up for me. Now go away, I need to focus."

He was shouting, and Millie realized that all of her attempts at subtlety and stealth were quickly being dashed against the stones.

"I'll be back," she said. She would go and get Nora. He would listen to his sister. There was still time.

"Don't bother," he spat. "And tell Kimball he had his chance and failed."

The clench of his jaw and the fire in his eyes told her his determination was unshakable. She would have to get out of there and regroup. She turned to slip out the door and walked right into a wall of a man.

"Well, if it isn't my guest from the other night," said Mr. Punch. "You're missing your red curl, though." He reached up and locked a giant hand on top of her head, squeezing and pulling the bald cap off and causing her hair to spring free.

"Hello there, Millie," he said with a predatory grin. "How nice of you to come see me."

Two men grabbed her by the arms and lifted her. She struggled, but was helpless to prevent herself from being carried down the hall in the wake of Mr. Punch.

"I should thank you, you know," said Punch. He sat behind a large desk in the office area upstairs, the very door she had seen him and his cronies coming through the night before. He had a new scar since the last time she had seen him, tracing down from his left ear to his chin, and it served to make him even more terrifying to behold.

She sat in a chair, false belly sitting in the corner behind Punch. The two men who stood behind her had ripped it from her in their search, along with the knives in her boots. The shirt that she wore was several sizes too large to account for the belly, and she held it wrapped tightly around her.

"How do you arrive at that?" she asked.

He squinted his cruel eyes and stared at her. "Because of you I ended up under the river for a while, and because of that I met a man named Pollard who told me all about his business. When I got out I looked him up and learned everything I could about the fighting world until his unfortunate death at the hands of some horrible villains."

Millie knew it had been Punch's hands. She could see him choking the life out of his benefactor, smiling as the man gasped for air.

"Fortunately, I was here to take up the reins and keep his dream going, so you see, if you hadn't betrayed me, I wouldn't be in charge of all you see."

He laughed then, that low, evil laugh that made her stomach churn, and steepled his hands under his chin.

"So, thank you," he said.

"Don't worry about it. Now if that's all, I'll just be on my way," she said, hopping to her feet. Four hands grabbed her and pulled her back into the chair hard enough to knock the wind out of her."

Punch feigned shock. "Gentlemen, be polite. Miss Mondegreen is our guest," he said.

"Your hospitality leaves a lot to be desired," she quipped.

Punch's fake smile reset to his usual scowl. "Why are you skulking around my business, little rat?" he growled.

Millie shrugged. "I just thought I'd see what you were up to, you know, for old time's sake."

He slammed his fist down on the desk so hard that all three members of his audience jumped. "Enough with the clever retorts, Millie. What are you doing here?"

She weighed all the options. She couldn't tell him why she was really there. If Punch knew there was something she wanted he would do all he could to keep it from her just out of spite. "I heard you were back in town and running this show and I thought I'd have a look around and make sure you were on the up and up."

He sat back and spread his arms. "Everything is legal. I'm completely legitimate," he said.

"Mmmm-hmmm, tell that to the corpse your guys hauled out last night," she said. She knew it was foolish to provoke him, but she couldn't help it. Everything about him disgusted her.

"Accidents may happen on occasion," he said with a shrug. "The fighters all know the dangers involved."

Down below the crowd roared and a bell rang. The night's events had begun. She wondered if Declan was fighting first, or if his first brush with death would come later.

"Well then, everything seems in order so I'll just be on my way," she said. Before she could stand she felt hands on her shoulders again.

"Why were you bothering my new fighter?" Punch asked.

"Just trying to get information out of him is all," she said. "He was the first one I came upon before you came along to say hello."

He stared at her and narrowed his eyes. "I think there's more to it. I think he means something to you," he said.

She shook her head emphatically. "No, he means nothing to me," she said.

"Well good, then you won't mind if he ends up getting carried out of the ring. Tommo, tell Dommer that the new kid should go up against the Bonecruncher. Tell him it's a one out."

One of the men behind her whistled and left quickly. The cruel grin on Punch's face spread.

"What does that mean?" asked Millie, afraid she already knew.

"Let's just say the new kid is either going to come in with a splash or go out with a splat," he said, and his laugh filled the room and shook Millie's spine.

Jeremiah had tried to stop her. He had explained the dangers and tried to convince her to wait for Ward and his men to join them, but Nora would not be stopped. In the end she had told him to either come with her or get out of her way.

He didn't know what the plan was, but he was grateful he had left his house prepared. He gripped his cane with one hand and patted his shin with the other, feeling the reassuring bulge there.

Nora stared out the carriage window with misty eyes but no tears fell.

"He's an idiot," she said finally, and Jeremiah was grateful for the sound of her voice.

"He certainly seems misguided," he said quietly.

"Ever since we were children he couldn't help but get himself in trouble. I've seen him in so many fights I've lost count. If only they didn't all happen because he was too blessed hot-headed to think things through." The tears that had been waiting in the corners of her eyes finally fell free, rolling down her flushed cheeks. She angrily wiped them away.

"Maybe Millie got him out of there," he suggested.

Nora barked a laugh. "If she went into that place trying to convince my imbecile brother not to participate in a fight, then she would have had more success telling a wall to fall down."

"We cannot go in there asking for trouble," he cautioned.

She looked at him and more tears fell. "He's my brother."

Jeremiah took her hand and nodded. "I know. We'll get him out. We just can't go in making demands. These are not people who respond well to being told what to do."

A pounding on the top of the carriage let them know they had arrived.

They stepped out onto an empty street, but Jeremiah quickly spotted a man as he slipped down an alley. His ears picked up the cheer of a crowd. "This way," he said, "but quietly."

They followed the man and heard him knock on a door, then say, "I'd like to buy some tulips," before the alley was flooded with light and noise and then he was gone.

Jeremiah looked down at his clothes and then at the nurse's uniform Nora wore. They would likely stand out, but nothing could be done about that now.

He stepped forward and rapped on the door with the head of his cane.

"I'd like to buy some tulips," he said to the eyes behind the hatch and moments later they found themselves in the hallway flinching from the cacophonous roar of the crowd.

"Prepare yourself, Nora. The fighting you see here will be much harsher than you have seen before. This is a no rules environment. Anything is allowed."

She nodded. "I've seen the after-effects of these sorts of places. I will be fine."

They made their way down the stairs and through the crowd. Jeremiah was trying to maneuver them to the section Millie had told him about, where the fighters waited, hoping to get Nora to her brother to talk sense into him.

One of the two men in the ring fell with a loud thud and did not get back up, rendering the other the victor. Jeremiah watched with worry until he saw the fallen man shaking his head as another man helped him out of the ring.

The fact that it wasn't a raised ring surrounded by ropes was very unsettling to him. The rough fence that surrounded the fight area was rusty and sharp in places and he wondered how often it was used as a weapon by an enterprising fighter.

Nora was saying something but he couldn't hear her. When he asked her to repeat it she waved him off, pointing forward. The crowd was too thick for them to push through since the next fight was about to begin and they were trapped with all the others as a man held his hands up and the crowd quieted.

"This place is vile," Nora said quietly, and then she gasped.

Jeremiah looked in the direction she was staring and saw the young man from the photo he held in his pocket standing next to the other man in the ring, who held a megaphone to his mouth and shouted, "Making his debut in the pit is a young scrapper from down the tracks who is already making a name for himself with his undefeated record. I give you Declan 'Fire Fists' Quinlan!"

The crowd cheered, drowning out the next thing Nora said.

"And his opponent, a crowd favorite, it's the Bonecruncher!"

At this the crowd erupted in such a loud cheer that Jeremiah almost had to cover his ears. He saw Nora's face contort with terror and was somehow able to hear her scream over the crowd as he turned and saw the walking behemoth that joined her brother in the ring. The man was enormous, towering over Declan by at least two feet, broad-shouldered and heavyset with a scar that ran from his neck down to his navel and others decorating both arms. He had half of his teeth, which he showed as he roared and threw up his bare fists.

Declan's smug grin melted into expressionless terror.

Chapter Eight

"Stop this, Punch!" shouted Millie. She was looking down at the ring through the window in his office. "Killing that boy won't gain you anything."

"It will entertain me, and isn't that the most important thing? The six months I spent under the river I sorely lacked entertainment, and now I can create my own. I get to watch a good fight, albeit a quick one no doubt, and I get to watch you suffer." He stood behind her and held her shoulders, forcing her to watch. She was alone with him now, the other goons sent off to collect bets.

"He's just a kid," she pleaded.

Unbeknownst to Punch, his goons had not found all of her weapons, and she slowly worked the long pin free from the front of her shirt.

"Make it worth it for me, Millie," he said, leeringly.

She glared back over her shoulder. "You're disgusting. I would never sink that low." The point of the pin finally came through the fabric.

"You will do that and more if you want this boy to live. I think you need to come back to working for me again. I think you owe me that," he said. The crowd below roared as the fight began. Millie saw Declan racing around the ring desperate to stay out of the way of Bonecruncher's meaty fists.

She saw Jeremiah then in the crowd and Nora alongside him. The two of them were trying to force their way to the side of the ring. She could see the heaving of the crowd and knew they would have a hard time of it.

"Please," she said, working the pin out more.

"Do you want to know what a 'one out' is, Millie?" he said. He was right behind her with his mouth to her ear. "It's when two men go into the ring, but only one comes out. That boy down there, if he stops running around like a headless chicken, is going to be beaten to a pulp." He laughed then, that cruel baritone laugh she remembered so well. "You can stop it all, though. One word from you and I'll tell them to stop. I'll call it off. All you have to do is say 'yes.'"

She had the pin in her hand. She could feel the length of it, only six inches, and knew that she only had one chance to strike. She hoped she could do what she needed to. She hoped Jeremiah would know she had no choice.

"Yes to what?" she asked.

"To whatever I want, Millie. Say 'yes' and the boy lives. Say 'yes' and you become mine again. Just say the word."

His hands were on her shoulders and his hot breath invaded her ear. She gripped the pin and prepared herself. In the ring Bonecruncher swung and connected with Declan's shoulder, sending the boy careening into the wall of the ring. She could agree to Punch's demands, but she knew he would never let her go.

"Say the word, Millie. Say it."

If she took out Punch the fight would still go on. Was it a risk worth taking? Declan was back on his feet down below and still avoiding the brute, but for how long?

She mumbled something low. Punch leaned in and placed his chin on her shoulder. "I didn't hear you. What was that? Say it."

She swung up as quickly and as accurately as she could, driving the pin into the face of her captor. It sank into his eye and he fell back screaming.

"You cow! I'll kill you for this!" shouted Punch, blood pouring out of his damaged eye socket. He was thrashing as he rose to his feet. She kicked, crumpling his nose and dropping him again.

"Stay down, Punch, or I'll make it worse for you," she said. She ran over to the corner and tore open the fake belly she had worn earlier. The revolver felt good in her hand, reassuring, and she turned and pointed it at Punch who had risen to his feet and glared at her through his one good eye.

"You won't make it out of here alive," he growled. "My guards will gun you down where you stand."

She stared at the man who had been her terror for so long and laughed. He looked pathetic plucking at his eye in an attempt to pull the pin out as he tried to look intimidating. He stood between her and the door.

The crowd below erupted in cheers. Punch laughed.

"Your boy is dead! Drop the damn gun and you might not join him."

"Big talk for a man who can't see anything," she said. She moved around to stand in front of the window, hoping to get a glimpse of what was happening down below. "Your reign of terror is over, Chester."

She could have shot him. She knew that. The world would have been a better place if she simply put a bullet in his head and called it a day. But Jeremiah was right. He was at her mercy and something inside her wouldn't let her execute him like that. But she knew Punch. She knew what he was like.

She also knew that he hated people calling him Chester.

He roared and charged at her, fists swinging and spittle flying from his blood-caked face as he sought to bowl her over and treat her to the same treatment young Declan had likely already suffered.

Millie had no trouble seeing, unlike the unfortunate Mr. Punch. She stepped aside as he came at her and cleared the path to the window for him.

His momentum unstoppable, Mr. Punch crashed through the glass and launched himself down to the floor below.

Jeremiah tried to pull her away, but Nora fought to stay where she was. "Get me to the side of the ring," she demanded.

He turned and began to push forward, parting the crowd with his stick, sometimes prying them apart. It was slow going and he chanced the occasional glance up every so often to see Declan was still standing. Nora was behind him, her hands on his back helping to push forward.

He could barely hear her voice over the crowd but he could hear the desperation in it and it urged him forward. More than once a man turned to confront him but backed down when they saw the look on his face and likely the look of the woman following.

"He's going to need more than a nurse," heckled one man after seeing Nora's uniform.

Declan was doing his best to avoid being pummeled, dodging left and right in an attempt to wear the big man out but it didn't seem to be working. Bonecruncher roared in frustration and his swings became even more brutal and wide-reaching.

He finally connected with Declan's shoulder and the boy went flying into the wall. Fortunately that was the moment they broke through the barrier of people and he happened to fall right in front of them.

"Declan!" shouted Nora.

He looked up and after a quick second registered who he was looking at, all context telling him that it couldn't be her.

"Stumps?" he shouted. "What are you doing here?"

"You idiot boy, that's the same question I have for you. Look out!"

Bonecruncher came lumbering over and swung his fist but Declan was quick and raced out of the way. The brute looked at Nora and grinned, winking at her before turning to continue the hunt.

"We can pull him out next time he comes this way," she shouted.

"You pull him out, and he forfeits, and if you forfeit on Mr. Punch, you forfeit your life," shouted a man who stood near them.

Jeremiah nodded. "I've heard the same about the man, I'm afraid," he said. "But there's nothing in the rules that says he can't have help." He began to take off his coat and Nora put her hand on his arm.

"No, I've got this." She waited until Declan was back on their side of the ring and shouted at him. "Declan! Are you here to fight or dance?"

He glared at her. "Have you seen what I'm up against here?"

She shrugged. "Reminds me of Mitch Haggard," she shouted.

Declan registered her words and his face broke into an enormous grin. He nodded and dodged again, drawing the brute over to the other side.

Bonecruncher charged directly at him, laughing as Declan climbed up on the wall of the ring. "Chickening out, boy? I'll still come after you even if you run all the way to Fleis!"

Declan glanced over his shoulder and waited, balancing on the wall carefully. When Bonecruncher came close enough, he lunged backwards, doing a backflip over the advancing hulk. As he passed over him Declan brought his fists together hard, connecting with both sides of Bonecruncher's head.

He landed on his feet and spun around, laughing as the big man wobbled and fell forward, slamming his head on the wall. He forced himself up and turned, but Declan was already in place and drove his fist into the side of Bonecruncher's knee. A sickening snap sounded over the din of the crowd, and as Declan dodged out of the way the mass of the man came crashing down, his knee shattered.

The crowd erupted in cheers, praising Declan and booing Bonecruncher. The big man pulled himself up, hopping on his one good leg, and lunged forward, but Declan was ready for this too, and he sent a hard uppercut into Bonecruncher's face. Teeth flew in every direction and the man fell forward, moaning.

Declan turned and held up his fists victorious. The referee ran forward and looked down at Bonecruncher.

"I won, right? It's over," shouted Declan.

"This is a 'one out'," responded the man. "You have to finish it."

Declan shook his head. "No, Mr. Punch said I would be doing regular fights. Nothing like that."

The referee shrugged. "You're welcome to ask him if you'd like. He doesn't look kindly on his orders being challenged, though."

The crowd quieted down as they watched to see what would happen next. No victor had been declared. Men held betting tickets in their hands and watched with great interest.

Declan looked over at Nora, his face pleading for help. She and Jeremiah climbed over the wall and ran over.

"Don't do it," she shouted.

Jeremiah looked around at the gathered mass of humanity and clutched his stick, ready to defend himself and Nora. Declan could clearly take care of himself.

"Do it!" shouted someone in the crowd.

Declan set his jaw. "Mr. Punch," he shouted, "I've beaten this man. I won't kill him."

The referee sucked air through his teeth. "It was nice knowing you, kid."

"What happens now?" Declan asked him.

"Now he'll come down here and sort you out himself," said the referee.

A loud crash grabbed everyone's attention as the bulking form of Mr. Punch flew through an upstairs window and fell to the floor, landing with a sickening crunch at Declan's feet.

Jeremiah looked up at the opening the man left behind and saw Millie looking down at him, her eyes steely and a smile on her lips.

She nodded and disappeared from view.

Chapter Nine

"Who is Mitch Haggard?" asked Jeremiah. They all stood in the center of the ring, the warehouse empty of all of its previous occupants. The Constabulary had come quickly at Jeremiah's summons, but not quickly enough to stop the violence that had occurred.

Nora laughed. "He's a boy from our village. He used to bully Declan until one day he decided to chase him onto our farm. Papa saw the chase and stopped the boys, offering Mitch the choice of either apologizing for harassing Declan or settling it in a fight."

"Not the usual approach," said Jeremiah.

"I think Papa thought it would toughen Declan up. Little did he know how correct he would be. Since Mitch was much bigger than Declan, Papa whispered a bit of advice to my brother which you saw recreated tonight, although the knee break was an unpleasant but effective addition."

"It was a clever move."

"Yes, but I think Papa regretted it from that day forward. Declan seemed to always find himself in a fight after that."

"You saved him, you know," said Jeremiah. They looked over to where Declan was being interviewed by Ward.

"No, he saved himself. I just reminded him that he could. He's a real idiot sometimes. Most times, actually."

Jeremiah chuckled. "So what now?"

She sighed. "He has agreed to come back to St. Dismus with me and talk about how we want to handle things. He's free to do as he pleases, as long as it's what I tell him to do." She smiled.

"When they're done I'll call for a cab to take you both back," said Jeremiah. "Or I'm sure one of the Constabulary carriages can take you."

"I'll come by your office tomorrow and settle payment for your services," Nora said. "In the meantime, I think your friend might need your attention."

She gestured to where Millie stood looking down at the crumpled mass that had been Mr. Punch. A tarp had been spread over the body after the constables had fully investigated the scene. Jeremiah couldn't see her face with her back turned, but he could see that she wasn't moving.

"Hey Stumps, ready to get out of here?" shouted Declan.

Nora groaned. "I hate that nickname."

"I can imagine," said Jeremiah, but his eyes were on Millie's back.

"Talk to her," said Nora gently, giving his arm a squeeze. "We can talk more tomorrow."

Jeremiah pulled his attention away from Millie to look at Nora whose face looked practically angelic to him after all of the horrors they had seen. He nodded. "I look forward to it."

Millie was standing with her chin in her hand, staring at the amorphous mass. "You didn't tell her, did you?" she said, when Jeremiah joined her.

"That? That is what you've been over here thinking about?" said Jeremiah.

She laughed. "No. No, I've been standing here trying to figure out how this pile of bones and fat ever filled me with fear."

"He was an intimidating man when he was alive, Millie. There's no shame in the fact that he made you feel afraid."

"I didn't kill him, Jeremiah. I want you to know that. I had my gun, and I had the drop on him, and I didn't do it." She stared at him, her eyes shining with suppressed tears.

"I know you, Millie Mondegreen. I know you are a good person. Whatever happened in that room that led to this end, whatever you did or did not do, it was necessary," he said. "It's over now. Mr. Punch will no longer be a phantom in the shadows stalking you through life. He is done, and you are free."

She broke down, then, falling into his arms as all of the fear and grief and pain poured out of her onto his waistcoat in torrents of tears. Jeremiah held her tightly, giving her the space and safety to release it all.

He looked down at the tarp and replayed in his mind the image of the man, arms flailing and face filled with hate, crashing through the glass and falling to the ground. He again heard the snap as Punch hit, guaranteeing that his life was at an end. Jeremiah remembered it again and again and felt satisfaction in it, because he knew that if that fall had not been the end of Punch, Jeremiah certainly would have been.

"I'm proud of you, Millie," he said.

She patted his arm and pulled herself together, wiping the tears from her eyes. "You say that to all the girls who take down crime bosses," she laughed. "Hey, where are Nora and Declan?"

Jeremiah looked and saw that they were gone. Ward stood talking with a few constables, directing them on the next steps in that voice he used that told all present that his instructions should be followed implicitly. He saw them both watching and headed over to them.

"Leave it to you two to find yourselves in a steaming pile of trouble," he said. He glanced past Millie and barked over his shoulder, "and get that body out of here."

"He's just a body now," said Millie quietly. Jeremiah squeezed her arm.

"How are you? Anyone hurt?" asked Ward. He was in full work mode, a far cry from the man who guffawed at everything as they sat outside Cobbler's Rest.

"We are alright," said Jeremiah. "I don't suppose you could provide us with transportation."

Ward clapped him on the shoulder. "Take mine. I'll be here for a while still. Just tell the driver to come back for me because I have no desire to go for a late night stroll."

Jeremiah and Millie headed out into the night. Millie didn't look back.

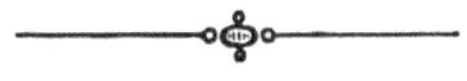

"I'm sorry, Mr. Mountweazel, truly I am," said Tarquin. He was pacing back and forth in Jeremiah's study. "I just didn't know what to do."

"And so you decided subterfuge and kidnapping were the best approach?"

"I wasn't kidnapped, Mr. Mountweazel. I went of my own accord. We love each other. We truly do." Elodie didn't look up. She sat in one of the chairs looking at her feet. She did not look in the slightest bit happy.

"We thought it would be better," said Tarquin.

"Well, my dear boy, you thought poorly and with no regard to anyone but the two of you. Mr. Panglossian was beside himself with worry, and that's saying nothing about the way you tried to derail my investigation to cover your unkindness." Jeremiah stood at the window but faced the boy. He was not shouting, merely speaking in his usual level tone, but Tarquin recoiled from his words as if he had been struck.

"What do we do?" he pleaded.

Jeremiah put his hand on Tarquin's shoulder to stop his pacing. "You are in a situation of your own creation, but you are not alone. Not only are you in this with Elodie, but also with everyone in yours and Elodie's life, and that includes me."

"Ivan will be so angry," whispered Elodie. She began to cry and Tarquin rushed over to rub her shoulders.

"I think," said Jeremiah after a glance down to the street, "that you will find him very forgiving once he is unburdened of his worry."

The door opened and Millie came in first, followed closely by Mr. Panglossian. At the sight of Elodie he let out a happy laugh and rushed over to her, hugging her and peppering the top of her head with kisses.

"My dear girl, I was so worried! I can't tell you how much it warms my heart to see you well and safe."

She erupted into tears and hugged him, trying to explain but failing to find the words. Mr. Panglossian shushed her and told her there was nothing to forgive.

He continued to stare at Tarquin but spoke to Elodie. "Miss Mondegreen has been kind enough to inform me of the situation you two have gotten yourselves into. She also explained why you fled the way you did. I'm so sorry, Elodie, if I gave you any impression that I would ever think anything but the world of you, no matter what."

"No matter what?" she implored.

He took her face in his hands and wiped the tears off her cheek. "I did not have children, so I will not have grandchildren, but you, my dear girl, are as much a daughter or granddaughter to me as if I had raised you myself." He kissed her forehead and stood to face Tarquin. "I do not know you well, young man, but I am told by our friends here that you are kind and you have been doing your best for Elodie, however misguided your methods were, and for that I am grateful and owe you respect."

He offered his hand. Tarquin stared at it for a moment as if it may explode before tentatively shaking it. "I just want them safe. I love her, Mr. Panglossian. And I will love our baby."

Mr. Panglossian nodded. "I have been informed regarding the condition of the place you are living in, and I would like to offer an alternative." He knelt down and took Elodie's hands. "Come back to your room, my dear. If you want him to stay with you he can do that. You are my family and are welcome to live with me as long as you would like."

She began to cry again and hugged him. Tarquin stood as though he wasn't sure what he was supposed to do next.

"You're not angry with me?" she asked.

"Not at all. Come, let us go downstairs and make you some food. Both of you."

He stood and helped Elodie to her feet. Tarquin dutifully fell into step behind them, casting a quick glance over his shoulder at Jeremiah, who gave him a smile and a wink.

When the door closed, Millie fell into one of the chairs with an exhausted sigh. "Well, that's all worked out. Pretty soon we'll be hearing the screaming of a little baby coming through the walls."

Jeremiah looked worried. "I hadn't thought of that."

A knock on the door startled both of them, and as Jeremiah moved around to open it Millie poured herself a drink.

Nora stood on the landing, her brother behind her. Jeremiah wondered how many sheepishly ashamed young men he would see that day.

"So lovely to see you again, and looking so well," he said, gesturing for them to come in.

"Thank you, Jeremiah. And I wanted to thank you again for helping me locate my errant brother," Nora said. She handed him an envelope.

"I'm not a child, Stumps," complained Declan.

She shot him a look. "What did I tell you?"

"Sorry," he said with a shrug. "Old habits and all that. I'm not a child, Nora."

Jeremiah looked at the envelope. "There really is no need. As I said, it was hardly any effort on our part."

Millie raised her eyebrows at this but said nothing. The smile that spread across her face said it all.

"Be that as it may, without your and Miss Mondegreen's help Declan and I may not have been reunited, and I am grateful."

"What will you do now?" asked Millie.

"We head for home this afternoon. Hopefully Papa is faring better, but if not, I will help to nurse him while Declan takes care of the farm needs," she said. There was a sadness to her face that was mirrored on Jeremiah's.

"I think I've had enough of the city," said Declan. "People are far too dishonest here. You know where you are with farmers."

Millie grinned and slapped him on the back. "You'll have some stories to tell, eh?"

Declan chuckled. "I'll be popular for a while, especially with the prize money."

"Prize money?" Jeremiah's attention was drawn from Nora's face at the mention.

"Inspector Ward said since I won the fight I was due the money that would have come my way if things had been done legitimately. Turns out it was a hefty sum."

"From which your fee has been paid," said Nora. "So I'll hear no more mention of it not being necessary."

"Will you be returning to Tamarind after sorting out your family?" asked Jeremiah. His eyes were full of hope.

Nora's, however, were full of sadness. "Alas, my healing efforts are still needed in Mellick. I was only meant to be here for a short while. Now it's time to return to my duties, after a bit of respite, of course."

Jeremiah's face fell, but he quickly recovered.

"I have no doubt you are needed wherever you go, Nora," he said quietly. He took her hand and kissed it.

"Well, sorry to put you all to any trouble. Our train is leaving soon, Stum—Nora, so we should get to the station," said Declan.

"I wish you both the best of everything," said Jeremiah.

"Safe travels," added Millie.

Nora smiled at Jeremiah. "If you're ever in Mellick, please do stop in," she said. "I am forever in your debt."

Millie walked them down and when she returned it was to find Jeremiah standing at the window. "I'm guessing you never told her how you felt."

"I knew this ending was inevitable, Millie. She has obligations, as do I," he said sadly.

Millie picked up the envelope and opened it, thumbing through the collection of bills it held. "Nice payout, though. Should keep us eating comfortably for a while. Oh, what's this?" She slipped a letter from between two bills and held it up. "It just has your name on it."

Jeremiah took it from her and tore it open. He sat down behind his desk and read the letter, then read it again. After the second time he slipped it into his breast pocket and sat back in the chair smiling.

He stood and rubbed his stomach. "I'm feeling a bit peckish, how about you?"

"You're not going to tell me what it says, are you?"

"You know Millie," Jeremiah said, still smiling, "I've been meaning to visit Mellick more often. Maybe pay a visit to some friends."

Millie grinned with him. "Sounds good."

They made their way down the stairs and were stopped at the bottom by a man with a large parcel wrapped in dark brown paper. "Delivery for Jeremiah Mountweazel," he said, holding out a clipboard.

Jeremiah signed his name, took the package, then turned to face the door they had just exited.

"Help me open this, would you?" he said to Millie.

She took the parcel and began to tear the paper as he pulled a screwdriver from his pocket. He removed the sign that had hung there for as long as she had known him. It read, in faded gold lettering, 'Mountweazel, Finder.'

He set it down and turned to her, reaching out his hand expectantly. She pulled the packing paper free and looked at the sign, then smiled as she handed it to him.

"About time you saw some sense," she said.

Jeremiah took it and screwed it into place. He stepped back and admired the gold and black lettering:

MOUNTWEAZEL & MONDEGREEN, FINDERS

"Too right, Millie," he said. "Lunch?"

Acknowledgements

I have to start by saying that this book is in your hands because of the incredible help and support of Dan and Jen at Firewords. I've worked with them for years on their magazine as a reader, and when they offered me the opportunity to publish this book under their imprint I jumped at the chance so fast I'm pretty sure the sonic boom was heard around the world. Dan's expertise made the cover I conceived a work of art, and all the editing, typesetting, and putting up with my endless questions was by no means a simple task.

I can't forget Paul and Sean, my gaming buddies whose antics in one steampunk-oriented game I ran led them to be on a train and kick off a series of events that would ultimately inspire the back story on the first adventure in this book. They were there when it all went down.

To all the people who have read these stories in their various iterations over the years, thank you for helping to polish the stone.

And to all the members of the writing communities on the various social media sites I still frequent, I want to say thank you for being supportive of someone who you have never even met. A rising tide lifts all boats, as we all know.

Finally, I want to thank my wife, Carrie, and my daughter, Katie, for supporting me while these stories poured out of my head, often at unexpected times. Carrie did the initial edits with endless patience, and reminded me often about the importance of commas. They both were eager sounding boards for story ideas, and I have to give partial writing credit to Katie for helping me work out some aspects of Gilgungate. I could not have done this without them.

About the author

Wm. Brett Hill grew up just north of Athens, GA where he spent most of his time with his head in a book.

His short stories have been published in a plethora of publications, including *Firewords*, *Bandit Fiction*, *Literally Stories*, and others. He self-published four sci-fi novellas under the pseudonym Thor Bozman before compiling them and re-releasing them under his own name as *The Thor Bozman Collection - Tales of Survival*.

His career in IT has spanned over two decades and keeps him from writing nearly as much as he would like, but also keeps the lights on so the writing can happen.

He currently lives on the Eastern Shore of Maryland with his wife and daughter, three bantam chickens who don't lay eggs nearly as often as they should, and a labsky named Lexi who also lays no eggs.

9 798218 756826